PRAISE FOR *THE LAUNDRESS*

"I enjoyed the company of tequila-drinking, bubblegum-chewing, dancing Lavinia, the laundress, who took me on a no-tech tour of San Francisco, getting her hands into clients' dirty laundry and cleansing family secrets, including her own. Sapienza elicits sympathy for her Italian immigrant heroine, who has more ups and downs than San Francisco has hills but whose travails and travels left me happy and hungry for Mexican food and espresso."

—ANN LUDWIG, freelance travel writer for *The New York Times*

"Spirited, quirky, and independent Lavinia Lavinia makes a life as a laundress in San Francisco. But she feels a painful void: her family history and identity have been kept from her. As we follow her, the mystery slowly unravels, with the help of friendship, love, and adventure."

—PATRICIA STEENLAND, College Writing Programs,
UC Berkeley

"Barbara Sapienza draws the reader into the life of Lavinia Lavinia, providing a blueprint for living and prevailing in the modern world of the twenty-first century."

—JOHN D BREDEHOEFT, PhD, member of the
National Academy of Engineering

"Set in the aliveness of the c'   f San Franciso, *The Laundress* gives us a story of the pow   to break open the human heart, he   d within others."

—CHERYL KRAUTER,   *rm:
A Workbook for Telling   story*

"Written from the heart and spiced with swirling dance, chiming clocks, steaming tamales, sculpted clay, and double espressos, *The Laundress* tells a beautiful story of lost family and the healing power of friendship. A rich and rewarding read."

—DIANNE ROMAIN, author of *The Trumpet Lesson*

"Sapienza weaves a tapestry of Old World customs with New Age therapies, cityscape with wilderness, and festering wounds with blossoming love that dances to life on the page."

—SHARMON J. HILFINGER, author of *Arctic Requiem: The Story of Luke Cole and Kivalina*

"Barbara Sapienza is masterful at creating a powerful story of a yearning daughter driven to know her distant father—not easy, as Lavinia was snatched away from Naples as a baby and brought to San Francisco, creating a chasm of time and place. Readers are not only swept into a passionate pursuit of reunion but by the author's extraordinary skill at sustaining mystery until we are dazzled by surprise—the best kind."

—JOAN MINNINGER, PhD, author of *The Father/Daughter Dance*

THE
LAUNDRESS

A NOVEL

BARBARA SAPIENZA

SHE WRITES PRESS

Published 2020
Printed in the United States of America
ISBN: 978-1-63152-679-4
ISBN: 978-1-63152-680-0
Library of Congress Control Number: 2019954309

For information, address:
She Writes Press
1569 Solano Ave #546
Berkeley, CA 94707

She Writes Press is a division of SparkPoint Studio, LLC.

Interior design by Tabitha Lahr

All company and/or product names may be trade names, logos, trademarks, and/or registered trademarks and are the property of their respective owners.

For Peter Sapienza, my love

She weaves the story
the gods change them into birds
so that they can fly away again

Fillamina and Her Mute Sister
Accademia dei Lincei, Roma

Chapter 1:

THE RINGS OF TIME

L avinia Lavinia walks toward Columbus Avenue in San Francisco from the Mission District wearing her work uniform: black straight-leg jeans, a men's tuxedo jacket, and her T-strap shoes. She carries extra bubblegum in one pocket and in another a few tiny fig leaves she harvested from a backyard tree.

Monday mornings bring a lazy feeling on the street—if people aren't late for work, that is, and she isn't yet. As she nears Columbus, she sees cars looking for parking spaces and people milling around doorways, chatting, espressos in hand. The scent of roasted coffee beans floats into the street from the small cafés, intoxicating and tantalizing. Lavinia pops a piece of bubblegum into her mouth and lets the sugar pool into a liquid puddle on her tongue before she begins to chew. The first bite quells the unease she feels as she walks farther and farther away from her studio in the Mission and toward her new client's home.

Zack Luce called only this morning, saying that since his wife died, his clothes have suffered. Now, only thirty minutes later, she is en route to his house in North Beach to discuss his laundry needs.

Anticipation for this first meeting has brought fear and trembling into her body; a nervousness about entering an unknown house makes her ears ring, and, as she recalls his soft, whispering voice telling her that his wife died, a flutter enters her heart. The way his voice caught, the palpability of his sadness, both touched and scared her.

Lavinia Lavinia turns her focus to laundry. She loves to wash clothes. It is only while washing and ironing and folding that she feels fresh and free and even unique. She feels blessed by her particular skills. She is a laundress. She enjoys ironing, sorting, and removing stains in people's homes, their own private sanctuaries; she likes getting an intimate look at others' spaces. But in the first encounter at the door, when time seems to stand still, she always feels afraid. She's not sure what to say or do, or who will greet her.

Once inside, though, she is in awe of these places where people live so fully—unlike her in her storefront studio, which is minimally embellished, empty of her personal touch. With its long, narrow front room, her space is like a barn, more suitable for a horse than a young woman.

She decides to stop for coffee at Café Falcone in the ten minutes she has before meeting Mr. Luce. The coffee aromas answer her misgivings and pull her inside the café, where she joins six people waiting to order. The wooden tables scattered about seem to say, *Sit down here and sip your latte.* She orders a double espresso and stands at the bar to drink it, the way they do in Italy. The espresso slides down easily. She pays the barista, a young, good-looking guy, and places a piece of bubblegum in the tip jar before leaving to find the small street off Columbus where Mr. Luce lives.

She's in the habit of tipping with bubblegum; it's something she started doing when she was in first grade. It endeared her to her classmates, and now it, along with the fig leaves, has become her signature. The good-looking guy's eyes seem to pop as they follow her hand to and from the tip jar. She can feel him still watching as she strolls back out onto Columbus.

The neighborhood is a revival in Lavinia's eyes. North Beach's Italian bakeries, cafés, and delis interlace with the Chinese restaurants, butcher shops, and outdoor markets. Every other place on the block is a patchwork of color, vibrant and seductive. Although Mr. Luce's place is near the café, its location—on a small cul-de-sac—brings it a sense of privacy as a neighborhood home. Lavinia enters the vestibule, presses the white buzzer next to Mr. Luce's name, then grasps a piece of her silky hair in the fingers of her right hand and begins to twirl it into a tight twist as she waits. He buzzes her in just as she snaps a bubble with her tongue.

She opens the door to the inner foyer, where mailboxes and a wooden table line the walls. The entryway floor is carpeted in beige wool. Her feet press into the luxurious carpet, soft and spongy under her feet, a welcomed contrast to the cement sidewalk outside. The carpet has a few mean stains that make her wonder who spilled or dribbled. Was it a kid? Lovers playing? An old lady with trembling hands? She immediately focuses on what she would do to remove them, should she get the job.

The aroma of dried lavender permeates the entryway. He told her on the phone to come up one flight and his door would be on the right. She notices an elevator on the left side of the hallway—old-fashioned, small—but she takes the stairs, as instructed. At the top of the stairway she knocks on the door marked #2 and waits with her ear to the wooden door.

Footsteps approach, and she jumps back a little. When the door opens, an elderly gentleman stands before her. He's tall and thin, with white, wispy hair and glasses with dark frames. She notices the crease in his pressed slacks and the starched collar of an otherwise soft blue cotton shirt. She imagines pressing its long sleeves, smelling the clean cotton threads.

Mr. Luce says hello and smiles at her, ushers her inside his flat. His apartment is an Edwardian—once a large home, now subdivided into condominiums. Creamy white gives a light feel. The décor is soft and clean, splattered with fabrics too flowery for her taste. Assorted family photographs adorn the furniture. On a side table sits a bouquet of fresh yellow roses. On a mahogany dining table, set in a small alcove by the window, rests a starched blue linen tablecloth. Beautifully ironed. She feels her body relax.

"Pleas-s-s-e, sit down." He points to one of the dining room chairs. His voice—soft, as it was on the phone—puts her at ease.

"Thank you, Mr. Luce."

"Oh, pleas-s-s-e, call me Zack. This work relationship won't be a formal thing, you know. I just want someone to help me keep up with the laundry. I used to do it myself, but since Elsa died I'm not up to it anymore. I think I did it for her."

Lavinia lowers her head at hearing his wife's name; it brings death too close for her comfort. The fact that this house has seen death scares her. She touches the smooth skin of the fig leaf in her pocket.

"What exactly do you need?" She eyes his cotton pants, his long-sleeved shirt.

"I like my bed sheets washed every week, and then there's the kitchen linens, the tablecloth, and napkins." He looks toward the blue-covered table.

Thinking how strange it is to keep up this business of linens with his wife dead, Lavinia says instead, "Nice flowers."

"My daughter Margaret sends them. She likes yellow roses and thinks that's a substitute for visiting me."

Lavinia doesn't know what to say so she stares at the yellow flowers. They complement the blue cloth.

"Margaret lives in Davis. She's an ED doc, too busy with her work to do my laundry, and I wouldn't ask her anyway." Zack fiddles with a hearing aid in his right ear, moves his head closer to Lavinia.

"I'd come to your home once a week," she says, then, stops to look around the apartment. "You have a washer and dryer here? Ironing board and iron? Laundry soap and bleach for the whites? I prefer eco-friendly cleansers, if possible, non-scented or naturally scented."

Zack nods. "We're well-equipped here, but—"

"I don't drive and prefer to work in the home where the laundry lives."

Zack stares at her, raises his eyebrows.

By habit, she starts to fidget with her hair. "I guess I didn't explain. I provide in-home service." She gets up, moving to leave, thinking Mr. Luce must want his laundry taken outside.

"Wait, miss-s-s. How old are you?"

Lavinia stops, turns toward him. "I'm twenty-six," she says, and takes a card from the small leather purse she wears on her back. She hands it to him and watches him examine it, turning it right side up to discover it's in fact a business card fashioned into the shape of a long-sleeved shirt.

He reads aloud, "Lavinia Lavinia Laundress-s-s. Full service in-home laundry." He smiles at her. "Cute card! But I'm not quite sure whether this will work in this small apartment. I don't like feeling like I'm falling over someone. I've become used to living alone."

"Perhaps it won't work then. I need my quiet, too. People generally leave the home while I work." She steps closer, extends her arm, reaching for her card.

"Unless you can come in the afternoon on Wednesdays-s-s. That is, when I'm out a good number of hours." Zack gets up and moves closer to Lavinia, so close that his breath touches her forehead as he speaks.

Just then, a cuckoo clock chimes nine times.

Soon other clocks begin to chime, ringing and buzzing, surrounding her and making her feel twitchy. She imagines being watched by all the faces of these clocks, which she doesn't see but only hears, as if they are spirits speaking in some strange language. She looks toward the blue cloth, remembers Elsa, and imagines her presence in the house. Lavinia is not so sure she wants to work for Zack and so close to all these gongs that seem to be marking time. She wonders: If spirits could speak, might they sound like this? And what if she should come one morning and find him dead? He's the oldest person she knows.

She moves her gum, which has been resting on the back of her palate, to the center of her mouth and starts chewing. When she looks up he's still facing her, his head bent close to her ear.

"Well, I'll have to check my schedule," she says. "How much laundry do you estimate? And will ironing be involved?"

He touches the collar of his button-down shirt. "Three or four shirts-s-s a week, two or three pair of slacks-s-s, the usual towels-s-s and underwear. Yes, I would like you to iron."

"Sounds like two loads of white, including the linens, and one dark. And the sheets, too. I'd say to wash, dry, iron, and fold would take about four hours."

"Did you say four hours-s-s?" He bends forward, places a pink ear with soft white hairs next to her mouth.

"Four hours. You have my references."

"I saw your name at my dentist's office. Dr. Brady."

"I've worked for Dr. Brady in his home for years." She doesn't tell Zack that they have a barter: weekly laundry service for dental hygiene. She chews hard on her gum.

"What's your fee, miss?"

"Fifty dollars an hour."

"Miss Lavinia, I'm curious about how you got into your trade."

"My trade?"

"Yes. Also, your tuxedo jacket. I like it. I used to have one with the thin lapels, too. Where is that thing?" He looks around the room.

Lavinia doesn't know what to tell him, though people have asked her this same question countless times before. "Ah, that's a long story to save for another day," she says. "I have another appointment now. I'll confirm for next week." She moves to leave.

"I'll expect a call about whether Wednesdays-s-s work then. You have my number."

"Are you wanting my services every week?"

He nods and walks with Lavinia down the long hallway she didn't even notice on the way in. He opens the door and waits on the landing as she goes down the carpeted stairway. When she turns back, he's waving good-bye to her exuberantly.

Outside she nearly walks into a young boy, tall and skinny, with the longest feet she's ever seen, who brushes past her and runs up the steps. He wears a Giant's baseball cap and pants that look too big for him, exposing his butt. And what a skinny waist! When he passes her, he keeps his chin tucked so she can't see his face. He seems to be headed for the apartment she's just left. She wonders if he's related to Zack, or maybe a resident in the first-floor apartment. Likely the one who stained the carpet.

Back on Columbus Avenue, Lavinia dips into the same café for another espresso. The barista looks at her with a wide grin. He has a classic Greek nose and dimples. He looks to be about thirty. He seems to recognize her. She snaps a bubble at him, which causes him to smile even more deeply. She stands at the bar.

"You were in here earlier?" He draws her out. "Do you always tip gum?"

"As a matter of fact, yeah!"

"What are you doing in the neighborhood?"

"I'm a laundress."

"What's that?"

"I detail people's clothes. You know, so they look sharp."

He looks at his apron and smiles. "I could use some detailing."

"You know the people who live around here?"

"Who's asking?" He leans over the counter up and close to her.

"I am. I'm about to work for an old man at number 365." She points to his apartment.

"Oh, I know that building. Yeah, it belongs to Zack. He's lived there a long time, as long as North Beach has been in existence. A little hard of hearing, otherwise a nice guy. He's famous, too."

Lavinia's eyes widen.

"He patented a coffee maker. A real coffee connoisseur. An inventor. He replaced the old percolators. You know, camp coffee."

She raises her eyebrows. Before she can ask a follow-up question, he changes the subject.

"So a laundress! That's not something you hear very often. It sounds so old-world, like something from a Victorian novel."

"Yeah, it's as old as camp coffee. I launder people's clothes. Keep them clean and tidy. I specialize in removing stains with eco-friendly suds."

"That's a new one, and I thought I'd heard everything."

Lavinia tips her espresso to her lips and drains it to the last drop. Then she unwraps a fresh Bubblicious, pops it in her mouth, and pays. Before she leaves, she places an extra gum in the tip jar for the barista. He reaches in, picks out the gum, and winks at her before she turns to leave.

Chapter 2:

THE BLUE STAIN

Bubblegum renewed, Lavinia walks up the steep hill on Chestnut toward Russian Hill and her next job. Thoughts of Zack and the cute barista float around like a summer balloon in a soft wind. The barista's interest in her lingers like a wind that might take her balloon away.

She never intended to do laundry for a living; she wanted to teach first graders at the elementary school on Bryant Street where she did her student teaching, where her friend Kinky Montoya teaches third grade now. But everything happened so fast. Soon after Aunt Rose died, Uncle Sal got it into his head to move back to Naples, which meant he wouldn't be at her graduation. No sooner did she drop him off at SFO than she cut her hair, sold the car, and withdrew from her last semester at San Francisco State. If he didn't care enough to see her through, why should she care enough to finish? After all, he's her only family. Sal scooped her away from Naples before she was five, brought her to San Francisco to live with him and Aunt Rose—the jealous stepmother—and now he left without a qualm. What kind of uncle is he to abandon her like that?

Some part of her knows that Sal loves her. After all, he set her up to be okay, took care of her needs all these years, even redid her studio apartment with her tastes in mind before he left—but it's just all too much. She seems to lack the resilience needed to be completely on her own, and she's been grieving ever since he left a year ago. She feels like she's lost her home, even though she still lives in the same place; she feels like an orphan.

At first, the laundry soothed her and provided a respite from the gnawing estrangement. She found the circling of the water and the way the stains just wash away to be quite comforting. The fresh smell of the bleach cleanses; the methodical folding straightens; the rhythmic ironing smooths the wrinkles. That it has turned into a steady income still surprises her; that so many clients have come to her through Dr. Brady confounds her. First Nina, followed by George, and now in a year's time, Mr. Luce.

The hill is steep, so she watches her feet. Stretching her calves gives her strength. She pushes on toward Russian Hill, telling herself that if she decides to take the job working for Mr. Luce, she'll combine it with this client, Nina. But that will take some maneuvering. Changing someone's standing time is never easy, and Nina is particular.

Lavinia loves seeing how other people arrange their personal things, which wasn't anything she anticipated about laundering for others before she began. Take Mr. Luce, with his pressed blue linen tablecloth and yellow roses sitting nearby and his many clocks chiming, calling to be noticed. Such a unique blending of choices—blue for his wife and the yellow roses for Margaret. As for the clocks, she's not certain. Some weird ritual, she guesses.

She's pulled away from her thoughts when a trolley heading toward Fisherman's Wharf screeches nearby. She stops in her own tracks, a bit woozy. Trolleys make her shudder—the way the metallic wheels scrape along the tracks. When she regains her composure, she sees tourists shining their big smiles and calling her to the moment. She waves to them, then takes her next right, up a steep hill.

She stops in front of a large apartment complex that's built right into the hill, maximizing the views of the Bay Bridge and Coit Tower. She walks through the complex's lush garden and looks up toward a large eucalyptus tree, where a flock of green parrots is perched. She seems to have entered the Garden of Eden, and for a minute she feels as though she is Eve, the first woman, stepping into paradise. But then a parrot with a cherry-colored head brings her back to the present with a loud squawk. He must be one of the wild San Francisco parrot population she's read about—abandoned pets whose numbers have now grown to near three hundred. She feels happy they found their freedom.

She rings Nina's doorbell and waits. Nina's a lawyer who works from home on laundry days until Lavinia gets there. Lavinia has only met her husband, Don, once in the year she has worked for them—a day when Nina was out of town. Remembering how Don stared at her, making her aware of the mole she has on her upper lip, still gives her the creeps. His gaze felt visceral, like metal claws attaching to her birthmark. She scratches at her jaw.

Lavinia slips her gum back into its small wrapper, knowing Nina wouldn't approve, and checks her watch. She hears footsteps behind the heavy wooden door, and then Nina appears, neatly coiffed, dressed in a long-sleeved silk blouse and beige slacks.

"Come in—right on time, too. Let me show you a silk blouse. You've got to get rid of these incredible stains on it."

Lavinia follows her into the bedroom just opposite the hallway. On the closet door hangs a blue silk blouse with stains that definitely call attention. Lavinia gently grasps one of the spots between her fingers, letting the fabric slide, noting that the spot is a darker blue than the pale fabric.

"Oil," she says.

"Hummus, last night. I'm glad you're here. It's my favorite blouse. I bought it in Southeast Asia. I tried dabbing baby powder on it to soak up the grease . . ." She frowns. "Something my mother used to do. But . . ."

"I have a remedy, you know, so don't worry. It will be as good as new." Lavinia swallows hard, not knowing for sure if her small soil stick will do the job, but she wants to sound confident.

"I feel better already," Nina says. "And how are you?"

"I'm doing great. You know, I . . ." She wants to ask Nina if she can change her day to Wednesday to accommodate Mr. Luce, but figures she'll wait to see if she can get the stain out first. "Oh, never mind, actually. Yes, I'm doing just fine, thank you."

"Good to hear. Just the usual today. Sheets, towels, and my personals. Oh, and the new silk pajamas. They're red." She raises her eyebrows at their mention and Lavinia nods her understanding that they must be hand washed. "And Don's clothes are in his special hamper and his shirts are hanging in his closet. Nothing fussy, but he likes the navy blue shirt pressed."

"Not to worry."

Nina gathers her papers off the desk, showing off long, unpainted fingernails as she snaps her briefcase closed. Once Lavinia hears the door close, she unwraps her gum, sits by the great windows on the indoor patio, and meditates on the view: a crooked street below lined with tourists, the Bay Bridge in the distance, and city streets down below. *What would it be like to live in an exquisite apartment like this?* she wonders, staring at some tourists who jumped out of their car to walk the crooked street. *Could a place like this ever feel like home?*

People like Nina seem to have it all together—silk blouses, travel to Cambodia and Laos, good jobs. She considers what Nina said about Don's clothes preferences when she left—"Nothing fussy"—implying that Don's clothes will be simple. Lavinia has found that laundering for men is, in fact, easier. Rarely is hand washing involved, and no consideration of loose colorants running during laundering—as with Nina's red silk, which must be washed separately and by hand—is necessary.

But her feelings about Don, after that single meeting, are anything but simple. When he opened the door that day, he nervously swiped his falling bangs from his eyes, straightened out the knot of his navy tie, and just stared at Lavinia's birthmark—a small, dark mole on her upper lip. Most people are polite enough to move their eyes quickly from that spot as they greet her, but Don lingered there like a sneak thief, stealing something from her.

Lavinia chews her gum more furiously and fights the urge to snap a bubble to break the tension.

Maybe laundering men's clothing is simpler, but are men simpler than women? It certainly seemed simple for Andy, Lavinia's boyfriend of five years, to leave her. One morning—a year ago, just before Uncle Sal left—she and Andy lay in bed at his place, where they lived together for a year. He casually got out of bed in his underwear, holding his pillow, and left the house. She imagined he dressed first. The note she found in the morning said, "I don't love you anymore."

The previous night, before he left, she'd been sobbing next to him, comforted by his arm stretched across her navel and chest. She was dreading Rose's impending death, which scared the hell out of her—and, worse, made her feel guilty for their rocky relationship. Sadness had bitten her, and she'd cried until her nose and tears were so full they'd dripped on Andy's shoulder, slipping down his arm. He'd gotten soaked!

After finding the note, she gathered her stuff in a large black duffel bag and headed back to Sal and Rose's place, just in time for Rose's death. Her aunt was dying and she couldn't stand watching it, but there she was! She closed the door and never looked back, and never once thought it strange that she never tried to get back together with Andy.

All she can see now is how funny he looked sneaking out in his undies with a pillow under his long arm. She knew in that moment that he was gone. He slipped away as easily as her tears had drained out from her eyes, as easily as Rose died, and as easily as Sal left soon after.

She watches the wispy clouds above Coit Tower, flowing like a white banner above the city and the bay. The house creaks, prompting her to get to work.

In the living room, she places her jacket on the silk couch that sits across from a Japanese *tansu* step chest, which in turn sits next to a small French commode with a trellis motif. Beyond this ornate piece is a regular-looking CD player with a stack of CDs. She places one of Nina and Don's CDs, an opera, into the player, admiring the polished hardwood floors and the Turkish kilims as she does. The richness of the sounds and the textures of the rugs lift her spirits. Something about the beauty of it all and the way one thing relates to another intrigues her. Who would put Asian furniture next to a classical period piece? This is part of the allure of working in homes.

The music flows from the tenor's voice through her, following her into the bathroom, where the his-and-hers hampers wait.

As she begins sorting the whites from the darks, she revels in the music. Dramatically and deeply, the tenor sings an Italian aria, "Nessun Dorma." He's singing about a princess in a cold room. The Italian words are magically familiar to her ears. *"Vincero, vincero, vincero"* fills an ache in her soul. When he sings these words, Lavinia sings them out loud, too, while she piles under-wear in the center of the bathroom and then loads them into the washer. She adds one cup of eco-bleach to the cold-water wash, then a cup of liquid detergent.

The aria takes her right through to the beautiful blue blouse and its center stain. She finds the silk stain remover tucked in her jeans pocket and first dabs it lightly into the fabric hem with a soft cloth from the hamper. If it works, she'll apply it to the actual stain. She watches the material as it sucks the chemical up, spreading and growing in size, responding to the substance.

Will it dry without leaving a deeper stain? Can one actually get rid of stains? Doubt fills her. She worries, but she dumps the stains of her life—Rose's putrid death, Sal leaving for Italy, Andy's escape with his pillow, Don's disgusting staring, quitting school—together in the cold-water wash and leaves the room with the question hovering. *A stain is a stain is a stain,* she tells herself as she turns on the taps to run cool water into the double sinks. She rinses the light lingerie in one and then the red pajamas in the other. As she suspected, the pajamas turn the water rosy, then deep pink, and finally red.

Lavinia checks the soiled blouse and feels a kind of reprieve in finding that her stain remover didn't leave a watermark on the hem. Feeling safe, she dabs directly onto oil blotches with the magic potion, blotting gently from the center outwards. When the spot is entirely covered she lets it sit to dry. All at once, she feels free to dance across the large living room, and does, pausing for a moment to look at the photo of the couple on the mantle, holding their surfboards, before twirling away.

The pulse of the music rises up through her feet and ankles and through her thighs into her very core as she glides around the great room. She holds one hand on her tummy, anchoring herself, while she circles the space, dancing toward the master bedroom where the master's shirts hang on a hook in his closet. As is his habit, he hasn't dumped them into the hamper but on the floor, so she collects the four shirts, checking the pockets for paper tissues. She never wants paper lint in the wash cycle.

Her hands stop on a folded piece of paper that looks like origami. She opens it. She tells herself she must read it to see whether it's something of value to Don. He works in financial services and holds a prominent position with a large firm. Yes, it might be something of importance, she convinces herself.

As the paper crinkles in her hand, a creepy feeling takes hold. Oh, how she hated the way he stared at her! She can't imagine how Nina puts up with him. She carefully opens the origami and reads, "Meet me at Velo Rouge on Saturday."

Lavinia looks around the room to see if she's truly alone, somehow feeling his presence. What if he intended for her to find this note? What if it's for her?

She dismisses the thought as outlandish. She's only met the man once, and yet the memory of him causes her to chew her gum more furiously. *What an idiot!*

She hides the note in her pocket, trying to decide what she should do with it. In the bathroom, the precious silk pajamas still sit in the blood-red water, waiting for rinsing. The pajamas and the lingerie will be hung separately on the retractable line she's set up in the shower stall. Lavinia watches the dripping water flow onto the plastic cover she's placed on the floor.

She checks the stains on the blue silk. Satisfied they're gone, she rubs off the white residue of the chemicals, steam irons the blouse with a fabric steamer to refresh the silk, and then places it back on a hanger in Nina's closet.

In the other room, she hears the music click to a stop. She surveys her work progress against the time. A second wash? Yes, she will still make it. She returns to the patio to look over the city scene and the wide-open bay. Then she closes her eyes and dreams her recurring dream of the seaside town near the Bay of Naples where she was born and spent the first four years of her life. The Mediterranean caresses the bustling city on its edge. Lavinia gets lost in the labyrinth of the old neighborhood as she remembers herself as a little girl in T-strap shoes playing in the cobblestone streets across from the grotto garden, delighting in the sounds of other children and women. The old ladies scream from their windows for *pane, prosciutto, mozzarella di bufala*, the groceries to be hauled up to their second- and third-story apartments. Then she hears her mother call, "Lavinia Lavinia, come home now," coupled with an insistent phrase that pulses through her: "No, Papa, *lasciami*."

This is the place where Lavinia always awakens from her dream, feeling a rumble in her heart as if a mini tornado has flushed through her. To have her mother's loving voice calling her to come home fade away to a determined insistence—like she is fighting for her life, refusing someone vehemently—is unsettling. Lavinia feels frightened and confused. She reaches her hand out to catch the meaning, but like her bubbles it breaks apart and disappears.

When the buzzer rings on the dryer, Lavinia moves to the laundry room to fold Don's whites—the undershirts, the BVDs, the cotton white socks bundles—with those words still on her lips:

Leave me alone, I refuse. Somehow with these words in mind, her workload goes easier. The pile stacks up, with the smaller items— face cloths, dish towels, napkins, pillow cases—first, and towels next. She hangs the final wet garments on the expandable line, where she orders the colors from red to orange to yellow to green (noting that most are beige and coffee tones), a rainbow prayer flag to mark the ritual of this ancient practice.

Lavinia imagines Nina's happy face at seeing the spot removed from the precious silk until a darker concern clouds over. What might Nina make of the note in Don's pocket? It occurs to her that no matter what happens, she now holds it in secret. Another stain.

She starts in with a light pressing of Don's shirts, her favorite of all her tasks. Ironing the cotton, pressing away the wrinkles of time, hoping the cloud will pass. She loves the ritual of pressing a shirt. She begins with the front side panels, progresses to the back, and then to the sleeves and the cuffs. Finally, the collar. She lays the shirt flat on the ironing board, buttons every other small button from the top to the waist, and then folds it again into thirds lengthwise, incorporating the sleeves as if the shirt is hugging itself.

But today she doesn't love the way the sleeves hug. She fights with them. Is it the note that makes her feel heavy and greasy like the blue stain? A burden she can't put down? Her heart feels tight, like something is pressing in on her. She can't get a deep catch on her breath. Repulsive feelings toward Don make her want to tie the sleeves together into a knot.

Aggressively, she pulls the sheets from the bed and puts them in the wash. Then she surveys the apartment, puts it to rest as she found it, before putting on her jacket.

She picks up the two hundred dollars in twenties and replaces it with a small fig leaf—to change the negative vibes she feels and to commemorate the ritual. She leaves just five minutes short of four hours.

The route home involves a shortcut down steps that lead her back to North Beach. She wants another coffee to mask the sour taste in her mouth. As she passes Zack Luce's house, she smiles at the thought of him. He's a spritely old gentleman.

But then, before she can help it, other thoughts creep in. What if something happens to him while she's working in his home? He's in his eighties, after all. What if she shows up one day to find him lying on the floor—dead or needing help? She breathes deeply to slow down these fears, reminding herself to simply be grateful for the new client. She reminds herself that she cannot control outcomes, and continues on her way.

"You're back."

"Yeah, those double espressos are killers. I'm about to explode." Lavinia clutches her heart, waiting for her breath to regulate.

He looks at her. "You look frazzled, like you've had one too many."

"My mind's playing tricks on me. That's all."

"I got it." He hands her a small cup of dark coffee.

"Busy?" she says, regaining some stability.

"Always busy, especially because of the afternoon tiramisu crowd."

"True to its name—pick-me-up."

"You know Italian?"

"My native language," she says, taking a sip of the dark coffee.

"I wouldn't have guessed."

She shrugs. "I moved to San Francisco before I was five."

"Did you grow up around here?"

"Yup, right around corner."

"Did you learn Chinese?"

"A little. *Ni hao*. That's it!"

He grins. "I'm impressed. So where are you off to now?"

"Home to the Mission."

"So you left the 'hood."

"I did, after elementary school." She lifts her cup. "But not the espresso." She hands her new barista friend a colorfully wrapped Bubblicious.

"I'm growing fond of this custom of yours," he says, reaching for the gift.

"Thanks," she says.

"How'd this get started? You tipping with gum."

"I don't know. I guess I started keeping a stash in my skirt pockets at school when I was little, to give as gifts when other kids did something for me."

"Hmmm . . ." he says, eyeing her with curiosity.

"Hey, Barista, let's keep this line moving," a patron yells from the back of the line that's forming.

Lavinia steps to the side and hears the next man in line whisper to the barista, "The girl with the tuxedo is pretty cute! The shoes, too."

Lavinia looks down at her feet and then brushes the slim lapels of her jacket with her free hand. She bought it at a vintage shop on Haight Street and wears it every day.

The barista nods. "She's vintage chic."

Lavinia turns to see him blushing.

"Come on!" comes a sneer from the man in the back.

"Hold on! Patience, buddy," the barista calls out. People in the line cheer in agreement.

Lavinia giggles, folds her hand around his, then turns to leave, facing the customers in line, feeling much better than when she entered. Was he flirting with her? And "vintage chic"! She likes that.

Walking through her old neighborhood on the flats of North Beach, she stops at a local bakery, caught by the smells of the warm yeast that's escaped outside and is now trapped in her nostrils. She imagines the bubbling and rising of the soft dough. She looks inside and sees five-year-old Lavinia as a first grader with a pleated skirt, white ankle socks, and shiny shoes.

She stares at the five-year-old standing on tiptoes, her nose level with the floured breadboard, her hair parted in the middle and pulled into two gleaming pigtails. Tony, the baker, is up to his elbows in flour, kneading a plump hunk of dough. She is waiting for him to see her, hoping he does and hoping he doesn't.

Look, he hasn't seen me yet. Only when my hand edges over the rim of the board, crawling slowly like an itsy bitsy spider does he scream, "Who is stealing my dough?"

I jump.

Then he raps my hand gently. I laugh out loud and begin the game again.

Lavinia watches through the window of the bakery and laughs at her younger self playing, wondering how long they went on like this before Aunt Rose realized she was not in her room; that she would be late for school; that she had taken off for the bakery downstairs by herself. *And where was Aunt Rose anyway, that I could sneak away like that?*

And the gum? She must have had a book bag or lunch box for the gum. At least a pocket.

Heading to Grant Avenue, she cuts through Chinatown to catch a bus on Market, and passes the meat market on Grant where ducks hang from hooks, their heads all facing east. She feels a taste of disgust, reminding her of Naples, where meat always hung on hooks at the outdoor stalls and scared her.

This memory makes her think of Nina's stained blouse, Don's note, and her mother's vehemence. She takes the note from her pocket and throws it in the gutter. Whomever the note was meant for, she decides, it's not right.

When she arrives home it's still light out. Located on the east side of Valencia Street, her apartment was once Sal's storefront insurance office; he converted it into an artist live-in space for Lavinia before he left. Sal, Rose, and Lavinia used to live in the flat above the office, until Rose got sick with lung cancer. By then, Lavinia was spending most nights at Andy's. When Sal closed up shop after Rose died a year ago, he closed the upstairs apartment, too—took down the navy canvas awning out front because he didn't want anyone thinking he was still in business to be a bother for Lavinia. Then he left. Lavinia had not been upstairs since then.

She unlocks the door and enters the vast open space with its newly painted walls. The color, called Payne's Gray, is a dark blue-grey; it's her favorite neutral color, the color of the knitted blue cap and skirt her stuffed doll, Raggedy, wore. Lavinia used to love holding her, smelling her. In fact, she went with Sal to Benjamin Moore to watch the color consultant mix ultra marine and burnt sienna to create this cool-and-warm color, all the time remembering her Raggedy. Aunt Rose was mean to her, taking away her doll like that.

The walls meet the sunset-orange hardwood floor in a clean sweep from the high white ceilings. Overhead track lights warm the empty walls. She walks to the back of the long, narrow room—twenty by forty feet—to the small den, adjacent to an even smaller kitchen, that serves as her bedroom. There's a double mattress on the floor.

She keeps this room dark, but not quiet. She always has music playing, especially during the transitions between day and night, like now, late afternoon. She puts on her favorite CD and changes out of her tuxedo outfit, moving the small stack of fig leaves from her pocket to the fridge as she does. Then she hops into spandex capris and a flowing nylon shirt—her other favorite outfit, the one she reserves for her private space.

She begins to dance. After beginning slowly, the music builds to a crescendo and comes down to stillness, bringing her easily into the night. As she dances, she thinks about the barista and wonders if he has a girlfriend. The music is calling Lavinia to listen, to interact with the beat of the drum and the pulse of the rhythm. She moves through the large room, riding the dance waves, letting this vibration carry her through and around the space, letting the music take her through a world of rhythms. Dancing with her shadow, she closes her eyes and imagines herself dancing with the barista.

Chapter 3:

TAMALES AND TEQUILA
AND RAGGEDY

"**S**ix *tamales de elote*, my mother's specialty!"
Lavinia hears Kinky's shout at the door as her friend lets herself into the apartment with the spare key and walks to the back of the long room. Waking from her dance reverie, Lavinia is happy to see Kinky in her studio. Kinky is wearing a mid-length skirt and Toms, her elementary school teacher uniform. Her hair is tightly curled around her beaming face.

Lavinia and Kinky met at State as freshmen. They were in a teacher preparatory program with ESL certification. Lavinia admired Kinky's pluckiness, the way she spoke about kids in the barrio and her own family, and how everyone seemed to be her family. And Lavinia felt Kinky's love for her. She remembers the day Kinky took her eyebrow pencil and penciled in a little chocolate chip–size birthmark on her own upper lip. They laughed and laughed. Lavinia attached herself to Kinky, and since that day they've been best friends. Kinky has seen her through Aunt Rose dying, her breakup with Andy, and Uncle Sal leaving. Kinky has taken care of her since they became friends, and she's continued nurturing her even since Lavinia dropped out of school, not graduating or getting the ESL certificate.

"Let's eat on the back patio—the weather is grand," Lavinia says. She grabs two plates and two forks and opens the back door onto a small yard with a single fig tree that produces twice yearly.

Her friend follows her outside, drops the tamales on the center of the round lawn table in front of the fig. "They're still hot," Kinky tells her. "My mother sends a *besito*. She misses you."

"Hot tamales and a kiss. Who could ask for anything more?" Lavinia leans over and gives her friend a kiss on the cheek. "I miss her, too."

"Tequila," Kinky says, taking two shot glasses and a skinny metal container from her oversized jacket and holding it out in front of Lavinia, who plucks it from her hands.

"Boy, can I use this. Just enough for me." She winks at Kinky as she pours the amber liquid equally into each glass. "Let's eat. All I had today was bubblegum and too many espressos."

The two friends sit in aluminum armchairs and sip the tequila, letting its warmth run through their veins.

"What a day." Kinky sighs as she cuts a tamale into small squares. "The kid I tutor over on Valencia—you know, the boy who doesn't say too much? He actually wrote a story."

"Armando?"

"Yeah, he wrote a story about a boy who walked through the Sonoran Desert all the way to San Diego."

"You think it's true."

"Of course!" Kinky looks at Lavinia. "Where do you think we get our stories? Plus, he's only twelve years old."

"I don't know. What about dreams? Or fantasies?"

"These kids I tutor are quiet. I wonder if it's because English is their second language, or . . ." Kinky brushes her fingers through her tight curls as if she's pulling a Slinky, unwinding and unwinding, and looks at Lavinia.

". . . or they've been traumatized." Lavinia finishes the sentence then bites into a succulent tamale, tasting the spices, as if to accent what she's just said.

"Lavinia, you are so smart." Kinky shakes her head. "I wish you were teaching school this year at Bryant."

"Yeah, we could chew gum during the break . . . or drink tequila," Lavinia says, making light of a small discomfort she feels inside.

Kinky seems to notice, as usual. "Why'd you go and quit when you were so close to finishing?" she asks.

"I'd prefer not to go there now," Lavinia answers, looking directly at her.

"Well, I'm ready to listen when you decide to face all you've given up. You're a *desaparecida*. It's like someone kidnapped you."

"Kinky, quit!"

They eat in silence. Lavinia thinks of the phrase she heard her mother say today in her daydream so clearly—*Leave me alone*—but still, there's some truth in what Kinky says. Lavinia chews on her food until she calms herself.

"Speaking of writing," she says, "I found a note in one of my client's pocket today. A note, all folded and crinkled, saying, 'Meet me at Velo Rouge.'"

"I know that place. It's a small restaurant near USF."

"Don't know it." Lavinia returns to her tamale.

"Yeah, a block or two away. You think that note was meant for you, Lavinia?"

"I don't know. It's just the way the guy looked at me, you know? The way he stared at my birthmark the first day he set eyes on me." She pushes her plate away and puts her hands on her stomach, feeling a little nauseous. "I've been wondering about it. Even though I know it wasn't meant for me, it makes me scared."

"Are you afraid of him?" Kinky asks.

"I'm not afraid of Nina, I trust her . . . but him, I don't know. He's disgusting. Maybe worse."

"You gotta trust your gut."

"Yeah, he was so gross! But seriously, there's no way the note was for me. I don't know why I'm tripping out." Lavinia looks to Kinky for support.

"Don't worry, we all do that," Kinky says, ever empathetic.

"I guess." Lavinia sips her tequila. "Thank you, I feel better." She looks at the tamale she's just pushed away. "I met a possible new client today. A quirky old man who lives off Chestnut Street in North Beach. Nice guy. Plushy rugs."

"He doesn't want you to wash rugs, does he?"

"No. The usual." She pulls the tamale back toward her and takes a bite. "Oh, this tamale is to die for. I'm so hungry." They eat quietly for a while. Then Lavinia says, "He's hard of hearing, just lost his wife. An old dude with a daughter who is a doctor."

"Nice."

"Have you been around very old people, Kinky?"

"Only my grandparents. They live in Mexico. When I visited, I met a whole village of elderlies. Of course, Mama feels old in her ways."

"And . . ." Lavinia looks at her friend, wanting to hear something that will make her feel more at ease around the eighty-year-old.

"They know a lot. Why?"

"I don't know. It makes me nervous, that's all. To be working in his home. What if something happens to him?"

"Like what?"

"Like what if he falls? Or what if he dies?" She winces as she vocalizes to Kinky the fear that's been nagging at her.

"Like Rose," Kinky says.

Lavinia is stunned. "No, not like that. She was sick for a long time," she finally says.

"Well, it's still very close to you, and maybe it's making you afraid he'll die on you, too."

"Who's a smartass now?" Lavinia asks, not wanting to think about Rose's slow and painful death. But she is. She sees her gray skin and yellow eyes, feels her clammy flesh, and then remembers the smells of decay. She pushes her plate away again, feeling nauseated.

She has to wait a while, gathering herself, before she continues talking about her work.

"I just don't know what to expect. That's all. Anyway, he wants Wednesday afternoons, and that would mean two jobs, back to back, so I'm not sure how I'm going to swing that, unless I move Nina to another day. And she won't change."

"Wouldn't be so bad to go to North Beach twice a week."

Lavinia sucks her fingers, "No, especially since I met this guy today at Café Falcone. He makes great espresso. He gets it just right. Cute, too." She pulls her plate back and takes another bite of the tamale, letting a soft hum of enjoyment come out through her lips. "This tamale is so good, Kinky." She licks her lips. "Your mom is super to have made these for us. I would have had to offer you tuna from a can."

"I figured. Just protecting myself. So tell me more about the guy."

"I don't even know his name. An intelligent face, long straight nose, dimples."

Kinky sips from her small glass of the golden liquid. "Is he interested?"

"Maybe." Lavinia raises her eyebrows, withholding the information about their flirtation from her friend on purpose. She wants to unfold it slowly. She drinks, feeling her insides warm up to the idea of someone being sweet on her and to the gentle, balmy weather.

They sit silently together, waiting for moonrise over the small patio, letting the sounds of the night surround them.

"Oh, it's the way he noticed me. I felt this immediate connection with him." She impulsively touches her heart with the palm of her right hand.

Kinky grins. "Come on, you more than noticed him, too," she teases.

"I went back there three times," Lavinia confesses. "And the last time we held up the line."

"Cool. I'm excited for you, Lavinia."

"I love hanging out like this, Kinky. This is it, girl talk. You and me." Lavinia reaches out her glass. The two friends clink their tumblers and sip tequila; the warm night caresses them. "Did you ever want to have a sister?"

"Yeah, growing up I wished I had a sister. I hated being an only child. It felt like some kind of disease," Kinky says, cuddling into her friend.

"Yeah, or like being an orphan," Lavinia says, feeling a lump in her throat.

"Are you okay, Vinnie?"

"Yeah." She nearly chokes on her words.

"You had Rose and Sal," Kinky says, squeezing her hand.

"Yes, and I lost them, too."

"You are mourning Rose, is that it?" Kinky says again. "And that awful way she went." She looks up behind her, toward the upstairs flat.

"Awful, but at least she wasn't alone! I do mourn her, I think. And I'm grateful for everything she and Sal did for me. But if only . . ." Lavinia stops herself, afraid of going down that slope, but can't help but continue. "If only I'd kept on asking Sal about my mother's story."

But what if she'd heard from him that she was responsible for whatever happened to her mother? She was petrified of that. Didn't kids feel that way? Maybe she didn't want to know some horrible truth. Maybe that's why she never pestered Sal and Rose to tell her.

"I like it when you call me Vinnie." Lavinia laughs. "Remember how Sal called me Vinnie?"

Kinky nods.

"Maybe if I had a sister she would've called me that, too," Lavinia says, coming out of her worry.

"I think so. What do you remember about your mom?"

Lavinia leans back into her friend and closes her eyes. She sees white clothes sunning on a line, fresh and bright, and her mother's smiling face. She remembers her warm and inviting eyes the most. She hears whirling water in a pool where Mama is kneeling, kneading a small dress in her hands. She sees a small child filling a red pail with water and splashing her tiny hands in it. Her mother laughs and sings out, "Lavinia Lavinia," which makes her feel so special.

"You have a smile on your face a mile long, Vinnie."

"Yeah, I'm just thinking about my mom, the sound of her voice, her laugh, her eyes. But today I remembered something new." She tells Kinky about her mom's strong voice to someone she calls Papa, refusing him, telling him she won't do something he's asking.

"Papa would be her father, no?" Kinky says.

Lavinia nods. "I don't know much more. I snapped out of the memory. I couldn't catch it. It's always the same: sweet, and then some rumble!"

"What was her name?"

"Angela."

"Nice. Did Sal tell you anything about her death and why you came here to California so quickly after? It seems odd to me, that's all."

"I stopped asking." Lavinia can hear Sal's emphatic voice now: *"Lavinia, don't ask anymore!"*

"I never had the courage to ask about it after those first few months, actually." Lavinia shakes her head, feeling sorry for herself, and sorry for Sal at the same time. "He wouldn't tell me much. Just that she died at twenty-one and he came to take me away to this safe home."

"That's weird," says Kinky. "He didn't tell you what happened!"

"Odd, isn't it?"

"Pretty young, huh," Kinky acknowledges. "Can you imagine? Being pregnant in high school?" She stares up at the moon for a minute. "But did Sal ever tell you anything about the day you were born? Surely he was there, or heard stories. Any pictures?" Kinky seems agitated on Lavinia's behalf. "I have a ton of baby pictures."

"No pictures of me as a baby. Only one from right when I left." Lavinia feels sadder and heavier than ever. This loss is another to add to her cart. She sighs. "Yup, no pictures of me as a baby, and never any mention of how she died."

"That's a shame."

"He just always said it was a tragedy, and that she was too young to die. Once he told me she made a mistake and she didn't deserve to die that way, but when I followed up with him, he wouldn't say anything more about it."

"So sad," Kinky said, mirroring Lavinia's thoughts exactly. Lavinia could see how exasperated her friend was and that made her feel better and bolder—but also she felt some regret. Perhaps she should have pressed Sal harder. In fact, the more she thought about it, the more she felt she had the right to know.

"You know," Lavinia said, "the first time I heard Sal say the word 'tragedy' I thought he was saying 'raggedy,' that Mama's life was raggedy. When I was young I thought they were talking about the soft little blue-gray doll with a red apron I carried around with me. I brought it with me to San Francisco from Naples. It was all worn and pilled like a cashmere sweater gets. The satin ribbon around her skirt was torn at the edges, but still shiny and smooth. Rose kept pressing me to hand it over to her so she could wash the thing. She even tried to bribe me to throw it away for a new pretty pink doll, but I could never part with her. Rose meant no harm, but she misunderstood what it meant to me. She was a no-nonsense aunt. She was . . . pretty mean to me."

"Maybe she never had a doll or a stuffed animal she loved like that," Kinky says.

"But for me the doll meant so much more. If I cuddled it close, I could feel Mama, smell and even hear her. It was the only connection I had to her."

"What happened to it?"

"Raggedy disappeared one day. I think Rose took her."

"Why?" Kinky says.

"I can't remember, but I went crazy with worry. I asked Rose every day for three days if she'd help me find her. I pestered her, and she got mad at me. She turned all red that third day and shouted for me to stop it. That night when Sal got home from work, I asked him, too. He helped me search for Raggedy, but we never found her. I hated the Barbie Rose gave me as a replacement, and I hated her for stealing Raggedy." She stares at the ground. "Worse, I never forgave her."

Kinky tightens her grip around her friend. There's nothing more to say. They sit like this and Lavinia allows herself to sob. It's a while before she can breathe evenly again. Soon after, the first chilled air of the evening comes in and they move into the studio.

Chapter 4:

WORKING LIKE A DOG

At seven thirty the following morning, Lavinia wakes up with coffee percolating in her brain. Did she and Kinky really sit up till close to midnight last night? She thinks about her friend, who's already been at school, prepping for her third graders, for the past half hour. She pictures all those kids running to get to her, excited to begin the day. She misses that. She recalls her student teaching, the children excited to have her as their teacher, running up to her, showing their work—a good drawing or a simple addition problem they just solved—smiling, and saying, "Miss Lavinia, look at mine." How children want attention and love to please. Both.

As she gets dressed, she puts away these thoughts, planning her schedule to include one full day in North Beach—that'll be just right. She can almost hear the barista's voice in her head . . . but first, her job in the Mission.

A half hour later, Lavinia is walking down Valencia Street, which is already alive and moving. In the midst of the street action—voices calling to each other as kids on watch whistle, a seeming alarm code—she's reminded of how ground squirrels watch their territory for intruders too and *kuk kuk kuk* to one another. *Am I an intruder?*

Small groups of teenagers in colorful T-shirts and baggy jeans smoke in doorways. Mothers with shiny black hair, dressed in flowing skirts and sandals, push their babies in strollers. Lavinia sidesteps past old cars parked on the sidewalks. In this neighborhood, some doors are barricaded with elaborately carved metal fences. Other doors are open, with people sitting on the stoops in front of them. She likes the activity here. It's the way North Beach used to be when she was growing up there, when families lived in the neighborhood and did their business close to the street. Now North Beach is too commercial, but at least the Mission still has that old San Francisco feeling. She's grateful to live here.

On Folsom Street, industrial buildings replace small multi-family houses. Warehouses with small businesses cram together against other converted live-work spaces. George Levine, a forty-six-year-old sculptor from New York City, lives on the second floor of a former factory. He called Lavinia twelve months ago to ask about her laundry service, having gotten her name from Dr. Brady. Because he works at the far end of his studio, he gave her a key so she could let herself in. He told her he did not want to leave his creativity, *his zone*, to unlock the door for her when she comes.

Her job involves pulling up his canvas tarps and taking them to be laundered in an industrial washer and dryer twice a week. He has eight tarps; each time, she's supposed to take four to be laundered.

Today, as Lavinia unlocks the heavy metal gate, a homeless man walks past, pushing a shopping cart filled with cans. She closes the gate and walks two flights up the cement stairwell of George's building.

He rents the entire second floor of the former box factory. His workspace includes the clay room with a large kiln that heats up to over two thousand degrees; the drying room; a workspace where he sculpts; and a large, open-floor living area similar to her space. As she walks through the apartment side, sparsely furnished, she hears music. George is playing his familiar oldies. She knows this one, the Beatles' "A Hard Day's Night."

Humming as she opens the door, she feels the heat from inside the studio. George, at the far side of the room, wears shorts as he kneads the clay. She watches the way he throws a slab to the rhythm of the music. Bare-chested and wearing flip-flops, he wildly slams down a hunk of clay, using the energy of the music to help him wedge the material. This habit of his always makes her laugh so she stands there in the doorway, watching, until he sees her, at which point he stops what he's doing, wipes his hands on the black cloth on his wedging table, and walks toward her, smiling.

"Hello, Lavinia," he says, reaching for her hand.

"Hi, George, nice music. I love this song."

"Yeah, me, too. It's good for kneading clay, too." He smiles again.

"Looks like you're 'working like a dog,'" she jests.

He laughs. "Ever try it?"

"Working like a dog?" she asks, thinking he's trying to make a joke.

"No, kneading clay," he says more seriously now, looking toward his wedging table, where a slab of chocolate brown mud rests.

"Not since kindergarten," she says.

George's eyes glow as if he's divining something. "Want to try?" he asks, taking her hands. Before she knows what's

happening, the two of them are waltzing around the perimeter of the cement table, twirling. He's done this before, so she's
not totally surprised. She doesn't mind, either. She appreciates
George's zest for life.

He holds her in a waltz position until they are both standing
in front of the clay slab. George picks up a delicate clay slicer and
cuts the hunk of clay in half, then slams the bottom half onto the
top half.

His gesture intrigues her. First the slice, then the slam. She
stays still, mesmerized by the beat of the thump on the table,
which seems to be in sync with the next Beatles tune that's loaded:
"All I've Got to Do."

George does this work quickly and with ease, repeating the
gesture over and over, throwing clay onto the hard surface and
kneading it to the beat of the music. He works on and on—cutting slabs, throwing them onto the marble table. All the time his
hands, muddied from the soft and malleable Cassius clay (the
dark brown earth he prefers), work their magic.

"The pressure of one slam on the other releases all the air
from the wedge," he tells her. "Would you like to try it?" He gives
her the hunk and the slicer.

Lavinia holds the wooden handles of the metal slicer and pulls
it through the seamless slab of clay, enjoying the slippery way it
cuts through the brown flesh. Then she picks up one half, the way
George has been showing her, and slams it into the other piece,
listening for the thump. The combination of the smooth, silky feel
of the clay in her hands and the slamming action onto the table
creates a kind of duality in her mind and a relaxation in her body.

"Brava," she hears him cheer.

She can't help but feel satisfied. Yet instinctively, she feels it's
time to go. She has a sense of overstaying her welcome, although

George seems to have indicated anything but that. She wonders if, were she to stay here all day, he'd ever say anything about the laundry. She doubts it. He genuinely seems to enjoy her company, and she feels more comfortable with him than with any of her other clients.

Before stepping away from the table, she carefully places her dusty fingers in her inner pocket, removes a tiny fig leaf she picked from her tree this morning, and places it near the clay when George isn't looking. She wonders if he'll know she left it.

She heads for the bathroom to wash off the deep brown earth from her hands and the sleeves of her hoodie. Then she takes the bag filled with the soiled drop cloths George has deposited by the door for her and heads for the laundromat down the street. She has four hours. Though she prefers working on the premises, she's happy to make an exception since George's laundry facilities don't include industrial-size dryers or washers—and besides he's a little kooky.

She wonders what he creates with all that clay. She's never gotten to see a finished piece of his sculpture.

The air outside cools her down after the dance and the throwing in the hot studio. Lavinia lifts the heavy sack over her shoulder and walks toward the laundromat in her neighborhood, which has one or two heavy industrial washers and dryers. After a few long blocks, the canvas laundry bag pulls on her shoulder so she stops to switch it to the other shoulder.

She walks on 14th Street toward Guerrero, passing trendy new restaurants with the twenty-five-pound sack of drop cloths weighing on her back. She feels like she's Santa—or worse, a junk collector. She hides under her hoodie, hoping she doesn't run into

Andy, who would surely feel pity, if not outright disgust, if he saw her carrying a big bag down the street like a homeless person.

What made him not love me anymore? Why didn't I ask him?

When the scent of coffee pulls her into a café, she drops the sack outside, right in front of the door. She enters the café.

After she downs a double espresso, she feels better; now she has the buzz she needs to carry the sack. She goes outside.

The sack is gone.

Frantically, she looks around the doorway, opens and closes the door, thinking maybe someone brought it inside for her. She's never on the lookout to be robbed; now she realizes she should be. *Fuck! Now what?* She looks in all directions before she sees a man scurrying up 14th Street with the canvas sack on his back. He's loping up the street, swerving under the weight of it.

She rushes after him. "Stop, you stole my bag!" she yells. "Mister, that's my bag!" He turns to look back at her and then increases his speed, running like a mad man, and crosses Mission Street at high speed. Lavinia runs faster but the light turns just as she reaches the intersection.

"You skunk!" She paces in place, waiting for the signal to walk. It's far too busy for her to attempt to run after him, into traffic.

When she finally crosses the street he's nowhere in sight. "Damn," she says out loud as she scurries from one doorway to the next. "Where did he go?" She slams her hand on her hip and stamps her foot. *Damn, damn, damn.*

"You all right, miss?" a man sweeping outside a small convenience store asks.

"No, I'm not! Have you seen a man carrying a large canvas sack?"

"Only in my dreams," he says, laughing.

"A man just stole my laundry from the café."

"Clean or dirty?"

"Dirty." Trying to explain is hopeless. "Never mind."

She unwraps a bubblegum and pops it into her mouth before heading back toward Folsom, hoping she'll find the man before too long. *What a mess! What will I tell George? That someone stole his laundry bag full of expensive ground covers? A lame excuse. I can't even be trusted with an old bag of tarps. I'm even a failure at taking clothes to the laundry.*

She wanders the surrounding streets for another half hour, but to no avail. She feels for the leaf she keeps in her pocket, then realizes she left it for George. She imagines its smoothness, the tiny veins. Then she screws up her courage to go back and tell George what happened.

When she gets to his workspace, she lets herself in, climbs the two flights of stairs again, and opens the door to a now-silent apartment. The music is off. He must have gone for coffee. The only sound comes from an old radiator, a humming of the ventilation system that expels hot air from other artist studios in the building. The fan system is old-fashioned.

"George?" she calls as she walks through a door into a place she's never been before. This place must be where George sculpts. It's an orderly space with rotating platforms and wooden stands on which sit large torsos up to four feet in height. Human-size, naked, and without limbs or heads, they still convey a gesture. The axis of their torsos, each composed in a twist or sway, is compelling.

Farther on, she stops short. The small fig leaf she left earlier has been placed in front of a bust of a woman who looks familiar to Lavinia. She even has a birthmark on her face the size of a mini chocolate chip—and that color, too. The face is young, maybe that of a sixteen-year-old girl; the smile gently curved; the eyes looking down; the lips full. The expression she wears is shy, yet open at the same time. Lavinia touches her upper lip, letting her finger fall on her own birthmark, circles it. Chills run through her body as she stares at the young woman. Slowly she gazes at her beautiful features, expecting to see a puff of breath emerge from her mouth. She reaches out her fingers and touches the young woman's lips, her smooth cheeks; she rests her pinky on the raised bump. Time has stopped and Lavinia feels suspended as she stares, forgetting momentarily that she's looking for George.

Waking up, she continues toward a drying room where several other busts wait to be fired. Astounding clay heads stare at her. A full-bearded man with kind eyes and high, rounded cheeks smiles at her with thin lips surrounded by hair. The clay hair reminds her of spaghetti. Another head is of a child, a girl with hair piled high on her head and long curved brows above opened eyes. Her lips open in a pleasant smile.

She stops longer at the third bust, a twenty-something woman with stray hair that has more fullness on the right side. Her eyes, dark and round, look right at Lavinia. Over her cheek is the small, raised, dark medallion like her own. The same woman from the other room, but she is older and has a dimpled chin and a graceful neck above small rounded shoulders. Again she feels the chills and her hand goes to her own face and lands on her mole. She stands in front of the woman in disbelief.

"Lavinia, is that you?" George is standing near the kiln. "Thank you for the beautiful leaf."

"What? How? This?" Lavinia blurts out. "But I've never modeled for you."

George stands now, facing her. He looks confused.

"But I never gave you my permission."

"That's true."

He moves closer, his hands raised. She steps back, suspicious now. He moves closer again. She moves back and backs herself into a torso, one whose body seems to swivel as if to look at her, whose fluidity seems to make it come alive.

She looks at the sculpture. "This one is nude!" She feels disgusted. "Is that me?" Her mouth opens so that her gum falls out. She stares coldly at George, like fired clay itself. "Is this me, too?" She's now looking toward another nude torso.

"I'm fond of creating sculpture in the image of people I know. That's all."

"But I never posed for you."

"I'm a gestural artist, and I sculpt from memory."

Lavinia screws up her face. "Is that why you wanted to dance with me?" she demands, her voice rising to a tight, squealing pitch. "So you could make a sculpture? I thought you cared for me. I thought I could trust you. But you've been using me for your own benefit."

George reaches his hands toward her.

"Get away. You're a pervert."

She sees his face flush, his eyes grow alert. She puts her hands over her eyes.

"How can you say that, Lavinia?"

"Have you been spying on me at home?" She squirms away from the beautiful work that feels too intimate, too intrusive. The space with all these figures feels too small for her and George's face appears too large. She backs away from him, feeling trapped. She wants to run, to get out of here. She begins to sweat and her chest feels tight. She puts her hand on her shirt, clutching it. He's talking. She doesn't hear his words. She feels dizzy, disoriented. All she wants is air and space. But he's still speaking.

"Of course not, Lavinia. This is art. I'm an artist. And this is the art that I make. I deduce from people."

"Deduce! It feels to me like an abduction. Is this even ethical?"

"Ethical, yes."

"You're immoral then."

"If I used my art to make money then I'd agree with you, but that is not my intention. What if I planned to give them to you as a gift, or to ask your permission to put them in my show?"

"I'd refuse you, of course." She looks away, wanting to leave. But then there is another thing she feels—an intimacy that holds her there in the room with all the faces that look like her. She feels paralyzed, though her heart aches.

George has seen her face, has molded her with his hands, has fashioned the smoothness of her skin without ever touching her. He has sculpted the small blemish and made it beautiful, moving the contours of the earthen clay. He has seen into her soul. No one has ever seen her this way, been this close to her. She can almost hear his heart beating, like soft wings. And yet she can't stand this feeling erupting within her. It feels like she might explode, break open, and even cry. She doesn't want to, so she turns away from him and covers her eyes and mouth with her hands, smothering her silent sobs.

When she comes back, he's looking at her. His eyes are seeing her again.

"Why'd you go and spoil everything? You could have asked me to model for you."

"I didn't want you to see them, not yet," he says.

"When then?"

"In good time."

"On your time, then?"

"Yeah, I guess." He looks at his big plastic watch and says, "You're back sooner than usual. I never expected you so early. You walked in on my space."

"Well, yes, I returned early because a street person stole my pack with your dirty tarps and rags. I came to apologize."

George starts laughing, bending over at the waist. On and on he laughs, hysterically.

"Stop it, George. Please stop it." Her voice tries to catch breath, like a soprano mid-aria.

She storms out.

Chapter 5:

THE TOOL SHED

Walking home Lavinia looks at everyone on the street, feeling less secure. Under normal circumstances, losing a sack of laundry would have sent her into a tailspin, but she's far more upset now about her discovery of the sculptures and her conversation with George. Perhaps she was meant to lose it so that she'd come back and discover those sculptures, see what George had been up to. She feels an odd sense of vindication for her carelessness—but the emotion is complicated by the loss she feels over George. And today she got into his clay for the first time, and it felt so liberating.

Twisted on the inside, with one cord pulling her away from him and the other pulling her toward him, she walks away. The result, a knot in her stomach that aches. A sense of personal violation mixes with the sweet feeling of being seen by another. She's confused.

To protect herself from the gaze of others, she places the hood of her sweatshirt over her head and lowers her face. Her legs feel jittery and her head feels light, making it difficult to beef up her pace. She wants to escape the eyes of other walkers. At the crosswalk she puts her hands in her pockets and finds a tiny leaf she didn't know was there. She takes it out and rubs it on her cheek, letting its coolness seep inside.

As she crosses the busy street, she expects a car to smash into her or for someone to snatch the black purse hanging on her shoulder. Finally home, she rushes inside, double bolts the door, and pulls the curtains tightly closed. She crosses the great, empty space to her small room in the back. The sun sets earlier these days with daylight saving over, robbing an hour of light in the evening. How she longs for spring to come.

She grabs her cell phone and sees a text message from Zack Luce: "You're A-OK, according to Dr. Brady, except maybe for that gum chewing. My time is flexible. Call me."

She sticks her tongue through a wad of gum, making a sheer lining for her tongue, then blows an enormous bubble and opens the door to her patio with its high fences and fig tree. She rushes outside and kneels in front of the sprawling tree, focusing on the roots and the dry mulch strewn carelessly on top, not the way Sal would have liked it. She hasn't cared for it well. That used to be Sal's job.

She looks to the foliage, where the leaves are vibrant but starting to change color. The small pouches of green figs, beautifully shaped, are hard still, not mature. She doubts a fall harvest.

"Will you yield a second crop?" She looks at the wide, sprawling branches, the large leaves. *I'll give you fertilizer and water you.* She waits. Maybe it will shake, or the leaves will whistle in the wind, or one small sack will fall to the ground.

"Tool shed," she hears inside her head. She's shocked. There again: *"Tool shed."* She looks at the tree and then over her shoulder to Uncle Sal's small shed, just tall enough for him to stand. He

built it under the stairs to the second-floor flat. She can see him unlocking it, opening the door, putting on his soiled gardening gloves, pulling out a twenty-pound bag of mulch, the shovel, and finally a small wheelbarrow—the one-wheel type—he so proudly bought at Ace Hardware on sale for $49.

She bends into the dry, neglected soil around the base of the tree and with her fingers scrapes through the hard dirt, making eight-finger tracks. She rakes through the soil until her fingers begin to bleed.

"Feed me."

She gets up and goes over to the shed. The key is still on a hook. She opens the padlock and removes the bag of mulch and the other tools and goes back to the roots, where she scoops out the moist black organic mulch and spreads it onto the finger-raked roots, piling it four inches high.

Then she fills the watering pail and begins to sprinkle water onto the mulch. She watches the sprays of water seep into the earth stuff and senses a sigh of relief. She doesn't know if it's hers or the tree's.

She pours herself some wine and sits outside on one of the aluminum chairs, waiting for Kinky, feeling satisfied . . . until she remembers what she saw at George's. Then she complains to herself that it's too warm for November, not at all right for San Francisco. "Earthquake weather," the locals call it, because of the famous quake that came on a hot night in October in 1989.

Last night a large golden moon peeked over the fence for her and Kinky. She wants the moonlight to shine on the fig tonight as much as for her and Kinky. Looking back and forth between the fence and the ground, she waits and grinds her teeth. She lies down to calm her nerves, stretched out on the pavement next to the wet mulch, searching the sky. Faraway birds caw and mingle with the sounds of traffic and people talking in low voices. The rumbling sounds of men's voices and a dog barking are broken by the ring of her cell phone. She simultaneously hears pounding at her door. She rushes to make her way across the studio.

There's Kinky, small and round and hidden in her oversized jacket, standing in front of the door with her cell in one hand and a brown paper bag in the other. Lavinia hopes she brought tequila. She unbolts the latch.

"What's with the lock?"

"Some creep stole the bag of George's laundry today."

"What?"

"A long, ridiculous story."

"Sorry."

Lavinia frowns. "What's worse than the thief is what I discovered at George's art studio."

"Oh, god, what now?"

Lavinia shakes herself to get the bugs she imagines to be swarming around her face and body off. She feels dirty.

"I need to shower, Kinky. Let me do that and then I'll tell you the whole story, okay?" She holds up her dirty fingers, which are also streaked with lines of blood.

Her friend looks at her with concern and nods. "The tequila will be here when you're done."

"You're an angel." Lavinia runs the shower. "Help yourself. My glass is outside."

She meets Kinky on the patio twenty minutes later, wearing a towel on her head. It's warm enough that she can let it air dry tonight.

She places her glass under the spout of the tequila flask. "Cheers." They taste the yellow liquid and sit quietly with the rising moon.

"What happened today?" Kinky finally asks.

Lavinia sighs. "When I came back earlier than usual to tell George about the missing tarps, I ran into some stuff that clearly wasn't intended for me to see."

She describes the first grouping of life-sized sculptures—the heads displayed in a circle—and how one of them seemed so familiar to her. And then about the other bust, a woman about her age with a mole on her face and a cleft in her chin.

"Me." She touches the mole on her upper lip.

"No!" Kinky is properly outraged, and Lavinia feels some relief.

"Then I saw another torso that was also me. A life-sized me, minus the limbs. Can you imagine?"

"You never sat for him?"

"No way, but I've danced with him before. And today he showed me how to knead clay to get out the air bubbles, and I loved it." Lavinia sighs and lowers her head so far that her chin touches her chest. She closes her eyes. She keeps still for some moments before saying, "I feel so exposed, like he's seen me too closely. He's a voyeur, and he's exposed me without my permission."

"I get it. I'm so sorry. You know I'd feel the same way," Kinky says. "But I'm surprised. George has been your favorite."

"Not anymore! And worse, he didn't see anything wrong with it. He just said he was an artist. He laughed!" She's getting outraged again as she recalls the encounter.

"He laughed?" Kinky's voice raises a notch as she asks the question.

"I don't know why. He didn't take me seriously. So I left . . . I had to walk out to get my breath. I'm not working for him anymore, obviously." Lavinia's voice shoots up with a high-pitched edge. She drains the glass of tequila.

"Maybe when you calm down you should talk to him about it," Kinky offers. "There must be some explanation."

"I don't think I can do that."

"How did you leave it, then?"

"I just left and came home. I didn't even take the cash. Just rushed home." Lavinia looks into the eyes of her friend—dark, warm and welcoming eyes. They compel her to tell her more, so Lavinia adds the other layer she's been dealing with, this feeling of tenderness she can't explain. "I don't hate him," she tells her friend. "It's something I can't explain. The way he taught me how the clay talked this morning. He acts like he genuinely cares for me. And I could see from the sculptures, too, that he does. It got all confusing! I mean, he's never acted weird. It's not sexual. It's something else. Maybe it is just his art . . ."

"Oh, Vinnie, I'm so sorry. I love you." Kinky wraps her arms around her. "You look so far away."

"I know. I'm sorry. It seems I can't shake my past."

How has she lived all these years so alone? She misses Sal—even Rose. They were her constant adoptive parents, and now they abandoned her. Why did they adopt her? Why was she whisked away from her birthplace? What she does know is that Sal loved her mother so much that every time Lavinia asked about her, he cried like a baby. Is that why she stopped asking him? She supposes she wasn't ready to bear his sadness, and yet now her questions eat her up. What happened to her mother? Did Sal know her father? Is he dead or alive?

Kinky gets up, goes into the kitchen, and returns with the brown bag. "Mama made squash empanadas." She takes them out of the bag. They're wrapped tightly in cellophane packs, two in each.

"Thank heavens for your mother, or I would starve to death."

"She misses your visits. She sent Mexican chocolate for dessert."

"I miss her, too."

They each unwrap their packages and eat in silence.

As Lavinia swallows her last bite of empanada, she says, "Kinky, can you stay again tonight? I feel a little shaky."

"Of course. I brought my jammies," Kinky says, smiling.

They sit and wait for the moon to rise.

Lavinia wakes up later in her own bed to the hoot of an owl. It's still dark. She doesn't even remember getting there. Her head feels clamped. *Too much tequila.* Kinky's arm is spread across her shoulders, protective. Lavinia listens to her friend's soft, whirring breath at exhalation. Outside, a car speeds by. The owl hoots again, and then comes a response from another one far away, like the way Kinky responds to her. Lavinia touches her friend's outstretched arm, noticing how the moon overhead casts a luminous light on her, reflecting silver dust on her beautiful brown skin. Moon dust magic, it is. Lavinia may not have a sister, but Kinky is her sister at heart.

She lets the moonlight caress her, knowing that as a child she would have been drawn to this same perfect moon. One moon. The moon didn't change just because she moved halfway across the world, away from her birth parents. The same moon comforts her as it might have comforted her dear parents. The thought that they, too, once gazed at the moon, experiencing its silver gifts, makes her want to see them. *Can they see me now?*

Lavinia imagines her mother sending food on an evening like this, the way Señora Montoya does. But not *empanadas*. She would send *pappardelle Napoletana*. Or pizza or cannoli. Foods she loves to eat. Her mother would send enough for Kinky, too.

Lavinia falls asleep in the bosom of the silvery moon mother with her best friend beside her.

After Kinky leaves this morning, Lavinia places a call to Zack and they arrange a time. He tells her he'll meet her at the house at eight and can go over the arrangements. The good news is he can change the day so she'll have the place to herself. "Eight, then?" he asks.

"Yes. I'll be there," she assures him. She breathes deeply, relieved she doesn't have to ask Nina to change her day.

She puts on her headphones and listens to some new age music intermingled with Nina Simone's deep rich voice while she gets dressed. Its bass quality contrasts with her own high-pitched voice and calms her. Lavinia wants to imitate that voice. She holds her nose and then sings along, hoping for the same effect. Maybe if she smoked. She'll buy a pack later today and it will make her look tougher, stronger, she's sure. It will help her ward off thieves, George's glances, Nina's husband staring at her chocolate mole.

For now she lights a match. The flame buoys her up and enlarges itself as if it is a dragon protector-torch she needs to blow them all off, to keep her safe. She imagines the brave warrior Brunhilde in Wagner's *Die Walkure*, who is put in a trance and protected by a ring of fire. She wants that for herself. To be protected.

Chapter 6:

THE NAME

Standing in front of Zack's house in North Beach, Lavinia presses the bell with a minute to spare. He lets her in. At precisely 8:00 a.m. she reaches his hallway and hears a chorus of chimes, gongs, and bells welcoming her.

Passing the bookcases that line the walls, she asks Zack, "Have you read all these books?" Then, stopping in front of a tall bookcase, she muses, "They're all about time."

"Theoretical physics is my vocation," he responds, nodding.

She's not sure exactly what that means, so she points one book out. "Have you read this one?"

"Of cours-s-e, all of them, but I don't remember when, so I start all over regularly. Do you know, I learn something new each time I read one? New eyes-s-s."

Lavinia hadn't noticed the wall of books between the entryway and the living room on her first visit. Zack's collection rests on shelves from floor to ceiling.

He surveys his library with a bright look on his face. "My first love, after Elsa," he says. But he doesn't dwell too long. "You want to see the laundry facility?"

She follows him through the living room to a small laundry room.

"Elsa wanted a Miele washer," he says.

"Honey," she says, staring at the smart-washer-and-dryer combo. Shelves above the washer contain various detergents and bleaches, stain removers, and spray starch. Whether or not Zack catches her reference to the Italian word for honey, he ignores it. He follows her gaze to the starch.

"That's for the blue tablecloth?" she asks.

"She used to starch and iron it every week, while I did the whites." His voice catches.

"Elsa sounds like someone I would have liked to know."

He looks away, sniffling, then takes a hanky from his pants pocket and passes it over his nostrils. He's wearing navy velour pants with two white stripes down the legs. On his way out, he grabs a black zippered canvas sport bag and a Giant's baseball cap. Why Lavinia cringes when she sees that hat on top of his old head she doesn't know. It doesn't fit her image of him, a preppy gentleman engineer.

He seems to have caught her expression because he offers, seemingly by way of apology, "A gift from Margaret. She wants to protect my lily-white skin. Precancerous growths. Silly to worry at my age."

"Sorry about that. I just didn't picture you wearing a baseball hat, Mr. Luce. Maybe a golf hat."

"I'd rather that, too. I like your sense of fashion. And call me Zack." He opens the door and then looks back at her. "I'll let myself in about noon. I imagine you'll be done by then, but leave whenever you're done. I don't need you to watch the clock."

Just then, the clocks in the living room chime on the quarter hour.

"*Ciao,*" he says.

When he's gone, Lavinia sits in his study/living room looking at titles in his collection: *From Cradle to Cradle, Seven Arrows, The Golden Bough*. She doesn't recognize any of them. The common thread of evolution runs through them, the evolution of time. Is it man in cyclical time? She's never thought of time that way. She focuses on the clocks of every variety and size, wondering what these intruding clock faces have to do with anything. The tall grandfather clock with the roman numerals and large shiny hands, the one that gives her a sense of dread— its deep ticks and gongs seem to breathe with her, making her aware of how shallow her breath is. She takes one long, deep breath and moves along to explore the many family photos that decorate the room.

Zack and Elsa sit on a picnic blanket, laughing; a wedding picture with her in a white suit and a pillbox hat with a tiny veil over her eyes and Zack with white creased slacks and a tailored jacket. White shoes, too. On the fireplace mantle sits a photo of Margaret as a baby, held by Zack; another of her as a toddler; and one from elementary school. Then Margaret appears in a cap and gown, standing between her parents, a wide smile of accomplishment spread across her face. Margaret's skin is fair, her hair is light. She stands tall and thin. In a current picture with Zack, she looks about fifty. She links her arm around his waist. Lavinia likes her wholesome looks and the way she resembles Zack. Margaret is as tall as her father and seems happy beside him.

That familiar homeless feeling overcomes Lavinia, resting behind her eyes like a ghost. She's suddenly envious of Margaret, for having a relationship like this with her parents, for completing all these milestones Lavinia has never known. She smiles at the images to chase away her sadness.

In a slight fog she turns her gaze away from the photos, orienting herself toward the tasks at hand. She surveys the apartment like an animal marking the ins and outs of a new space, sniffing it out before she begins her cleansing ritual. She washes her hands, beginning what seems to her a dedicated act of purification.

In the bathroom shower, she finds bathing caps hung alongside bath towels. On the showerhead hangs a Speedo swimsuit and goggles. A swimmer. That makes sense to her; it accounts for his lean, tall body type. She immediately delves in, filling the water basin, then adding the suds before hand washing this paraphernalia. Performing her prescribed cleansing routine, knowing what is expected, makes her feel more grounded. But more than that, she believes she is participating in a solemn ritual. A rite of service—or is it a sacred ceremony?

Then she walks into his bedroom, a large room shielded from the sun. Like her, Zack seems to prefer to sleep in a darkened room. His bedside table is piled with books and magazines about the Long Now Foundation. She wonders what they do, so she picks up one of the magazines and skims it. She reads that Danny Hillis is the founder of the Long Now Foundation. There's a picture of him. He looks young, not too much older than her. With others, she reads, Hillis has conceived of a clock that will ring every day for ten thousand years. How strange, she thinks, and *who cares?*

She reads on. "We are at the very beginning of time for the human race. But there are tens of thousands of years in the future."

Suddenly, she feels dizzy. All this time on her hands boggles her mind. She sits down on the side of the bed and holds her head in her hands, wondering how she can bear tens of thousands of years without her mother. When she recovers, she pulls creamy white sheets from his bed. The Egyptian cotton is soft to her touch. She rubs the fabric across her chin then pulls the feather pillows from their covers and fluffs up the comforter. She considers how wasteful it is to wash the sheets when only one side of the bed gets used. As she carries the sheets to the laundry room, she passes another quiet but brighter bedroom with sun oozing through a half-opened door. She peeps in to find what looks like a child's room. Flowers and trees color the bedspread and matching curtains; a white desk and a blue striped easy chair and matching ottoman perch upon a soft green pile rug. She wonders if he's kept the décor Margaret favored as a child and again feels touched by this sign of fatherly connection. If only she had this.

In the laundry room she sorts the whites from the darks and places the darks in the washer, but not before searching the pockets for papers or tissues. Her Kleenex-can-wreak-havoc obsession comes to mind—one tissue messes up an entire load of clothes. The note she found at Nina's house in Don's pocket surely wreaked havoc, in or out of the machine. She can't believe she thought the note was meant for her. There's just no way it could have been. She'd only met the man once, after all.

She reaches inside her own jeans pocket, pulls out a piece of Bubblicious, pops it in her mouth, and places the wrapper back in her pocket. The flavor she loves explodes on her tongue and down her throat and soothes her agitation. There's no way she's going to let Don's lousy behavior corrupt her focus on her important task. *Back to work.*

The morning progresses easily despite the chiming clocks surrounding her, marking the time in her work cycle. And all the books mark time, too. What if she does have all the time in the world, or she is "at the very beginning of time," like the Long Now Foundation says?

When the colored clothes are finally dry, she pulls down the ironing board and sets to ironing. The shirts iron beautifully. The soft fabric meets the steam with its soft purr over the side panels, the back, the sleeves, the cuffs, and finally the collar. What a breeze!

She stays in the apartment until just before noon because she doesn't want to hear the bells chime out again —she especially wants to avoid the grandfather clock's gong, and the cuckoo's singing. It's too much like a chorus of clock beings speaking in some foreign language. Crazy!

She picks up her cash and leaves a tiny fig leaf on the starched and pressed blue tablecloth, right by the flowers.

Walking down Chestnut toward Columbus, she hastens her pace. She enters the now-familiar Falcone Café quietly, eavesdropping on the barista, who hasn't yet noticed her behind the long line of customers. From this vantage point she gets to study him in the same way she peruses her clients' homes, trying to get close but from a distance. She watches how he moves swiftly, with the certain grace of an athlete; how he sways from his waist, side to side, all his vertebrae involved, each one communicating with the next. She figures he's her age, maybe older. His hair is curly and black, more like Kinky's than her own. She didn't notice that before. His eyes are dark and intense, separated by the lovely straight slope of his nose. Some stubble dots his face. Would that bother her if she were to kiss him?

She's imagining their first kiss when she hears his voice.

"You're in the 'hood again," he says, turning. "Mondays. Zack, the timekeeper."

"It's like a church in there with all the bells."

"Of course, he has a house full of clocks." He chuckles. "Are they driving you nuts?"

She hesitates, but decides to tell the truth. "They're weirding me out . . . it's like walking around in a time machine that's going off," she says, flapping her hands.

"You're certainly concerned about time."

"I guess I feel like I'm running out."

"But you have all the time in the world. You're still young," he says.

Lavinia never feels she has all the time in the world—it's always seemed more that time is lost to her. She just looks at her new friend, trying to conjure up something that might make sense to him, or to her, for that matter.

"He's something else, isn't he?" she says, not knowing what else to say. "And the books he reads!"

"What are they about?" he asks.

"Guess," she teases.

"Time?"

She giggles and nods.

He looks toward the back corner of the café. "A double for you today?"

"Yep, a double." The handle on the espresso machine reminds her of Las Vegas. She's never been but she's often dreamed of playing the slots and winning a barrel of money.

The barista sets her small cup on the counter in front of her. She watches his muscular hand on the handle. Lingering, she watches his moves, feels an attraction for his body, likes it, and feels surprised by her reaction.

When there is a lull in customers, he walks back to her, facing her from the other side of the bar. Just looking.

"Do you dance?" she asks, breaking the silence.

"Dance? Well, sometimes. What makes you ask?"

"You have a dancer's body."

"How's that?" Smiling, he moves closer.

She twirls a clump of her hair. "You know. You sway; you're connected."

He approaches even more now, so close his nose almost grazes her face. "How about you?"

"I dance alone in my own space," she says, thinking about how she dances with her shadow.

"Well, let's change that," he says, winking at her.

Lavinia smiles before taking a serious sip of espresso. "I'll consider your offer, Barista. But, I'll need to know your name if we're going dancing."

"Mario," he says. "And yours?"

"My name is Lavinia Lavinia."

"Lavinia Lavinia. First and last?"

"Yes, an old custom in Italy."

"Well, I'm pleased to know you, Lavinia Lavinia. You so fit your name."

"How so?"

"Lavinia was the name of the daughter of King Latinus in Roman mythology."

"Ah, yes, she was a princess. I've heard of her."

"And then a queen. Did you know that Ursula Le Guin wrote a book from Lavinia's point of view, published in 2008?"

"No! Wow. You astound me, Mario. I'll have to go check that out. Thank you."

"You know, Lavinia married Aeneas, the son of Aphrodite," he says.

Lavinia can hardly believe how much he knows about this myth, one that she's never bothered to look into even though it's her namesake. She just stares at him, feeling overwhelmed with happiness.

"Somehow it fits that you're a laundress, Lavinia Lavinia. I'm glad you got a job in the neighborhood."

She smiles. "Me, too."

Chapter 7:

LA QUERENCIA

It's late afternoon, and Lavinia walks in the Mission thinking about Mercedes Montoya, Kinky's mother, who touches a soft place in her heart. It's not just the food she makes; it's something else, too. She quickens her pace, heading for their house on Florida Street. She knows Kinky's not home from work yet, but it's Mercedes she wants to see.

She knocks and waits at the door of the old-style Mission cottage.

Mercedes opens the door. "*Pasa adelante!*" she cries, and greets Lavinia with her usual warm hug before leading her into the den in the middle of the house. "Sit, *mija*," she says, gesturing to a soft chair with round, padded arms. "I have a story for you about the bulls in Spain."

Lavinia is intrigued by Mercedes, who always seems to have just the story she needs to hear. She figures the older woman is gifted in this way.

Mercedes begins with her hands solidly placed on her knees. "*La querencia* is a safe place in the bull ring, the place where the bull goes to stay alive, to stay away from the lance of the matador. But more, *chica*, it's a place to regain his power."

Lavinia stares at the floral plastic oilcloth on the side table. She's not sure what Mercedes is saying, or why she's telling her about bulls and matadors, but she listens.

Mercedes continues, "The matador doesn't like this place because he will not be able to kill the bull if he stays there. But the bull"—she stops to laugh—"he likes it there because he can gather his strength. Sometimes a bull might sit down and won't fight, or he might stay so close to the gate that the matador can't get close to him."

"*La querencia.*" Lavinia says the word slowly, allowing its four syllables to melt on her tongue. "*Querer* means 'to want' in Spanish, doesn't it?"

"The wanting place, *mija*. The bull wants to stay alive and to feel safe and strong, too."

"He knows when he is in danger, then, and does something about it." Lavinia looks down at her intertwined hands.

"Yes, this is the place you will find within yourself. It's the place where we rest in the midst of the turmoil."

"And out of the bull ring?" Lavinia asks. "There's danger there, too."

"Yes." Mercedes nods sagely. "We can even find the safe place here in our lives when we are in the midst of danger."

"I have a hard time finding that place," Lavinia confesses. She feels like Mercedes can see right through her, as if they're talking about what Lavinia is going through, although she hasn't told her anything about it.

"You can find it because it's within you."

"When I eat your great food and hear your stories, I find that place." Lavinia smiles and looks through the doorway toward the kitchen counter, where two bowls of the red and green salsa sit.

"Of course, *mijita*."

Little daughter. Lavinia loves that Mercedes calls her that.

"Not to worry," Mercedes says. "You have this place."

Lavinia hears the front door open, and within seconds Kinky enters the kitchen, puts her bag on the counter, and rushes into the den to kiss her mama and then Lavinia.

"*Besitos,*" she says, placing a kiss on her friend's cheek. "I'm glad you came to see Mama. And now dinner together."

"So many kisses in this house!" Lavinia exclaims.

"They are whispers sent from God," says Mercedes.

"Mama, have you been telling stories again?" Kinky asks, rounding the table to take a seat next to Lavinia. It's more of a rhetorical question, and Mercedes doesn't answer. Lavinia can't remember a time she's ever come to visit Mercedes when she hasn't told her a story.

"She told me about the *querencia,*" Lavinia tells her.

"Ah yes," Kinky says, looking pensive. "Well, that makes sense."

Lavinia smiles. "I'm learning to let them sink in and then the light bulb goes off."

"That's how it goes with Mama's stories, isn't it? I'm jealous. I could use one of her stories right now," Kinky says, eyeing Mercedes and then Lavinia. Lavinia wonders for the first time if she might be taking up too much space in their lives. "Speaking of stories, Armando had a bad day again today." Kinky grabs her friend, leads her into the kitchen, and sits at the table next to her.

Lavinia knows that she takes on Armando's burdens as her own. "Still writing his story of escape?" she asks.

"Oh, it's one step forward, two steps back. He looked like he might cry today."

"Slowly, slowly." Mercedes places her small hand onto Kinky's arm. "He will need his time—not to worry, not to push too hard, *mijita.*"

"My mother's a guru." Kinky smiles.

"I'm beginning to see that," Lavinia says. "She reminds me of Strega Nonna, a nice witch from a childhood story Sal used to read to me. Strega Nonna can make pasta out the door to feed the entire village. Her generosity drowns the town in pasta!"

They all laugh.

"And chef extraordinaire," Kinky adds, accepting the large burrito her mother is serving her.

They hold hands in a prayer of gratitude and then, as usual, all goes silent, except for the sound of chewing and swallowing and a little hum Mercedes makes as she tastes her food.

"And your day?" Mercedes asks Lavinia, breaking the silence.

Lavinia relates the pleasure of her first day in Zack's apartment—the stacks of books to the ceiling, the clocks.

"God is with him."

Lavinia looks at Mercedes, not knowing what to say to that.

"Have some *agua fresca, sandia, mijitas*," Mercedes offers. She pours the watermelon water.

Lavinia sips the sweet, cool drink, which is refreshing after the spicy salsas. "*Gracias*, Mercedes."

The meal finished, Lavinia readies herself to go to her flat but hesitates. A fear flutters inside her heart, pressing her to ask if she can stay the night . . . but she doesn't. She feels a deep, empty space inside her that can't be filled so she thinks of the story of the bull who manages to find his strength. She inhales the image of the self-protective bull, gathering her own strength.

What she really wants is to be Mercedes Montoya's daughter and Kinky's sister, to be part of their family. She admires Mercedes's round and powerful body, her latte-colored skin. She kids herself that she could pass for a brown girl. Mercedes's eyes are deep brown like her own. They both have round faces—Lavinia's with a chocolate chip stain and Mercedes's with large dimples on her cheeks that seem to rotate when she moves her full, rosy lips. Doesn't Mercedes call Lavinia *mijita*? Just that affectionate nickname alone fills her with love, even if she has to go home to an empty flat.

"Before I leave, Mercedes, how did you mean the story to be for me?" she asks.

"You will find your way," Mercedes says. "Don't worry. The path is just beneath your feet."

"Thank you. I guess I need patience."

Mercedes nods.

"I made this CD for you, Lavinia," Kinky says, placing it in her hand.

"Thank you." The jacket reads, "Dance Your Heart Out, Love Kinky."

When she turns to go she hears Kinky whispering to her mother—something about how they're spoiling her, how she needs to get it together.

Lavinia's heart sinks a little at this, but she shakes it off.

The air is still warm for November. Lavinia could walk miles like this but soon she's at her door. Before unlocking it, she looks to both sides to make sure no one's around. She slips easily into her studio and bolts the door.

She puts on the disc Kinky gave her. Kinky put it together by using something called Sound Hound. Lavinia can just see Kinky listening to her music, then dashing to her app and pressing the orange button to enable Sound2Sound to activate. It's an incredible matching technology to a never-ending database of music. She's touched to think Kinky made this with her in mind. It's true she is spoiling her, but Lavinia likes to think she's welcome in the Montoya household and not overdrawing on their generosity.

She listens to the first song. It's called *"Fare L'amore"*—"Making Love." She wonders if Kinky is encouraging Lavinia to open up to the new guy. Then she thinks how hard it was for her to open up freely to Andy; how she never felt relaxed in his bed; how sex was scary and tense; how when she did open up and let him see her cry, he left.

The staccato beat pulses and then her feet pound the wooden floor, calling her to bounce and press her feet into the floor, stamp away these thoughts, unearth her own *querencia*.

If I dig far enough, maybe I'll find it—or China.

She opens the patio door to the warm outside evening, where the fig tree, dressed as a black señorita, stands nobly in the moonlight. Lavinia dances in front of her, letting the ground of her small yard absorb the pounding of her feet, wondering if her shaking will cause the almost ready figs to drop. With the earth below and the moonlight above, she dances freely. A ripple of energy pushes up through her feet to her ankles and calves, then moves on up to her hips and pelvis, then up to her tailbone and to her spinal column, neck and head. She imagines the noble fig tree as her mother. *Have you followed me here, Mama?*

She dances until the music stops. Feeling satisfied, she goes inside to her darkened room and falls asleep.

She dreams of her mother—or is it the time before her mother? Cradled in water, her head and tailbone tucked in, her fists are closed tightly, as are her eyes. It's dark in this watery sea. There's a swishing underwater sound. She can hear the beat as an underwater muffled sound. Sometimes the sea is gentle and then it shifts like in a storm, maybe even a tidal wave. What is the tidal wave?

Lavinia opens her eyes. She's sweating but her sheets are dry. Though the dream unsettles her, she tries to grasp it, but it just slips away like a fish, leaving nothing but a deep yearning, a fluid feeling that is unfamiliar and yet as old as milk. She wonders if the noble fig has given her this dream.

Then a smile comes. *La querencia.*

Lavinia wants more time with Mercedes, with Kinky. "Who else do I have in my life?" she asks herself out loud. "Zack and Mario, whom I barely know? George?"

She misses him, though not without some agitation. He betrayed her, didn't he? But why doesn't she have deeper connections in her life? She can't help but think it's something about her. Why isn't she speaking more with people? She feels tongue tied, like the curled-fisted fetus in the dream. *Is that me? An embryo? Is that the dark shadow?*

Days pass and she can't get the dream or Mercedes out of her mind. On a late afternoon she leaves her apartment and walks down Valencia Street, passing the writing workshop where Kinky volunteers after a full day at school. The place bustles with kids of all ages working on computers, alone or with tutors. Lavinia looks at her watch: 3:30. Kinky won't be leaving here until 4:00 p.m. from tutoring.

She pops a Bubblicious like it's an injection, then quickens her step. Her body is leading her toward the guru *Strega* Mercedes. *Onward*, she tells herself, walking toward Florida Street, passing parked cars on the sidewalk. A man's legs hang out from beneath a Ford pickup truck. She thinks of George's sculptures of body parts and feels an anger rising up in her. She remembers the story of the bull who outwits the matador, and she moves on toward the house.

Then she's standing there at the Montoyas' door and knocks, anticipating the warm woman inside, knowing she is welcome.

"*Pasa adelante, mijita.*" Mercedes shows Lavinia into the familiar spot in the den, where she sits in the white chair with the soft round arms. Lavinia is beginning to experience the chair as home.

"Hmmm!" she whispers in recognition of her comfortable place.

"Sit down." Mercedes looks at the watch she wears on a gold chain around her neck. "Kinky will be here at six, in time for dinner."

"I wanted to see you today." Lavinia covers her face with her hands. A rash of sadness rises. She feels her throat tighten and then just as easily release. She continues, looking up at her and continues, "I wanted to ask you . . ." She mumbles, covering her lips, because what she wants to ask Mercedes is, *Are you my mother?*

She doesn't.

"You're sad today. Don't hide." Mercedes sits down next to her, placing a hand on hers.

"I came here today to see if you can help me understand something. Because I can't figure it out." She's choking back tears now. "Why did this happen to me? Why did my mother die?"

Mercedes rubs Lavinia's arm with her small, leathery hands—not abrasive, just rough and strong, like turtle skin. Lavinia watches her face, but Mercedes doesn't answer her question. She just sits with her in strong silence.

"This is the only place I feel safe," Lavinia tells her. "Otherwise, I feel so alone."

"I'm not able to tell you why this happened to you," Mercedes finally says, pulling Lavinia closer in, embracing her. "But you have Kinky and me, and we are one of your safe places."

She cares for me. Lavinia knows this to be true. The place behind her eyes gets tight and her eyes fill with a stinging sensation. She imagines a waterfall being held back. She waits before speaking, but the words don't come, only the tears. She sobs, leaning her head against Mercedes, noticing the cotton apron getting wet.

"Lavinia, Lavinia," Mercedes says, rubbing her back. This affectionate embrace only makes her cry more. "I miss my mother. I have nowhere to turn. I have no family."

"I know. I know," Mercedes says, stroking her head. "Tell me about your mother."

"All I know is that I left her when I was nearly five, when Sal brought me to San Francisco. And I don't know what happened. I don't know why we were separated, or how she died. I don't know if she died before we left, or if I'm the reason she's dead. Sometimes I feel that it was my fault. Sometimes I think she was arguing with someone in our house in Italy and maybe she was mad at me. I don't know. Sal told me that she had me when she was seventeen. I can't imagine. It's all confusing in my head."

"*Pobrecita* Lavinia."

"Something is happening inside me, like a whirlpool spinning."

"A whirlpool will spin you around and shake everything up. Sometimes it is just what we need, *mijita*." Mercedes massages her arm.

When Lavinia hears *mijita* again she feels a little bee buzz in her center and welcomes the soft touch of the woman beside her. She wants to memorize this feeling, to have it imprinted on her brain, but she doesn't even know what to call it or where to store it. All she knows is that her center is fluttering. She focuses on the folds of the floral apron at her bosom, which look like smiling faces of clowns with multicolored pointed hats made wet now by her tears.

"Lean back on this chair, my child," Mercedes says, pointing to the backrest of the soft upholstered chair with low arms. "I will massage your head the way I learned in my country."

Mercedes pulls up her straight-back chair near Lavinia's head. Lavinia adjusts her position, letting Mercedes' capable hands move slowly to her head, and takes a deep breath, lets herself relax.

Mercedes gently touches with one hand the top of her head with oil-scented fingers, moving around the crown, massaging points close to her scalp. While she presses her fingers, she hums. Lavinia allows herself to receive her gifts, accepting the way Mercedes holds her head in her hands and gently moves her neck to the left and then to the right, applying gentle pressure to her neck and shoulders. The humming relaxes her mind. She pictures the figs, smells the rich mulch under the fig tree, and sees the little green pouches filling with seeds.

Maybe thirty minutes pass this way . . . or is it an eternity? With her small hands Mercedes kneads, then cradles her head and just sits. No massage. No humming, just a quiet holding.

"This reminds me of just before I fall asleep," Lavinia says. "This is a space where I'm at peace."

"Sí, sí, my child. And your dreams?"

"I've been dreaming of a watery place where there is turmoil and swishy sounds; where I am all bundled, with tight fists."

"The womb. You're seeing yourself in your mother's womb."

Lavinia tenses her legs; her head jerks backwards. "Really! It seems so dark in the womb."

"Ah! The great mystery of connection," Mercedes says, still cupping Lavinia's head in her hands.

"I think my mother is whispering to me through the wind, the water, even the fig tree, but I can't hear her words." As Lavinia listens to Mercedes's hum, she begins to feel her legs relax and her body rest.

"You are in Mercedes's hands now. Not to worry, Lavinia," Mercedes says. "Your mother, she fell in love with you before you were born. And each time she held you, her love grew. She could only stare at you, *mijita*, marveling at the miracle of your birth. Out of lovemaking, you were born. She knew you were of her life and not of her life and that she must part with you someday, dear child." Mercedes voice gets dimmer, more serious. "Too soon," she says softly.

"I wish I could see my mother's face clearly. I only see white sheets hanging across clotheslines strung between old buildings. They are flapping like white wings of a great bird. Then I hear her voice, a sweet soprano, calling, 'Lavinia Lavinia!'" Vague images of a beautiful young woman standing on the balcony looking down at her, waving and smiling, her eyes gleaming like a bright sun, appear in Lavinia's mind as she says this. But then the sun is eclipsed and it all goes dark. Something black and scary blankets the sun.

"Mama," Mercedes says, cradling Lavinia's head. She whispers this over and over, all the while holding her head in her small oiled hands that smell of spring onions. Tears form in the corner of her eyes and begin to move down the sides of her face and onto Lavinia's forehead. "Mama, Mama, Mama," she prays, and the tears mingle with Lavinia's own so that Lavinia doesn't know which drops belong to whom.

Time stands still.

Lavinia hears stirring in the kitchen—sounds of a pot being moved from the stove, a spoon scraping along its insides, ice cubes against a glass, plates rattling, the closing of a cabinet door. Kinky must be home and getting things set up for supper. Lavinia was so immersed in the cradle, she didn't hear her friend come in.

The dinner tastes more delicious than anything she's ever eaten. Frijoles seasoned with chili, tomatoes, and garlic tickle her palate. The masa is soft and sweet on her tongue. The salty taste of the *queso* reminds her of her own tears. As they eat together, she doesn't even mind the silence. Then Kinky begins to talk of Armando lovingly.

Lavinia looks into Mercedes's deep, dark, fluid eyes and smiles. She feels safe and held, and free to leave her friends. It's early evening and still enough time to visit her friend Mario in North Beach.

Chapter 8:

THE FIRST DANCE

Lavinia walks into the Falcone Café. A man in line in front of her says she looks like she drives a Ferrari, the way her hair is so mussed up. Another patron adds that she looks like Sophia Loren with that dimple in her chin. Then another high-pitched voice asks if she just got laid. She looks around for that voice just as Mario locks eyes with her.

"Whoa! Who just said that?" Mario glares at a thin guy who works cleaning the glasses.

"How rude!" Lavinia says.

"He can be an asshole!" Mario says to her in a low voice, eyeing the skinny little guy in an orange T-shirt and baseball cap.

"I was thinking the same. Thanks."

Mario looks into her eyes. His seem inflamed to her. Or maybe it's her own fire she sees reflected in his eyes.

"I'll talk to him. You do glow, though, Bubblicious."

"I had a massage."

"I'll be off at nine." He looks directly into her eyes again before hesitantly moving away to the espresso machine, where he pulls the handle, froths the milk, and pours it to make heart designs in the lattes. Lavinia watches his quick, purposeful moves but mostly his body, so alert and strong. *What made a stranger say I look like I just got laid?* Truth be known, she hasn't been laid in a long time—she's been off that drug for a while. Since Andy left, she's shied away from men. And even with Andy she never felt free.

Sidling up to her at the bar for a brief moment when things are quiet, Mario puts his face near hers. He smells like he's been rolling around in the roasted beans. She inhales him.

"You want to hang out?" he asks. "Dinner?"

"Oh, sorry, I already had dinner with a friend earlier."

"You going with someone?" he asks—but when she frowns, he says, "Okay, no more questions. Are you too full to try a slice of the best pizza you've ever had?"

"Yummy!" She relaxes. She can't stay annoyed with him.

"I'll show you my favorite haunts in North Beach and we'll take it from there." He gets up and moves to his machine, where he begins to clean cups and glasses in a hot wash.

His replacement—a younger, shorter guy—stands next to him, examining her with big eyes.

"She's pretty cute. Yours?" the guy with the high-pitched voice, the one who insulted her, asks.

"Not mine, I don't own her," Mario says.

"Ha ha! I bet you'd like to."

"Steve, you're out of control. Quit it! Or you're fired!" the barista snaps before going behind the bar to a closed room.

The guy moves toward Lavinia. "I'm Steve Crow. You're new in the 'hood."

"And you're rude!"

"Guy talk! Sorry, if I offended you."

"Get over it," she says. "Guy talk is absolutely out of fashion!"

"Truce?" he asks, putting out his hand.

She looks at his hand and then toward the door Mario just disappeared behind.

"Mario's a good boss," Steve says. Then, "You don't know much about him, do you?"

"No, I don't."

"He's a bro. Fair. Pulls the shots straight."

"Does he have a girlfriend?" She can't help asking.

"Maybe." The coworker winks at her just as Mario comes toward them.

Lavinia regrets having asked him about Mario, feels disgusted. Why didn't she diss him totally? She turns away from him.

Mario's, hair slicked back with grease and parted in the middle, makes him look like a movie star. He wears blue jeans. Walking towards her, he buttons a peacoat over a collared shirt. His shoes are stylish. Lavinia stands up from the bar stool. They are about the same height, though his body is fuller and more muscular than hers.

They walk onto Columbus Street toward Vallejo, where groups of young people laugh and talk. Occasionally an older couple mingles with small groups of men and women, women only, men out for fun. Party animals! She delights in being one of them—out for fun. They merge with the small pockets of restaurateurs and bar hoppers.

"What did Steve tell you?"

"Nothing." She tells a fib and walks in step with him. "Thank you for speaking to him."

Mario takes her arm as they cross a busy intersection on Columbus where several side streets converge with traffic going in all different directions.

They walk toward the pizza place. People are queueing inside for pizza by the slice. Behind a long counter, a man is throwing pizza dough into the air. Deep inside the small pizzeria, seats line the walls. Outside, people sit at sidewalk tables with aluminum seating.

"You're not chewing gum tonight," Mario comments.

"No need tonight."

"You beam. That's what I was trying to say," he says, as if to explain the bad behavior.

"I had a beautiful head massage this afternoon from my friend's mother." She looks into his eyes.

"That accounts for the glow."

"How do you keep so clear and direct? Usually, I mean." She squeezes his arm.

"I try to stay in the physical world—present," he says.

She's not sure what he means but doesn't ask him to explain, either.

"And your secret, Lavinia Lavinia?" he asks.

"I don't think of myself as direct at all," she says, staring at Mario. If she were direct and clear, she would have finished State and not impulsively quit; she would have confronted Andy; she would not have indulged Steve's desire to tell her about Mario; she would have spoken with Nina about Don; she would have insisted that Sal tell her about her mother. The list goes on.

"Fair enough." Mario points to the menu. He orders two slices of pizza with mushrooms and sausage for himself. "A beer for you?" he asks.

She nods.

"And two Morettis," Mario tells the guy behind the counter.

Lavinia orders a slice with mushrooms. Soon they're eating at an outside table, their hands dripping with olive oil.

"Delicious," Lavinia says. "You'd think I never ate."

Mario grins. "The best in North Beach, like I said."

They drain their beers. When they stand to leave, Mario

nudges her, pressing his shoulder into hers. "You want to dance tonight? I know an unusual music venue."

"I love to dance." She slips her arm through his.

"Let's go to my favorite place. Not the usual," he says.

He tells her it's more a gestalt practice where you dance to five rhythms developed by a dance therapist named Gabrielle Roth. He warns her that a teacher-DJ might stop the music at some point and ask everyone to contemplate and pay attention to themselves.

"It's like a groovy meditation," he says, "or a yoga practice."

Lavinia considers it. "Not sure about it!"

"Well, it's different and not for everyone." He pauses and looks into her eyes. "If you want to leave before the two-hour deal, I'll leave with you."

"Fair enough," she says, consciously repeating his familiar response, trying it out.

Mario and Lavinia join a line on the sidewalk outside a large, gray, fifties-style building—a relatively nondescript building on Columbus Avenue, one she's never noticed before. It's more like the Masonic Lodge than a rock concert or a dance hall—but then, according to what Mario told her, it's not the usual club. She's amazed to see such a long line at 10 p.m. People wear flowing costumes; Lavinia pulls at the lapels on her tuxedo jacket, perceiving her attire to be a little stiff, picturing her own flowing shirt at home, the one she reserves for dancing alone.

People laugh and hug each other in greeting. She smooths down the front of her jacket. Several women and men offer their cheek to Mario, as if this is his special club. She can't help but feel a little jealous at his attention to others.

"This is the hardest part," he says, whispering in her ear, "hugging all these people. Dancing for two hours will be a piece of cake."

"I bet!"

Lavinia's not so sure this venue is for her. Actually, she feels a familiar tension in her gut—the one that makes her want to bolt or make an excuse to get away for a few minutes, like she has to pee—but she thinks of the bull and stands her ground as small groups continue to gather together around Mario. The energy in the line is one of excitement. Everyone but her seems to know each other. She steps closer to Mario as a dramatic-looking woman in a gypsy skirt and a guy wearing soft, flowing pants approach them.

"What a night, like summer," the woman says, leaning into Mario's shoulder. "The DJ's from LA tonight."

Lavinia feels a pinch in her gut. Maybe she has to shit.

"She's the best," the woman continues, "she really cuts it up. Do you know her?" She mentions a name Lavinia doesn't catch—but then, she wouldn't recognize the name anyway.

Lavinia stands quietly, twirling her hair with one hand and resting the other on her stomach, which is growling. Mario steps closer as if to shield her, allowing their shoulders to touch, reassuring her as the line moves into a small interior room with bright lighting.

Two people sit behind a small counter, wearing big, smiley faces, collecting money. Mario pays for the two tickets—forty bucks total. Lavinia is surprised by the reasonable entrance fee. He gives her a ticket and they walk arm in arm to the far end of the small room, where a man stands retrieving the tickets.

"Want a hug?" the man at the entranceway asks.

This seems odd to Lavinia—off-putting, or worse. *How can I be here in this awful place?*

She looks down at her T-straps, avoiding his arms, and pushes into a large room the size of a gymnasium. On the far side from the door, a woman stands with her equipment—a musical console and mixer.

Mario leads Lavinia closer to the DJ and the music center as a slow piece of music fills the room like a billowing cloud. People move slowly, mostly alone, letting their heads sway gently from side to side. "Lets find a place," he whispers.

She follows him, passing people doing stretches on the floor, some in yoga or meditation poses. Others stand face to face, or alone with their eyes closed. Lavinia wants to find a safe place in the corner and not in the center of the grand-sized room. She thinks of the bull, who stays by the gate. As the overhead lights dim, she dares to look into the faces of the dancers. Some seem lost; others seem happy, with wide grins. One woman walks the periphery of the room as if in a trance, eyes down. Lavinia notices a very short man wearing a silver bracelet engaged with the slow beat like a baby fawn with its mother. His rhythm is so grounded, maybe because his center of gravity is closer to the ground. But now everyone is dancing or moving to this slow, even-paced rhythm, their heads swaying ever so gently from side to side. It's as if the music pulls for a kind of movement. She deduces from what Mario told her outside that this is the first rhythm.

Mario stops in the lower corner of the room, left and center from the DJ. Lavinia stands beside him, beginning to let the beat move though her ever so slowly, allowing her feet to connect with the wooden floor. It's like she's dancing in her own place, where she lets the music speak to her. Forgetting for a moment all the people around, she lets the beat guide each step.

"How about staying here?"

Lavinia nods and faces Mario as the room fills. A sign reads, "Capacity 150." Another sign reads, "Talk with your dance."

"Mario, we can't talk?" she asks.

He nods, moving in closer to her, staying in sync with the slow, flowing sound. She follows him, getting closer. When one song ends she hears short connecting beats that fade into the next mix. Most of the music is instrumental and new to her, but then a vocal piece plays. Someone is singing, "Are We Humans or Are We Dancers?" She loves it, hangs onto the words, sings aloud. Some of the dancers are singing. The round clock above the DJ reads ten thirty. With two hours to go, she can't imagine what surprises lie ahead.

But the music speaks its own language, pulling her into its wave, moving her closer to other dancers. At times someone pairs with her momentarily and then moves on into the deeper part of the sea of dancers. Lavinia is content to stay in her place close to the wall. *For right now, this corner is where I feel safe.*

With each change of music comes a mini crisis for her. As one song ends and before another unknown piece begins, there is a pause or transition during which she feels in limbo. Where to go, how to move, what to do? Day turning to night, in the in-between times, always makes her anxious. But the dancers still move. She shifts her weight from foot to foot, trying to anticipate the next new and different beat so she can ease into the flow. But she only feels uncertainty. Restlessness replaces safety. A man who dances through the space like a galloping colt scares her. She doesn't understand his beat. Again, fleeting thoughts of leaving or going to the bathroom compel her.

She looks for Mario. His eyes are closed, his body is responding to the music. She moves close so that she is almost touching him. He opens his eyes and gathers her close. They are in the flow now, their bodies touching. She stares at him. He smiles like a child who's happy to see her—a smile so warm and beautiful she can't take her eyes off his lovely face with its high cheekbones and full lips. He nuzzles her face with his nose. She can't leave.

Her heart fills as the music informs her feet, her legs; her hips sway; her waist swivels; her torso rolls; her arms fly as the beat picks up. She feels like a puppy wagging its tail and finds she is more connected to herself.

The music shifts. This must be another rhythm. The pizzazz of the increasing vitality of the music enlivens her, freeing her from her constraints. All of the dancers seem to respond with rotating shoulders and bobbing heads, then flying arms and feet. She is in this sea of joyful dancers, each safely in their own boats, bobbing on the same ocean—or are they each their own wave? The waves bring buoyancy and uncontrollable joy to her being. She finds her tight-lipped mouth opening into a wide smile.

A man wearing a kaftan bobs beside her. They are in sync, and he is a complete stranger. A young woman wearing a midriff top joins them. They are laughing. People come together on some unspoken cue. Each speaks a unique language without any words and dances near or by her through the open space, allowing her to make contact with so many new people. No words. Only the vibrational threads connect her with others. She feels deliriously happy. Her feet fly to the crashing sound of the escalating music. Her heart is laughing.

Now here comes a tall, galloping woman who seems to match the running colt Lavinia noticed earlier. She doesn't feel so afraid anymore. She looks over toward the short man, who is enmeshed in a dance with a yet shorter woman. Flying, circling repetitions! They are so closely connected. She envies their intimacy.

The music slows down. She hears the DJ ask everyone to stay purely in the physical world, letting all stories and thoughts melt away. Lavinia remembers Mario saying that what makes him clear is staying in the physical world. The DJ asks them to imagine the entire space and then the space before them and behind them.

These words stick. Lavinia keeps repeating, *The space behind you and the space in front of you,* in her head.

The music has started again. Mario playfully engages her now, bringing her back into the sensate world. Their eyes meet. He gently pushes her raised hand with his palm. She responds to the light contact with a similar touch, following this pressure, making circles in the air. They stay attached hand to hand, arm to arm, playing. When he pushes, she meets his energy. Then she places her other hand at his shoulder and pushes, and he rotates in that direction. Soon they are engaged in an ongoing push-pull. It feels like a tango, except they are both leading.

Now she is leading, pulling him toward her and then pushing him away from her. Her legs shoot out. She loves this awareness of actually staying attached to his moves, which allows her to follow them likewise. They are engaged in a playful dance, coming and going, expressing some primal language. She imagines two polar bears playing without words.

Then the rhythm slows—still playful, but more mellow. The music moves from its peak into graceful, silvery rivulets toward a still pond. As their breath catches up with them and their heart rates slow, they flow on an ebullient cloud across the room, turning and swirling, promenading themselves in some grand pas de deux, until the music slows again and eventually stops, leaving only the pulsing in their veins.

The room is a silent hum.

The DJ says, "Now bring this practice into the physical world."

"Already? Where did the time go?" Lavinia whispers to Mario, not believing two hours have passed.

"Time, there you have it," is all he says. He holds her hand as they leave the dance hall and walk out into the cool night. They hop a cab to her house. He asks the cabby to wait for her to get safely inside.

She peeks out her window after closing the door behind her, just in time to see the cab pull away with Mario inside throwing her a kiss.

Chapter 9:

THE WOLF

Monday morning comes too fast for her. After dancing on Friday night, she spent a beautiful weekend on the coast with Kinky, beach combing, chatting, and eating seafood at Puerto 27. And then they bought a pumpkin for Mercedes, something Kinky and Lavinia do every fall to celebrate the changing light of November days before heading home.

Lying in her bed, Lavinia fingers an abandoned shell she found, wondering whether the snail might have found a new home. A bird sings the answer with a cadence she can almost decipher, so familiar a song, but can't quite make it out. She decides the birds are telling her to take some more time and not go to work today. Her phone beeps—a small, clacking noise. She reaches her arm to the floor and looks at the screen. It's a text from George: "Are you okay? Are you going to come back to work? I don't care about the missing laundry."

Lavinia's stomach turns. *I'm not ready to deal with him.* She turns her attention to Friday night and her time with Mario when they danced, flowing in and around the space they created, sometimes like birds in flight and other times like cubs rolling around a grassy knoll. Without their even exchanging words, she felt so understood by him and like she'd gotten to know him better, too. She wants to hang out with her thoughts of him a bit longer. She's grateful for her Monday Zack day that will bring her to North Beach.

On Wednesday Lavinia picks herself up, dresses, and packs her special cleaning potions into her small leather purse, remembering to add a few fig leaves she stored in the fridge. She nods to the mother tree, which has become a sentinel with a prescience of the divine in her mind.

When Lavinia arrives on Russian Hill, Nina's greeting is brusque. She's quick to tell her the spot is still there. Even before saying hello, she grumbles her sour complaint, then pulls on her blazer, fiddles with her briefcase, organizes papers—all with a sharp pencil in her mouth. Lavinia wonders if the pencil is all that's keeping Nina from biting her head off.

"I'll drop it off at the dry cleaner on Hyde Street before I leave today," Lavinia says, taking it from her hand and stuffing it into her small shoulder purse.

Nina seems to cringe at seeing the blouse handled so roughly. "Okay, then today, a few blouses, a skirt, some linens. Don wants his running clothes laundered this week. The vest, lightweight jacket, sheets, tablecloth." Nina runs through the checklist as she moves toward the doorway, pushing past Lavinia like a great storm ready to wreak havoc. Lavinia wishes she had the guts to interrupt the tirade to tell Nina her husband is an asshole, but she can't. Nina's a client, after all, not a friend.

After Nina leaves, Lavinia sits on the patio trying to center herself. Coit Tower reflects the light. White. Pristine. The Bay

Bridge in the distance shows off its new span, a triangular wonder glistening in the sunlight. When she looks into the dining room she sees dishes still on the table. Is that the linen Nina described? She breathes deeply, looking outside to see Nina get into her car. Her skirt is above her knees, exposing her generous thighs, and Lavinia feels embarrassed.

When Nina finally shuts the door and pulls away, Lavinia is left to her thoughts. How can Nina live with him?

Once again she studies the framed pictures on the mantle above the marble fireplace. Nina's graduation photo—like Margaret, Zack's daughter, she wears a hooded cap and gown, the tassel hanging over her eyes, while Don stands beside her wearing a wolfish grin. In another photo Don is crossing the finish line, number 21708 on his chest. His teeth look too big for his mouth. Like a wolf, he seems to be gloating over his accomplishment. Then they stand together at the beach, each of them holding a surfboard. Nina wears a sports bathing suit that covers her thighs, and he wears a wetsuit.

Lavinia feels at a loss when she looks at these photos. She has no accomplishments like these that she wishes to commemorate in photos she'd place around her home. She herself didn't even finish undergraduate school in elementary education. She doesn't even have an ESL certificate. She can't imagine running a marathon or surfing in the rough Pacific. Still, she's more alarmed by Don's success than envious.

She turns to the mess in the kitchen. She's not a maid, but she removes the breakfast dishes from the table—raspberry muesli, coffee, and a plate of toast. She places the butter in the fridge, where an open bottle of champagne sits in the door shelf. She pulls the linen tablecloth and napkins off the table and moves toward the laundry room.

She stops to reflect on her ritual, allowing her mind to focus on this cleansing as a practice. The ritual of going down to the river to purify clothes is as old as time and near to Lavinia's heart. It promises a renewal, a freshness, both for her and the wearer. Today, both Nina and Don's laundry bags rest on top of the washer—sheets and pillowcases and sports clothes, mostly. Sorting, she pulls out the light colors first, comparing the piles of lights and darks to each other. *Quite a bit to do today.* She puts the lingerie and one shirt in a basin to soak. Then she puts in a load of whites, which include Don's underwear, running socks, Nina's white cotton panties, two towels, and the white linen tablecloth—a full load. The rushing sound of the running water brings her to that river; she immediately slows her pace to savor the experience.

Hanging on a hook in the closet are T-shirts and a pair of men's slacks. On another hanger, there is a pair of jeans. She checks the pockets as usual, but with trepidation this time, remembering last week's note. In the small pocket, she finds another note. She's tempted to throw it out, but she can't. Her curiosity gets the better of her. She unfolds the piece of paper, hoping that it will perhaps explain the last one.

"When you didn't come, I figured you decided not to go through with the deal I proposed. I'll call you."

Lavinia shakes her head wondering how she could have ever imagined the first note was intended for her. Now the second note intrigues her. What? Who? If it is meant for her, it's some kind of a delusion. Maybe even psychotic. She tears it into small pieces and flushes the pieces down the toilet. Then she proceeds to do the hand washing at the sink, adding soap and swishing the few things, listening to the sound of the water and the churning of the washing machine.

When she turns around upon completing her task, she's surprised to see Don standing in the doorway. His lips are stretched across his face in a wide, closed-mouthed grin. She jumps. She wonders how long he's been standing there. Has he been home the whole time, hiding in wait?

"You scared me," she says, fearing he saw her rip up the note and flush it down the toilet.

"I forgot something." Don moves toward the bedroom, where she can see him looking in his dresser. He finds his sports jacket and rummages through the two pockets.

"Damn," he says. He's taller than she remembered. He sighs and then walks toward her, flipping his hair off his forehead, "You didn't see a handwritten note in my pants pocket, did you?" His fists clench. When Lavinia's mouth drops open, he stares at her mole. "You took it, didn't you?" He's too close now, breathing down her neck.

"Move away from me, don't touch me!" she shouts. She backs up against the sink.

"Maybe you'll come across it. If you do, you can rip it up." He smirks.

She stands perfectly still. He's staring at her still, looking intently at her birthmark, but he doesn't say anything more. His lingering stare kills her. She's furious; she wants to slap him. He turns away down the hall. She hears the front door slam. When he leaves she runs to the window and looks down to see him get into a waiting car. The driver, a woman, pulls away.

More angry than confused, she resumes her work, wanting to get the hell out of there as soon as possible. There is no way to make the cycles of washer and dryer go faster. She pokes around, killing time.

She rushes after work and gets to Falcone in half the usual time. Not even noticing the garden or if the wild parrots are perched in the trees, she gets down the hill and dashes inside like someone is chasing her.

"You look scared," Mario says as soon as he sees her. "Are you okay?"

She sits down at a table, hoping he'll take the cue that she wants to talk to him privately. She waits a few minutes, and when he comes out from behind the bar, he's carrying an espresso, her favorite. He sets it down and she takes a sip.

"Thank you. Just what I needed." She sighs. "It's my clients. They're lunatics, that's all. I had an encounter today with the man at the house."

"Zack Luce?

"Not him. The runner-husband lunatic on Russian Hill. A strange guy who leaves handwritten notes in his pocket."

"Not to you."

"At first I thought so, but now I don't know. He was lurking around today. After his wife left, he came back and we had a run-in. He accused me of taking the note. His energy frightens me."

"Did you take it?"

"No, I didn't steal it," she says, automatically. *But I ripped it up and flushed it*, she says to herself, biting her lip. When her lip trembles, she lifts her drink to her mouth, trying to hide the twitch behind the small cup. *But did I steal it?* Isn't that her job—to check the pockets before submerging the pants into water? She sees herself checking Don's pockets, a standard procedure; finding the folded paper note, which had the same quality as the first; feeling alarmed, as if there were an urgency; wanting not to read it, but at the same time needing to know if it was meant for her. Then, in her desperate need to clear her mind, to drop the nagging question, to find an abdication or a plea of innocence of any involvement with Don, doing the deed—taking it and reading it and then disposing of it in the toilet.

She knows he saw her do it. He was lurking like a snake in the corner. She knows it by the way he smirked. In some twisted way of thinking, that makes her an accomplice.

She feels a sticky involvement with Don. And now she's lied to Mario. *Ugh!*

She hears Mario talking; he's asking her something. She puts the small cup down, uncovering her lips.

"Why don't you tell her?" he's asking.

"That's a hard thing to do. She already seems so irritated with me. I feel like I could be fired any day, if I don't quit first." She sighs, looking into Mario's kind brown eyes. "I've had some weirdos lately. Maybe it's me?"

She tells Mario about having the bag of tarps stolen and returning to George's studio and finding busts of women who looked like her; how strange to feel her employer was sculpting her without her permission; how she quit.

Mario takes her hands, rubbing them. "You're so cold."

"I've taken to sipping tequila to warm me up," Lavinia confides. They sit close together in the corner of the café, away from the eyes of the others. "I loved dancing with you on Friday night," she whispers.

Mario smiles. "Me too. What did you like most?"

"Our *pas de deux*. Did we really float across the room?"

"We did."

"And you?"

"Pushing hands with you," he says.

"Yeah, that was amazing. I love what we had together."

"And what about that vibration at the end?" he asks.

"A hum."

"That's it exactly," he says. "It was palpable."

"Yes, just a hum and the tingling in my hands and feet. I feel it now with you and me, like this."

"You rock, Lavinia. I love the way you moved your arms and your hips and shoulders, like a beautiful windmill." Mario puts his nose close to her mouth, inhaling her breath.

She moves closer in to feel his breath on her upper lip.

"I smell your gum," he says.

Lavinia reaches into her pocket, pulls out two pieces, and hands them to him. "A double for the barista," she says as they move away from this moment of closeness.

He walks back to his station. She waves and then leaves for home.

Chapter 10:

A LETTER FROM SAL

When Lavinia opens her door, she sees mail scattered on the floor. Immediately she spies Italian stamps and Uncle Sal's unique script. Her heart skips at the sight of the formal letter, having only received monthly postcards announcing his travels since he left. She puts away the thought that he might be ill.

She misses him, and can hardly make sense of a letter from him lying on the wooden floor in front of her foot. A bit of Uncle Sal right here in her studio makes her feel frozen. She hates him for leaving her, yet she loves him, too. She surveys her apartment as if looking for something to hold onto, but the walls in the long, empty front room are bare. Her eyes survey the tiny back living space with its small couch and coffee table, but there's nothing there. Only the darkened bedroom with the mattress on the floor and the old fig tree outside ground her.

She kneels on the floor close to the letter and carefully picks it up as if it is too fragile to withstand the heat of her hands. The silky paper slides into her palm; she stares at it as if it is alive. Then she carries it out to the patio and sits by the tree.

"We'll read it together," she says, fingering the curved letters of her name. She notes how his ones have little flags on top of them and the sevens have lines through them. She smells the waxed paper and carefully opens the letter, not wanting to tear into the body of the work for fear she might lose one of his words.

November 9

Dear Lavinia Lavinia,

I am writing to you from my new home on Via Toledo in the old part of Naples. You probably are wondering why I haven't communicated sooner, and I don't blame you. It's been too long since we talked.

It took me a while to settle into this place again after my long absence. I wasn't even sure my decision to leave was the right one, and each day I considered hopping on a plane and coming home. So, I'm slowly trying to find my ground here on my native soil like a cat staking out his territory.

I tried and tried to pick up the phone, but every time I went near it I felt a magnet repelling my hand away. You see, what I was afraid of was that you would hear the sadness in my voice. I didn't want you to hear my voice for fear that you would hear me cry.

When I first arrived here, I had to pick up the pieces of the crumbling life I had left when everything had crashed and was in ruins. Pa was gone and Ma, your nonna, was one lonely cookie. Your grandma looks old. It's been over twenty years since I last saw her. She lives in Salerno on the Amalfi Coast, a beautiful place, historic town, too, from WWII. She lives with her younger sister, Giuseppa.

When I found her, she was sitting on a balcony of her sister's apartment decked out in a shroud. She looked like the ghost of herself, but when she saw me, her eyes lit up. That made me so happy.

You know what she said, Vinnie, when she reached to hug me? She said, "What a waste, Salvia!"

I said, "No, Ma, it's not a waste. Vinnie's a teacher now." She smiled and repeated your name as if it were a song.

I miss you, but I know that you are settled in your studio with the Payne Gray walls, ragazza. I see you teaching school. I see how those children adore you, your beautiful face. "Faccia mia," the face I love. I hope you are not ruining those teeth with that bubblegum you chew. Ha! Ha! Just a joke.

Lavinia gets up with the letter, shakes it at the tree, then goes to get a glass of wine. Back on the patio, she resumes reading.

Soon after I got here I found the house where you were born, where I first met you. It was not an easy thing to come by but there it was on a narrow cobblestone street in the old section. Not exactly as it had been when I was here last, when I first laid eyes on you, ragazza. Time had grown the house, and I half-expected to see my mother and father and sister still living there. But all was gone and the house had been sold.

The new owners, a young couple, took down the balcony on the second level, changed the small window with the white lace curtains for a large, expansive window with double sliding doors. Your mama wouldn't have liked to see the balcony gone, nor that clothesline, the one strung between your house and Malvina's across the way.

But the new owners were nice enough and they let me come inside to see the apartment. The place has been divided up into several units, so it's smaller than I remembered. What struck me is the way the dining room and living room were all one room and the kitchen so small. I guess something like the one you have now. In there I remembered your mama making pastry on a wooden pastry board she placed on the sink. Gone!

What a baker she was! Mamma mia! *That sister of mine fried dough and then dipped it into honey, piled high. She called it* struffoli. *She liked to bake late at night after you were asleep so that when you woke up you could pull off a dough ball smothered in honey and chew it, smacking your lips, Lavinia Lavinia.*

I guess I never told you about her being a baker. I'd forgotten until I saw the old kitchen in my mind as it had once been, before all that happened. All that ugly stuff I pulled you away from. I wanted to save you from any of it!

That's what I remembered when I was in the flat. I could see you and your mama, my beautiful sister, Angela, making struffoli. *But it was just my imagination, because the place was remodeled so that the very small kitchen now has every convenience, even marble pastry board counters, a microwave oven, and a grill on the stovetop.*

But I am writing so much my hands and my fingers are stiff. I guess I could've gone to the internet café and dictated this letter. But I'm a little private about my thoughts.

Now I have a small apartment near all the restaurants. I even hooked up with an old school chum, Giovanni. He knew your mama and your father. He wanted to talk about her accident and told me his own feelings about this sad misfortune. He's a storyteller, too, and a widower. We hang out together and drink espresso and play cards at the sidewalk tables. Gamble a little, too. Have you gotten to Las Vegas yet? You'll love it.

Well, let me put a little something in this letter for your chewing habits. My new address is Via Toledo, #9, Napoli Italy 84121. I don't have a telephone yet. Love from your uncle,
Zio Salvatore.
PS: Are you still dancing? Watering the fig?

Instead of bringing her comfort, Sal's jokes make her mad. Her body agitated and her mind restless, her stomach contracts. She gets up from her chair and paces around the patio, holding the letter in one hand and her stomach with the other, but she can't stay mad at him. If she stays mad at Sal, he'll dissolve. He'll cry. Worse, he'll leave her. There won't be any more letters—at least, that's what she believes. She takes the letter to her chest and holds it there, trying to keep the buzzing of his words alive. He's the only connection she has to her mother. She feels like a bee on a summer day inhaling a flower. She smells the paper, rubs her fingers over the carefully written words, tracing the small, round letters.

A check for five hundred dollars falls from the sheets.

Lavinia savors the image of the piled volcano of fried dough dipped in honey—*struffoli*, he called it. He said her mother baked for her as a child. Her mouth waters as she thinks of the sweet pillows of dough. She wishes she could remember.

Closing her eyes and borrowing Sal's imagination, she sees the kitchen he remembered: small, like hers, he said, but with a pastry board sitting on the sink. She pictures the volcano of sugared dough prepared at night. Then she sees herself, little Lavinia.

It's morning. She's just woken up in a twin-sized bed. A wing of light shines through the half-opened door to her bedroom. It's a pretty room. She imagines herself barefoot, wearing a nightdress with butterfly patterns and tiny smooth buttons on it. Her mama will have slept nearby, in the bed next to her, but in her reverie, Lavinia wakes up and Mama's not there. She listens and hears her humming a pretty song. She slips out of her bed and goes toward the sweet voice.

"Lavinia, you're just in time. I have a surprise for you," her mamma says, "something to go with your latte." Mama peels off a small piece of fried dough from the top of a mound of pastry in the shape of a peaked mountain. "*La cima*," she says, placing the tip of the mountain on Lavinia's tongue.

The sweet, buttery pastry melts in her mouth. She chews and sticks out her tongue for more.

Lavinia smiles. She can almost smell the dough, feel the sweet honey sticking to her lips and fingers. She slips to her knees in front of the fig, now grateful for having had a lovingly sweet mother.

She thinks about Sal, imagines him sitting on the old, narrow street with his buddy, sipping wine and weaving stories. He loved to tell stories, and yet he's never told her anything about her mother or her father before now. The sweetness dissolves into a big zero—like Sal, who kept her in the dark. This is the first time he's ever mentioned Giovanni, a man who knew her father. Fear and thrill grip at her. Questions pile up. Sal knew her father all

these years and never told her? And what is the sad misfortune—
the accident—that Giovanni alludes to? And her poor Nonna,
what did she call it? A waste? She wants to know every detail. Sal's
going slowly, still keeping this secret from her. Yet again! Damn!

She takes the watering pail, fills it, and waters the fig, talking
to it as if it is a person. "Seems to me he made the big transition
from a man who lost his wife to a boy-man, playing cards with
friends in his hometown, six thousand miles away from us. At least
he's thinking of us." She looks at the soft spray wetting the thick
layer of mulch. "Could he get any farther away?" she asks. "There
he is, living in my hometown that I know so little about. I don't feel
connected to that place. Home is here in San Francisco, with you,
and Kinky, and Mario, and Mercedes." She looks at the tree, then
pictures Sal sitting at the table, sipping and eating and playing chess
with his old friend, perhaps wearing his woolen fisherman hat, like
the one he wore when he lived here. She misses him.

She kneels down again in front of the tree. "I wish he and
Giovanni were here sitting with us, gabbing and eating. Then we
could ask them all our questions." She hugs the base of the fig.

Chapter 11:

UPSTAIRS

"*Upstairs, go upstairs,*" she hears. She swivels around, acci-dently kicking over the watering can.

Again, the voice, "Upstairs, in the bureau. Rose. Go."

She looks up at the tree. The broad leaves shimmer in the light breeze.

"Don't be afraid, Lavinia."

"But I am afraid!" she says aloud.

She's flooded by new memories, helping her to understand the complex relationship between Sal and his father, her grandfather.

She sees the first house in North Beach. Uncle Sal and Aunt Rose are arguing in the kitchen. She remembers sitting under the table with her new Barbie. She's listening. Sal enters the flat from the back stairwell off the kitchen and slams the door. He places his briefcase on the counter and bends to give Aunt Rose a smooch, a quick and hard-sounding kiss. Aunt Rose crunches a crisp toast she's eating in response.

"How's the kid?" There's worry in his voice.

"She asks for that raggedy thing. She can't let it go, Sal."

"You stole the kid's doll, Rose!" his voice thuds. Crunching toast cuts the air. "She's only a kid who lost her mother. Give her a break." Uncle Sal bangs the table. Thud! Thud! Thud! The legs of the table wobble.

Lavinia sits very still, holding her breath, listening for every word and watching Uncle Sal from under the table. His legs make a whole circle around the table, and stop again in front of Aunt Rose. Lavinia hears only the munching, a staccato beat in her ears.

"My father used to do that to me, take what belonged to me. He'd steal my life if he could. You know what he did, that bastard?" Another pound on the table scares Lavinia. "He insisted I take over the family business. Me, the only son of a garbage collector, should pick up people's shit. *Merda*," he hisses. "Merda. Merda. You know what, Rose? He punched me on the day I told him I was going to study accounting. You know what he said? He said, 'No son of mine will leave the family!' *Mai!* Never, never!"

Lavinia hates to hear her uncle's voice like that. The way he's talking, so fast and so very strong, scares her. It's too loud. She covers her ears, but she can still hear him ranting about his father.

"'Hit me, Pa. Be a man! Hit me, Pa!'" he's saying. "'You want me to carry shit the way you did? Me a shit carrier? Well, forget it, Pa.'"

"It's okay now, Salvi. You got away from him. Calm yourself, dear husband." Aunt Rose slides her chair away from the table and Uncle Sal.

The rumble of Uncle Sal's voice alarms Lavinia under the table. He's making her upset. She starts hitting the Barbie, rapping her against the floor, spanking her hard, peeling her slim pants off so she might better feel the spanking. Finally, she hits Barbie's blond head against the wooden floor. Uncle Sal doesn't hear the drumming because he's still yelling.

"You know what he said, Rose?" He stops to catch a breath before he shouts, "My old man kept repeating, 'On my grave, on my grave.'" Uncle Sal is crying now, shouting and crying. "I should have known, I should have known. *Mannagia!*" Under the table little Lavinia is shouting, too, "*Man na gia*, dolly! On my grave, Dolly!" They don't seem to hear her. She wonders if Barbie can hear her or if she has shut down, too.

Now Uncle Sal is silent and sitting next to Aunt Rose. Lavinia can see their knees touching from under the table. Aunt Rose is saying, "It's okay, Salvi. You didn't do nothing to your sister, you didn't do nothing to her. You don't need to damn yourself."

The argument is over now, and Lavinia uncovers her ears. Aunt Rose is softer, trying to calm him down. She wants him to feel better. After a while, they get up and move to their room. Lavinia watches their legs go away. They aren't yelling anymore. Lavinia likes when Aunt Rose has that soft voice to help Uncle Sal calm down and stop pounding the table.

But the voices Lavinia hears in her mind now shift. No longer is she in Sal's and Rose's North Beach apartment. The house is not even in San Francisco. It is far away, but the sounds are just as strong.

She's in a different house, the one with the breadboard on the sink. She's four and hiding behind an older woman who wears a black dress and black tie shoes and smells of garlic and basil. The old woman is making pasta. Lavinia holds her hands over her ears, trying not to hear the gruff voice speaking in Italian—swearing, boiling over, saying *mannagia* and *mamma mia* over and over again.

The gruff man is yelling, "*Io non ti lascero andare*"—I won't let you go.

The woman, a gentle voice, says, "*Non stai in pena per me*"— You don't have to worry about me.

The gruff man says, "You won't go."

She says, repeatedly, "*Lasciami, io non ci sto.*"

He says, "On my grave!" and then storms out of the house.

The little girl is screaming, clutching her mamma's legs, wanting to bite the old man's legs, do something to protect her mamma, so that he won't be able to hurt her anymore.

The older woman drops the pasta on the floor and covers her eyes. She doesn't see how the pasta has landed on her shoe, how it winds like a snake.

The scenes disappear but the rumbling words beat at Lavinia like giant wings. She covers her head. She feels wretched. She bends forward toward the tree and barfs in the thick mulch, expelling the gross, curdled stuff, watching it absorb into the rich soil.

"I'm sorry, dear tree." She sits there under the tree with an acid taste in her mouth. Thinking of the tree standing above her helps her locate her *querencia*.

Again she hears, "Don't be afraid. Upstairs."

She's confused. She hasn't been upstairs since Rose died. She looks toward the green fig leaves dancing gently in the breeze. They are large and wide-leafed, a triple leaf. A jay squeals and flies away.

Stuffing the letter into its envelope, she goes inside to her dark bedroom, to her chest of drawers where she keeps the key to upstairs. When she opens the small top drawer, she sees the photo of her and Sal taken in Naples the day he came to take her to America. She's looking down at a piece of candy, wrapped in colorful shiny paper and twisted at the ends. Raggedy sits on Sal's knee.

She places the picture back in the drawer, takes the key in her hand, and turns on her heel. "Upstairs," she says.

She takes the wooden stairs slowly, unlocks the door at the landing, and leaves it open. Old fried food smells breathe out from the kitchen where once they ate as a family, smothering her. Stuffy. How Sal loved fried fish.

She enters the bedroom where Rose died. Mint green curtains match the chenille bedspread. On one wall is an apothecary console with many small compartments, on the other a mahogany dresser. Rose loved this heavy furniture. Sandwiched between them is the bed. In Lavinia's mind's eye, she sees Rose on the bed with gray skin and shrunken eyes, dying. It's as if she has been here all these twelve months, just rotting away with the smells, waiting for Lavinia to visit. Their last supper together would have been ten months ago, the fish fry Sal made before she took to her bed. He hoped it would perk her up. It didn't.

Lavinia's stomach heaves. Dry heaves, since nothing is left in it.

She walks closer to the bed, remembering that last day of Rose's life when her friends Kate and Mari Karen gathered round her bed, singing their song. Lavinia recalls their sweet voices, singing like angels all around her. There was a beatific smile on Aunt Rose's face.

Now, as Lavinia approaches the bed, she sees Rose. Alarmed, she squints. Rose lifts her head off the pillow, staring at Lavinia, nodding. With a frail finger, she points toward her bureau.

Lavinia feels a combination of fear and awe. *I must be going crazy.*

The finger is wriggling now, so Lavinia walks toward the mahogany dresser and opens the middle drawer. She steps back, places her hand over her mouth, and sighs.

In a zippered plastic container is a blue-gray stuffed doll with a frayed satin trim.

"Raggedy!" she cries, kneeling before her treasure.

Before she unzips the bag, she looks toward the dead woman, who seems to be smiling now. Lavinia makes a small bow of gratitude to the no-nonsense woman and clutches her doll. She closes the drawer and then finds her way back down the creaky wooden steps to the tree, which seems to be smiling, too.

Nesting in her studio on the wooden floor with Raggedy in her hands, Lavinia puts away intrusive images. She hugs her, smelling almond and lemon scents that she associates with her mother. Stretching her legs and arms, she tends to her breathing, minding her heartbeat, which seems out of time. Held in a mother space, like the one in her dreams, Lavinia has a new regard for Rose. Rose wanted to love Lavinia but didn't know how; she, a forlorn woman who made her best effort to teach Lavinia about the hard knocks of life. Maybe she was hell-bent on teaching her about adversity, trying to help the lost child make it in the tough new world. Lavinia's memory has helped her to see her aunt as a woman who had to support gruff Sal in raising his niece. Lavinia holds her Raggedy close to her and lets herself be wrapped in a blanket of forgiveness.

Maybe Rose had never been tended to like a young fig might be.

Something Lavinia cannot name flips inside her. Outside is inside and inside is outside. She can't tell what, exactly, is different as she inhabits this new awareness of her other mother, Rose, the one who had the tough job of filling in for the too-sweet young mother who gave up to the external forces of life as a twenty-one-year-old. Aunt Rose hung in there. She did her best. No matter what.

Lavinia's phone vibrates, bringing her back to the present moment. It's a text from George. "When are you coming back to work? Don't worry about ground cloths. I bought new ones."

She deletes the message. Not George. She knows she owes him some money for the ground cloths, but it doesn't sound as though he expects a payback. He just wants her to come back to work.

No, not yet. She's not ready to see what else might show up on his clay table.

Chapter 12:

KINKY AND LAVINIA

Lavinia freezes when she hears a knock on her studio door. Because the curtains on the front window are drawn shut, she can't see who's there. Maybe it's George. Her cell phone vibrates. It's Kinky, so she gets up to answer the door.

"I was on the floor."

"What were you doing on the floor?" Kinky asks.

"Relishing this," she says, holding out the doll for Kinky to see.

"Oh my God! Is that Raggedy?"

"It's her. Feel. Smell. Like my mother." She shakes her head. "From Rose. She kept it hidden in her drawer all these years."

"Another secret. Why would she have done that?" Kinky asks. "I thought she liked you."

"I think she was jealous."

"She wanted to be your mother," Kinky says.

"When I first arrived, I thought she liked me. I have memories of her trying to be nice, doing stuff like plaiting ribbons in my braids, but I didn't like that."

"So what happened?"

"That's a hard one. I'm not sure. I can't remember, and over time we settled into a better rhythm. But she was never very loving toward me."

"But what was with all the secrets?"

"Their MO!" Lavinia holds up her cell phone to show Kinky George's text. "He wants me to come back to work."

"He wants something from you."

"That's exactly my fear."

"Don't go back, Lavinia. You don't owe him anything." Kinky takes a flask out of her jacket pocket, followed by two more packages. "Food from Mama." She points to the letter. "Is that from Sal?" she asks as she unloads her offerings onto the counter.

Lavinia smiles at her friend. She feels a cloud has lifted today, and now Kinky's brought her dinner.

"Mama's been asking for you."

Lavinia puts her hand over her heart, grateful for this friend and her willingness to share her dear mother.

"Mama's a *curandera*."

"You're like her. You both make me feel better," Lavinia says.

"Today she told me about a woman from her village who lost her husband and began to steal shoes from the closets of the other women in her village."

"Why?"

"Well, she believed that if you stand in someone else's shoes, your loss will be reversed. She thought if she did it, he would return."

"What?"

"Go figure."

"Why do you think she told you that story today?"

"Because I was complaining about my shoes."

"Then give me your shoes."

Kinky looks at her and laughs. "It doesn't matter. Sometimes nonsense is better than fact."

"Where is Mercedes from?" Lavinia asks.

"You know she came here from Spain through Mexico," Kinky says with a perplexed look.

"Alone?"

"No, with the sad, deep *cante*, and the *alegría*," Kinky says. "The *cante* was my father, who taught her the low songs—and the happy sounds, too." Kinky's voice halts. "Papa died in an accident when I was eight years old." She bites her lower lip.

Shock runs through Lavinia, startling and jolting her body. Of course she knew Kinky's father was not in the picture, but how could she not know this information? How could she not have asked about it? She's been so focused on her own pain, she's never seen or asked. She sees more clearly now than ever before how Kinky has always soothed her. How has Lavinia never asked her about her father? She's been obsessed, needing her own mothering. She feels selfish. She doesn't want this part to be true.

Kinky is looking at her.

"I'm sorry, for you and Mercedes." Lavinia takes her friend in her arms and listens to her soft whimper. When she settles, Lavinia says, "You never said anything. How could that be?"

"You know, Lavinia"—Kinky pauses as if hesitant to continue, but she does—"didn't you lose your mother in an accident?"

"Yes, we have that horror in common, Kinky, but you . . ." Lavinia stops. "You seem so much more well adjusted than me."

"But I have my mother. I am not an orphan."

Lavinia feels the bolt. One hand crosses her heart.

"I'm sorry, Lavinia, I didn't mean to say something to hurt you."

The two friends look at each other. It's as if they have passed through a deep chasm together. Kinky reaches over to grab her friend's hands. Their four hands wind in a garland with their two dark hearts at its center.

Kinky begins plating the carnitas and tortillas on a large platter sitting out on the counter.

"Sal thinks I finished State," Lavinia says, watching Kinky prepare their food.

"He doesn't know you left?"

"Apparently not. He sent me a check for five hundred dollars."

"That's not even enough to cover your book expenses."

"I know," Lavinia says, her face dropping.

"You can still finish," Kinky encourages her.

"I'm not interested. Sal pictures me teaching elementary school to kids on Bryant Street."

"I do, too."

Lavinia ignores her friend's comment. "He told me he visited the house where I was born. He remembered me cooking there with Mamma as a four-year-old." Lavinia gets up and goes inside to her bureau and returns with the photo. Kinky puts down her fork, wipes her hands on her oversized sweatshirt, and carefully takes the small black-and-white photo with its fluted edges. She stares at it for a long time.

"Look at you with your T-strap shoes." She looks down at Lavinia's shoes. "You still love T-straps."

Lavinia shrugs. "I'm still a baby."

Kinky laughs. "Sal's pretty dapper with those creased pants and leather shoes."

"He prided himself on the way he looked. His hair was always slicked with some kind of grease, and then he'd wear a hat. He worked at a small accounting firm when I was little, and I always wondered if he took his hat off at work."

"Look how he only has eyes for you," Kinky says. She places the photo on the clean side of the outdoor table.

"His friend Giovanni told him something about my mother," Lavinia says, her voice deep and throaty, thick and edgy. She stops, can't go on.

Kinky sits quietly and reaches out to touch her hand. The warm night air seems to hold them in some protected space—the fig tree, a shadow guide. The carnitas and tortillas wait.

Lavinia breaks the silence by picking up her small tequila glass and clinking it against Kinky's. "*Buen provecho.*" They both take a sip and then eat Mercedes's carnitas and tortillas, spicy and sweet and salty all at the same time. They eat slowly and in silence, their only soundtrack the evening sounds of crickets left over from the late summer. Or are they newly born?

Street voices rumble. A bus pulls away from the curb. When Lavinia finishes eating, she musters her courage to speak of her mother.

"Giovanni told Uncle Sal that Mom and her family had some misfortune."

"Sal must know that." Kinky sits up tall in the metal chair, invigorated.

"He never told me what really happened, what prompted him bringing me to the States. He only said that Mamma went to the angels. It wasn't until I was ten years old that I realized that being with the angels meant she must've died."

"Then you have no idea how she died."

"None."

"You must be curious."

"Furious."

"To my mind, Lavinia, that's the sadness." Kinky looks at her, her eyebrows drawn together. "Maybe it would have been too much when you were four or five, but they owed you an explanation as you got older."

Lavinia stares into the dark fig tree, tears glistening in the corners of her eyes. It's as if Kinky's proclamation is the first she's ever heard or understood the degree to which she has been wronged. The pieces are fitting together now in some mysterious way.

Kinky fidgets with her glass, swishing the liquid gold. Lavinia feels that if she listened carefully enough, she could hear the sap seeping from the agave. She could swear the fig is producing its own milky white sap—crying, too.

Chapter 13:

THE CONTRAPTION

Lavinia goes to North Beach every day now, passing the places where she grew up—one above the bakery on Columbus and another on Vallejo. She never sees anyone at home. The Vallejo house sits like a big fortress, shut off to the world.

Stopping in front of the bakery, Lavinia inhales deeply, smelling the sweet aromas of Italian bread baking in the downstairs oven, sweet creams and butters, rum-flavored cream. Although Maria, the baker, is gone, the new memory of Lavinia's own mother arises in this moment. She remembers her mother's offering, a latte and a bite of fried dough, in the kitchen of her birth home. She takes a moment to savor this memory before hurrying off to Zack's house. She carries the sweet smell of dough lingering in her nostrils—her mother's dough, *struffoli,* she imagines.

Zack Luce is waiting for her at the door, dressed in his gym clothes. A small duffel bag waits near the door. Lavinia feels welcomed, grateful that someone is at home to greet her, even if he is her client. His smile and zest for life gives her a sunny, citrus feeling inside. He is a contrast to Nina, who barely says hello. Zack waits at the door for her wearing a genuine smile.

"Ss-so, we're off to a good s-s-start," he says with a big smile. "I'm glad it worked out with your other clients."

"Oh, yes, Don and Nina White. Nina didn't switch times." Lavinia looks up to see the tall, slim man open his mouth. "You know them?" she asks, surprised by the small world.

"Yes, we once worked together on a neighborhood project." His Adam's apple pulses as he speaks about them. She hasn't noticed that before, nor has she noticed his long, thin hands with their shiny fingernails.

Zack directs her to the living room. The wall-to-wall books give her the feeling she's ascending into some great library, only interrupted by the singsong s's of his speech. The ambience of his place and his speech please her. She stands near the divan across from the Boston rocker with a floral print pillow. He rocks it forward with his long hands.

"Please," he says, "sit and lis-s-s-sten to the eight fifteen chimes of the clocks with me."

She sits on the couch and he slides into the rocker, resting his hands, wrinkled by time, on the arms of the black wooden chair, studying her, making her feel mildly self-conscious. She shifts her weight as if she's in a rocker, too. *He's a quiet man,* she thinks. This thought eases her mind. "I've never seen or heard so many clocks," she says.

"My collection. Elsa loved them as well. Be sure to check out the granddaddy of them all." He looks over his right shoulder to a large wooden clock with a silver pendulum, its medallion moving back and forth. "We got that in Germany when we lived in Munich."

"And the book collection?" Lavinia wants to hear a summary of the books, but more, she wants to know about the man who collected the books.

"Mostly mine. Bought over the years. I don't make many purchases now."

"And all about time," she says.

Zack nods. "Most of them, anyway."

She waits for a long moment, but he adds nothing more. The silence seems to underscore time until, a moment later, they hear the eight fifteen chimes, each clock seeming to speak to the next.

Zack rises and says, as if in a hurry, "Speaking of time, I must get to the gym now. A water baby, you know. I feel most alive suspended."

"I don't swim."

"Too bad. But then, that means you have a lot to look forward to. It's never too late to learn." He stands up. "Oh," he says, as if he's forgotten something, "the laundry is pretty simple today. The soft creases you ironed in my chinos are just how I like them. I rigged a clothesline in the shower for you. It's one of my own inventions—like a tape measure, but it has a crystal on the end of the fluorescent blue tape. Crystal is what it's all about for me. Moving through the water is like moving through the facets of a crystal."

What Zack said about crystal lingers in Lavinia's ears. She runs the water into the washer. Faucets splash into the spinning tub and gushing water fills the blue basin, churning a world full of colors with foam at the top. She imagines each splash of water as a facet of a crystal, reflecting color. She watches, mesmerized.

While the clothes soak in the bathroom, she pulls one of Zack's books off the shelf. The author announces, "This is not a tree. This paper is made from a combination of recycled materials. and you can make good choices." This idea seems to be the gist of the book.

She considers what a person's book collection says about them. She tries to imagine Zack reading these books, and considers how they've informed his life. *And what does he mean about swimming in a crystal? Is that even possible?* She has never before thought about liquid crystals; she has always associated crystal with mass and light. Light is *luce* in Italian, she remembers. Light relates to crystal, and to Zack, who seems to reflect light. "Hmm!" She feels happy, like she's uncovered a deep mystery.

The washer begins its turning cycle, swishing round and round. Sorting through the laundry hamper, she finds at the bottom assorted water gear: bathing trunks, Speedos, swim caps, booties, even a pair of gloves. She carefully pulls the damp, already musty-smelling garments from the dry ones, placing them in the sink basin to wash separately. She will use her skills to cleanse this important gear for the old man, get rid of that mildew smell. She wonders what Elsa thought about doing the laundry, knowing as she does that most people find it a burden.

"Coo-coo," she hears, and looks toward the grandfather clock. It's ten minutes before the hour. *That's odd*, she thinks. Looking around the room, she realizes the cuckoo sound is coming from the washer, signaling that the cycle is done.

On her way to move the laundry to the dryer, she passes the bookshelf again and is drawn to another title, *The Long Now*. Curious, she sits down on the couch and begins to flip through its pages.

She's not sure how much time has passed or how many books she's flipped through when Zack knocks on the wall from the kitchen.

She startles. She's been so immersed she didn't even hear him come in.

"I'm just returning for my gym bag." He smiles at her but she feels like she's been caught. He chuckles—at the expression on her face, no doubt. "Are you interested in the clock?" he asks, pointing at the book she's reading.

She closes the book and looks at its cover: *The Millennium Clock*. "Yes, I am."

He stops, seeming to listen for something.

"Time fascinates me. The way it feels so long and at times passes without a moment of awareness," Lavinia says.

"Yes, there it is, you've hit it. Time has no substance. We don't even know if it exists."

She nods, never having heard about this—the possible nonexistence of time. She's heard a man at the museum say time is life or time is beauty, but that's different. She looks at Zack, waiting.

"Have you read *Cradle to Cradle*?" he asks.

"Yes, I keep coming back to it. What do you make of it? Are those words of wisdom? A Buddhist koan?"

"You might say they are. In Buddhism time is the main teaching, isn't it?" he says.

Lavinia doesn't know. "Can you tell me how they're related?" she asks, experiencing a wave of excitement about learning something new. His interest in teaching further sparks her interest in the clock.

"Impermanence. Things appear and then seem to disappear. Time."

"How interesting. I've never thought about time in that way," she says, her mind bubbling over with enthusiasm.

"Everything rises and passes away," he says.

"Like thoughts?"

"Yes, and time," he says.

"So all there is . . . is change," Lavinia says.

"Exactly. You get it!" he says excitedly. "That's not an easy concept. And we haven't even mentioned that we are timeless."

His eyes fill with what seem to be tears, but gleeful tears or laughing tears. "And more. Deep ecology to save our dear planet from us," he adds.

"Are you an ecologist, too?"

"I study deep ecology."

"What's that?" she asks.

"The easiest way to explain it is that everything is related to everything. Interdependence. We need each other. The trees need our breath, and we need theirs. My love is time. Time is love. Your work here is time, and your time and commitment is love." He looks around the room at his many clocks.

"I'd love to hear more about the millennium clock," she says. Just then the grandfather clock drones out the deepest and heaviest drawl, a *basso profondo*, announcing the half hour.

"Follow me," Zack says. "Let me show you something." He heads toward the guest bedroom and opens the door.

With the curtains pulled open, a massive machine reveals itself, its shiny panels reflecting light.

Lavinia steps back and puts her hand over her mouth. It's so impressive with the sun pouring in on it, glinting on the metal. "Is it a robot?" she asks, twirling a piece of her hair and stepping closer to Zack. Whatever it is, it takes up the entire room.

"Yes, you might say that. This is a model of another machine—a smaller version of the main millennium clock that will be buried in a limestone mountain."

"Another what?" He's going too fast for her and she wants to understand.

"A clock."

"This is a clock? But I don't see any dials." She moves toward the contraption, searching for anything that might reveal that it's actually a clock. She steps up to its base and sees a three-pronged wheel with metal knobs at the end of each spike. Mid-range she sees a circular dial sitting on a spiral of coils at least a foot in diameter.

"This is the replica, a smaller version of the 10,000-year clock, designed to keep time for that long."

"But how can it do that?"

He hands her a small framed quote from the man whose brainchild this clock project was, Danny Hillis.

Lavinia sits on the footstool and reads in a soft voice, "'I want to build the clock that ticks once every year. The century hand advances once every one hundred years. Cuckoo comes out every millennium for the next ten thousand years.'"

"It chimed two times when we went from 1999 to 2000," Zack says. "Soon, the Millennium Clock will have a new home." His voice rises as if he's singing a glorious chant. He's on his toes now, looking very much to Lavinia like a little boy dancing with excitement. "If I could have one thing in the world before I die, I would visit the site where the real clock will rest."

He looks at her with a yearning that she knows well, but her longing, a burning feeling, relates to family wishes and not a clock. And just now she wants to have this connection with Zack.

"The final clock?" She faces Zack, whose eyes light up like the early sun.

"Yes, the one built for the Ely, Nevada site will be embedded in white limestone on top of Mount Washington—with a glorious view."

Ely, Nevada? "Zack, can you tell me more? I want so much to follow you."

He looks at her, his face soft and in reflection. "This is like an Egyptian pyramid. Something that will continue to be alive even though there will be no ears to hear it. The idea is that the future goes on—and the clock will symbolize that."

"The future goes on? Even after we're dead. Is that so important if we are dead?" she asks, surprised by her own question. "Yes," he says firmly. "For the children's sake, we must believe in the future."

"Yes, that makes sense . . . and did you say Nevada?"

He nods. "Ely, Nevada."

"Is that near Las Vegas?"

"No. Ely is nearer to the Ancient Bristlecone Pine Forest in the White Mountains here in California. Have you heard of it? Oldest trees in the known world, some 4,800-year-old trees-s-s."

Lavinia sighs. "I've never been to Nevada." She feels an ache in the pit of her stomach as she realizes she's never left San Francisco—that her life here has been rather sheltered. She always begged Sal to take her to Las Vegas to play the slots, but now that no longer appeals to her as much as seeing a 4,800-year-old tree.

"Let me propose something," Zack stammers as his long hand rests with curved fingers on his cheek.

"Okay." Lavinia hesitates.

"I wonder if you might drive with me to the bristlecone forest, and then to Ely. Of course, I'd pay you for your time. I think it's worth . . . four thousand? How does that sound?"

The excitement she feels about this offer runs through her like colored ribbons flying into unique patterns, tickling her mood. And what about the generous fee! "Why would you invite me?" she asks.

"Well, I have a car, but my daughter says I shouldn't drive on my own to Ely. And Margaret's a bit too busy right now with her practice."

His head bends, and Lavinia senses his sadness. Her instinct is to comfort him but she stands still, waiting. He's looking at her; she keeps staring at all the weird coils at the base of the machine, observing the strong feelings within her body. It's a pinch in her heart that makes her feel sorrow for Zack and her own loss. She aches with him.

Margaret has this home and this father. Why wouldn't she want to make his dream come true? Lavinia would do it for her own father, if she had one.

When she comes back to the moment, Zack is spouting off some data about the first prototype of the clock, which was built with Monel metal and brass.

"Monel?"

"An alloy of nickel and copper. Brass for the moving components. The four-inch pendulum is made of tungsten, an indestructible metal—strong enough to last ten thousand years."

Lavinia looks into the old man's eyes. He seems to be pleading with her.

"*The Long Now*," she says. "The long view of time."

Just then the grand cuckoo breathes out nine long cuckoos. Has a half hour really gone by?

Zack looks toward the doorway. "Well, I best be going for my swim now and leave you to your work. Don't worry too much about doing the laundry today. I'd rather you look at the books and consider the drive to the bristlecone forest and then to Ely."

"I'll think about it," she says, smiling.

His eyebrows arch up in a half circle; he is smiling. "Do you drive?" he asks.

"Yes, I have my license."

"Good," he says, nodding, before leaving the room.

She hears the front door click a few moments later, and she's alone with the massive clock.

After Zack leaves, Lavinia reflects on her world, feeling more expansive and lighter. Not knowing about the books, not knowing about the machine, not even knowing her mother or her father seem less consuming of her thoughts. The labyrinth she lives in seems to be less tight. That she can neither see where she entered nor its center or path of return doesn't bother her. She brushes herself as if she's clearing some disturbance from her body, making room for something new.

Maybe going with Zack will free her; illuminate her path as she moves into her own future; teach her how to swim in crystal waters; free her up from her fears of dying. And then there is the money offer, more than she's ever handled.

She wants to walk in the dark the way Mario does, without her morbid fears of loss; to be like Mercedes and Kinky, who make a place for their dead at their table while they sing and dance.

The granddaddy chimes, freezing her to the spot with its *basso profondo.* Counting each chime—one, two, three, four, five, six, seven, eight, nine, ten—intensifies the old, familiar feelings of being trapped and time passing. *No,* she thinks, *I don't want to be trapped in time, I want to remember this new feeling, the expansiveness of time, the future of time. Please,* she begs the clock as if it were a foreboding god. Then she is flooded with questions. *Do I have time? Is time on my side? Am I living in the time of my life or out of time? No time, or timeless?* She doesn't know the answers.

Look at the space in front and the space behind you. She hears the DJ's words.

Her life moves past her and yet stands still, too, as if she's taking two steps back and one forward, going backwards nonetheless. What are her accomplishments? Sal thinks she finished school. And what instead? Ironing and washing. Sorting the dark from the light, the wet from the dry. Hanging and drying. Making crisp pleats in an old man's pants. She pushes at this lost feeling, fighting with herself. Time in front. Time in back. Time to the right, time to the left. Time now feels frantic. *Time to visit Kinky!* This thought grounds her.

Although Zack has let her off the hook for the day, she finishes her work—cycling out the load from the washer to the dryer, pressing his pants, and ironing two shirts. Thinking of his generous offer makes her feel good. She hangs the swimwear on the pullout clothesline of azure and crystal, picturing Zack swimming in deep, crystalline waters, considering his offer. Envisioning the eight-hour car ride, followed by an adventure in the mountains, lightens her mood. As she rinses Zack's plaid swim trunks by hand, she decides she will travel with him to see the old forest and the site of the clock.

When the wash is done, she places it in the drier, sets the timer, and lets herself out.

Chapter 14:

FLAMENCO DAZE

Lavinia watches Kinky pour a jigger from her mother's Don Eduardo Tequila, 100 percent *de agave*. The bottle of tequila reflects the late-afternoon light and makes her wonder if it's liquid crystal. The two girls stare at the small shot glasses on the floral colored tablecloth. One empty glass waits for Mercedes, who is doing her afternoon harvesting and pruning at the community garden nearby.

"Armando talked today," Kinky says.

"What'd he say?"

"He told me how boys don't cry. When a boy cries, he gets hit. That's what his dad told him."

Lavinia raises her eyebrows in question as she sips her tequila, then waits patiently, aware of her friend's affection for the boy, seeing that she's upset.

"Not that I've seen any visible bruises," Kinky continues, the crease of worry in the space between her eyebrows deepening. "He's using the time now to talk about his family and whether it's right to complain about his fears." She bites her lip. "He's worried his mother will have to return to Mexico."

"Oh, no. That's horrible."

"He's heard about the immigration officers doing raids in the city and feels scared they'll come and get them. The mother of one of his friends had to return to Mexico."

"The poor boy," Lavinia responds quietly. "How to live like that?" Then she pauses, feeling a quiver in her heart. "I can relate to his fear of loss."

"You miss Sal?" Kinky swirls the tequila in her glass.

"Encourage Armando to complain," Lavinia says, not wanting to talk about Sal, or about how she knows about having a mother snatched away mysteriously.

"His Sunday school teacher told him he must love everyone, even his enemies. I wanted to tell him, 'You get to protect yourself, Armando.' You know, be safe—but six-year-olds depend on others for their safety."

"That's advice I need to hear, too, since I'm surrounded by all these weirdos!" Lavinia looks to her friend and thinks about the snake on Russian Hill. "Why do I keep attracting these nuts for clients?" Lavinia looks around the homey room, the table set with a place for her; this, combined with the anticipation of Mercedes's bounty, makes her smile, and a feeling of ease fills her body. "I'm glad I have you and Mercedes in my life."

Kinky reaches for her hand. Lavinia lets her hold it, appreciating the warm gesture from her friend.

"I think there are just a lot of weird people around. I don't think it's your fault, Lavinia, or that you're attracting them. Nuts are attracted to San Francisco, that's all. Sometimes I think you take too much responsibility for shit happening," Kinky says confidently.

"That's something to think about. Thank you." What Kinky says is on the mark, though Lavinia could never have expressed it herself with such clarity. She sighs, feeling her eyes fill up at being so clearly seen. As the heaviness in her heart lifts, she focuses on the green diamond center of a square floor tile, which pulls her in.

"*Buenas tardes, mijitas,*" Mercedes says, coming into the dining room from outside, carrying her harvest bag with beet tops hanging over the edge.

"Let me help you." Lavinia rushes over, takes the heavy bag of veggies from her hands, and puts them by the sink.

"*Gracias,*" Mercedes says as she takes her purse off her wrist and moves toward the table. "You're relaxing for a change," she says, looking back at them as if they are still sitting at the table, the way she first must have seen them when she walked in. "You both work so hard. I like to see you taking time in the afternoon to sit together and talk about your day."

"Mama, you're home in time to help Lavinia. She wants to roar like a lion."

Lavinia laughs out loud, swiveling around toward her friend. "Where'd you get that idea?" Kinky astounds her. Is it just that she knows her so well, or is it that she's truly clairvoyant? "I actually want to dance," she counters.

"*Claro,*" Mercedes says. "*Bebemos,*" she adds, lifting the small crystal glass to her lips. Her upper lip reflects beads of sweat. She stares at the drink before she sips. It looks to Lavinia as if she is consulting with the magic fluid. After some moments, she walks toward a wooden cabinet on the far wall of the kitchen where she keeps her musical stuff: bells, castanets, all sitting in two large bowls. She picks up a small, pleated fan with brightly colored flowers and waves it in front of her face, then brings the bowls stuffed with the instruments to the table.

"How can I pass up this offer?" Mercedes says, sitting down at her table. She places her hands securely on her knees. Kinky pours some Don Eduardo into Lavinia's empty glass and then into her own. Now three gleaming golden tequilas shine on the table.

After they each take another sip, Mercedes says, "Let's play music."

She removes the instruments from the bowls, then places the bowls on the table in front of Lavinia. They look like salad bowls to her and she can't imagine what the older woman has in mind. When Mercedes leaves to get water, Lavinia taps at the hollowed out bowls.

Mercedes returns and pours water from a yellow watering pail into the larger of the bowls. Lavinia watches, mesmerized by the stream of clear water filling the empty vessel. When it's two-thirds filled, Mercedes gently sinks the smaller bowl, upside down, into the bowl of water. It floats. "This is a Mexican water gourd drum," she says, placing her two small hands on the top of the small head of the gourd and tapping it with her fingers, then with the palms of her hands. The water drum makes deep sounds.

"Try, *mijita*," she says, placing Lavinia's hands on the gourd. At first Lavinia is afraid she'll tumble the top gourd, but she holds onto the floating drum as if she's in a dream, surfing a perfect arc, all fluid beneath her, the way she imagines a surfer riding a big wave. With her hands rolling around the head of the drum, she begins to tap with her fingers. She has never experienced anything like this fluid drum with its resonating sounds before.

The partially submerged bowl, decorated with red roses on a glossy black ground, fascinates her.

Mercedes takes two black wooden castanets and hands them to Kinky. While Kinky slips the elastic bands of the small clappers on the thumbs of each hand, Lavinia taps on the floating drum.

"A warrior woman needs to drum to find her heartbeat," Mercedes says.

Lavinia likes to think of herself in this way and feels encouraged to place her hands on the round belly of the drum, using her knuckles and then her palms, trying different, simple rhythms, enjoying the deep sounds that seem to pull her to sway in her chair.

With her embroidered silk shawl hanging on her rounded back—black tassels hanging over her arms, embroidered roses cupping her shoulders—Mercedes goes to the CD player and cues up flamenco music. That done, she sits back at the table with her feet flat on the linoleum floor, closes her eyes, and relaxes in stillness. Lavinia hears her breathing in the song of a *malaguena*, a folk tune played by a guitarist who alternates rapid fingering with slow picks.

Mama Montoya's head bobs fluidly on her neck as her face transforms. The round woman seems to inhabit the music. She holds her upper lip muscles taut, bringing about rosy red, full lips, as if an invisible finger has painted them. Lavinia can't take her eyes off her. She has never seen such focus of attention before. Mercedes wears a regal concentration, which brings a nobility of posture: she sits with an erect spine that seems connected to the earth energy. Lavinia thinks of a queen, a warrior queen, who can protect herself and give sustenance to the daughters of the world. She feels in good company.

Lavinia listens to the guitarist's loose fingers strum as Mercedes remains in stillness with her eyes closed and a smile on her face. Lavinia is overcome by the notion that the guitarist playing on the CD is Kinky's father. Could it be Mercedes is calling up the spirit of her husband? Or maybe she's having a visit with his memory. It makes her think that we don't really lose our dead— that somehow, instead, they're always with us.

Lavinia holds the small drum fluidly but steadily under her hands. Only when Mercedes's foot begins to beat out the rhythm does she begin to forget herself and allow the music to move her, too. One-two-three, one-two-three—a sweet trail of music complements her foot stomping, sending her to a place where her heart and her feet dance as one. Lavinia is only faintly aware that her face is softening, her cheekbones relaxing as her chin drops to the sound of the castanets that accompany the flamenco music—the black wooden castanets that have become an extension of Kinky's fingers.

"*Ay, ay, ay, ay, ay,*" Mercedes begins. Is she singing to her daughter, to her lover, to God? Lavinia doesn't know and it doesn't matter. Mercedes's foot thumps on the floor as her arms rise and snake over her head, her fingers gracefully extended to answer the music. Now the guitarist is singing, calling to her. Mercedes seems embodied in the music as the tapping and clacking and stomping increase into one great riff.

Without realizing it, Lavinia has begun to stamp her feet, too, and then suddenly Mercedes gets up and stands by the table, dancing a *torque de lavarte*. She moves rapidly, standing mostly in one place, stamping and tapping her feet as her hands clap the beat. This gypsy woman seems in a trance as she chants, creating a spell and pulling Kinky and Lavinia along.

Lavinia's elation wraps around her like a beautiful emerald shawl that shimmers like the sea. Her heart and pulse dance through her, sending her into an ecstasy of joy. "*Alegría!*" she yells out. She imagines a line dance in which all her ancestors from the beginning of time line up. Her mother and Aunt Rose are at the head of the line, and then all the nonnas and papas, all the way back to before the Norman conquest. Then the line stretches way back to the cave people, short men and women wearing loincloths, carrying baskets, the women with babies on their backs. Time is fluid, moving backward and forward at the same time. Like a psychedelic drug? Like liquid crystal? She has a vision of a DNA thread she carries in every cell. She strains to see her father there, but she's never seen him and she can't conjure up an image of him.

Mercedes claps and stamps her feet with her raised arms above her head, her face proud and strong. She is showing Lavinia what a warrior woman looks like, dancing her soul through her feet. Kinky is clapping. Lavinia feels *la querencia* once again with Mercedes, this lioness right before her eyes. Here in this moment, Lavinia stands before the eyes of her ancestors within the beat of the dance. She's not alone now but fulfilled by the presence of others, and her new family fills her with their blessing.

When the music stops, Mercedes sits again in her chair at the kitchen table. She places one foot on her knee and begins to rub her small toes, looking at Kinky and Lavinia. "Now you have seen the warrior woman," she says, looking exhausted, as if she's pulled some images from the deep recesses of time.

Lavinia wonders if the *curandera* intentionally produced the images of ancestors who passed in a long line through her mind during the dance, and then watches Kinky, who's inching her chair toward her mother.

"Mama, let me massage your feet," she says, reaching over and taking Mercedes's foot into her hand. She tilts her head. "Whose shoes have you been standing in?"

Mercedes looks at her daughter. "In God's shoes."

When Lavinia leaves the house, she carries with her the blessed feelings of being part of a human family. She has a sense of being connected to the Montoyas. A thread runs through her, one she hasn't ever experienced before. Maybe she left behind her longing on the kitchen floor, right there in the center of the green diamond pattern on the linoleum tile.

She thinks of her Nonna Caterina, who wears a shroud instead of a colorful mantilla like the one Mercedes has. *What kinds of rituals does Nonna make?* she wonders. As she walks the streets toward her studio, she revisits her thought about how Kinky's father is with them and how they aren't lost just because he's gone. This is what she feels she can have from her own human chain. Her recognition is in how to live a full life even when you feel these absences.

Then her attention turns to Uncle Sal's letter from Italy. *Why did he decide to write to me now, after a whole year has passed? And why drop that bomb about my mother suffering a great misfortune?* She's very conscious of how much sadness she's been carrying with her since she received the letter.

Shouldn't her mother's misfortune be something he talked about with her face-to-face? What a stupid ass he is! She wants to blame him for all her discomfort.

At home, she gets out of her costume. The tuxedo jacket she wears every day feels too tight. Tonight when she visits Mario, she'll wear her bomber jacket instead. She hugs Raggedy, then takes a pad of white paper from a small desk and a pencil and scribbles out a letter.

> *Dear Uncle Sal,*
> *You'll be happy to know things are turning around for me. I have a job and Kinky remains my good friend. Señora Montoya feeds me in so many ways. I visit North Beach every day. I have a friend there.*
> *But the letter you sent me is like a train wreck! How can you drop this on me? Better to deliver this news in person.*

She puts the pencil down. She has to bite on something to quell the wild horse running through her body. She chews on her gum. She begins again.

> *Uncle Sal, your letter upsets me and touches off great longing for my mother and many despairing memories. What happened to her? I want to know. My heart is breaking, and I must know about my parents. Why didn't you protect me better?*
>
> *Because of the fig tree, I found my doll. My connection to my mother was stuffed in plastic in Rose's middle drawer in the same way I've been stuck in plastic all my life. The way you let her rule you. You never protected me. You let her steal my Raggedy, the way you stole me from my early home. You're a coward, uncle. I hate you! And I didn't finish at State. I wash underwear and clean dirty tarps and men stare at my birthmark.*
>
> *The fig tree talked to me and today Aunt Rose appeared from the dead, returning my doll to me. I am grateful for that.*
> *Love from your niece,*
> *Lavinia Lavinia*

She folds the short letter, places it in a stamped envelope, and addresses it to Via Toledo, No. 9, Naples, Italy. She places it on the stoop by the front door, leaving it for the mailman to pick up in the morning. Then she sits in the darkening living space of her home. No matter how many bubbles she snaps, she feels an agony creep inside her, dark and thick. Her breath feels tight as she dresses hurriedly, pulling on the bomber jacket with the sleeves rolled up over a slinky top. She leaves the studio, stepping over the letter that will go to Sal in the morning on her way out.

As Lavinia closes her door, she catches the glimpse of the shadow of a man rushing off. Her heart races as she crosses Valencia, heading away from the man and toward the restaurant scene on 16th Street, where she knows there'll be lots of people and traffic. She looks behind her only once as she jaywalks across Valencia.

She walks briskly, her cell phone in her hand, ready to dial 911 or Kinky. She swallows hard. *There's no one I can call*, she tells herself. *I'm alone and no one cares.*

She reminds herself to stop. *Those thoughts don't ring true anymore*, she tells herself.

Not after her time with Mercedes and Kinky, not after her connection with Zack and his time machine, not after what she's experienced with Mario. *I am loved*, she tells herself. Something inside her, insistent and demanding, won't let her believe that old story any longer.

Yet on and on the thoughts come, rampaging through her mind. At the bus stop she's riding the horse, trying to tame her passions, but she keeps bucking. It's not until she hops on the bus heading for North Beach, focuses on the other miscreants sitting alone and staring out the window or slumping half asleep in their seats, that she admires her new outfit in the mirror and finally takes a deep and relaxing breath. She will be with Mario soon.

Chapter 15:

A NIGHT WALK IN THE WOODS

She reaches North Beach by 7:00 p.m. It's already dark. From the end of the line, she stares at Mario, who's making espresso. She wants to see his expression when he first notices her presence. That will tell her whether he belongs on the list of people who love her. He looks up at her, meeting her face, meeting her eyes. His eyes glisten. A wide smile parts his lips. He tilts his head as he pours the coffee into a small cup, placing it on the bar for her. His eyes say, *What are you waiting for Lavinia? Come closer to me.*

What he says out loud is, "Long time."

She places herself at the bar and looks into his soft, happy eyes. "I know," she says, "I've missed you."

"Been dancing lately?"

"Sort of, flamenco dancing." She tells him about her time with Mercedes and Kinky, remembering the odd feeling of having been in a trance or on drugs. Thinking about Mercedes as a *curandera* with magical powers gives her goose bumps.

"That sounds fantastic!" he exclaims.

"After it was over I felt pretty lonely, though," she confesses.

"Well, you're here now," he says, bending toward her at the bar.

She nods. Her lips part in a shy smile.

"How about a walk in the woods after my shift? There's a little patch of redwoods in Golden Gate Park," he says.

"When are you off?"

"In ten minutes."

She smiles at how unique Mario is, loving the idea of strolling in the woods in this otherwise dense city.

Ten minutes later, Mario emerges from the back looking more like a customer than a barista in his navy-colored, wool peacoat. He chats in the line with others and then excuses himself to go over to her and give her a peck on the cheek.

A little abashed, she points at his feet. He's wearing Nikes. He, in turn, points to her T-strap shoes and then acknowledges her jacket. "Cool!"

"Same-same but different," she answers, referencing their two jackets—her bomber jacket, worn by military pilots, and his peacoat, worn by sailors. They laugh as he slips his arm through hers, and they walk onto Columbus Avenue.

At the corner, as they wait for a cab, she tells him about Zack's proposal to accompany him to Ely. "What do you think about my going?"

"I think it's a fantastic offer. He's rich. Interesting and stable, too," he says, as a cab pulls up. "I mean, he's a good guy . . . I think you should do it."

En route to Golden Gate Park, where the small redwood grove lives, they sit in silence. Lavinia looks out the window into the darkness, wondering about going off into the woods at this time of night. Seven thirty. Darker still.

"First time for me," she says.

"Best time."

His hand squeezes hers gently, and she feels safe. When he

looks at her with his warm and inviting smile, she trusts the good feelings in her heart. These feelings are trustworthy—her own *querencia*, a special kind of knowing, the one Mercedes said she would find in herself.

The cab pulls up on Tenth Avenue at the corner of a long dark block of woods that extends three city blocks toward Park Presidio. As they get out and walk slowly, adjusting to the darkness of the night, Lavinia recalls a line from Dante's Inferno. "*Lasciate ogne speranza, voi ch'intrate*": "Abandon all hope, ye who enter here." A foreboding thought, and yet upon entering the woods she feels a sense of softness, a deep hush within her being, a letting go of all expectations, as her feet squish into the spongy cushion of the pine needles. She smells the deep resin from the trees, clean and spicy, and it gives her a sense of well-being. She feels relief and her breath sags deeply. It's as if she's remembering another time when there was no time, when time rested in timelessness. Maybe all the ancestors at her back are protecting her.

Streetlights on Fulton reflect on the wide path that runs diagonally through the grove of trees and away from the busy street. She takes another deep breath, this time smelling the fresh, fecund earth. Walking slower, she wonders if she's standing still. The scent of the rich dirt works its magic. She imagines an underworld of *funghi* nourishing the earth with their paths of undergrowth twining and tunneling under the forest floor—an entire city of nourishing networks and tendrils she can't see. A city under the city! Maybe even reaching for the fig tree in her back yard.

She focuses on the darkest groves of trees ahead of her, wanting nothing more than to go inside, lie down, and let the earth hold her.

She looks at Mario. "Can we sit a minute?"

He nods and follows her into the center of a family of redwood trees. Several stand in a circle, surrounding the original trunk of a dead tree. With her foot Lavinia finds the center, an old stump filled with fallen pine needles, and moves into its cup.

"Come sit with me," she says, reaching a hand toward him. "This is so soft, I could stay here forever." She inhales the moist smell of the earth and listens to the silence of the special stand of tall trees as he sits beside her.

"We're sitting in the womb of the tree," Mario says. "I've never done this before."

"Really!" She feels touched, like they are breaking bread together.

"This is the parent tree. Those are the daughters," he says, moving a hand up the length of the tall trees toward the dark sky.

"You're kidding." Lavinia's nerves seem to be jumping. Something is taking hold inside her, and she feels ready to burst. "Please, tell me more."

"When the mother tree dies, it stimulates seeds and creates a circle of daughters."

"A circle of daughters, I love that."

"And you're the most beautiful of them all," he says.

Her eyes fill. She bends into him, feeling something like joy.

"You're not crying, are you, Lavinia?"

"No," she says, the tears receding. She recalls her experience earlier today with Mercedes and the line of ancestors. The three women—Mercedes, Kinky, and Lavinia—are a circle of daughters.

"A fairy circle," he adds to the pot. "Have you ever danced in a fairy circle?"

"No," she says. She wants to feel his body. Her nose twitches.

"Let's do it," he says, standing up and reaching out to her.

She nods her head. He pulls her up and soon she is in his arms in the middle of the fairy circle. She hears him humming as they sway gently in one place in the midst of the whispering trees. For another song he sings *la-la-la*, and they dance. She's dancing in his arms and not with her own shadow, as was her custom in her long room before meeting him. Then they move out again onto the larger path, skipping hand in hand through the forest like two children, until they stop in front of a large granite stone. Mario takes her hand and places it on the face of the stone. It feels cold compared to his body heat. She touches the etchings in the granite, rough marks engraved in the smooth granite surface.

"Someone's carved small letters into this hard material," she says, stopped by this act of remembrance and the skill exercised in the carving of rock. She fingers the list.

"This is a memorial," he says, still cupping her hand.

She runs her hand down the list slowly; his hand stays on top of hers as she moves it across the rock. He lets her lead until she stops on the polished side of the monument.

"Wow! A shrine." She imagines once again the long line of ancestors from her trance with Mercedes, wishing to see their names on the list, but this is different. This hard rock carved by hand with tools is for others. Her focus is on Mario, her new family, and the family of trees.

"'In memory of sons and daughters lost to war from 1917 to 1921,'" he reads.

"That's a hundred years ago!" She's in awe.

"I love this place," he says, still holding her hand, looking up at the trees. "Redwoods. I hunt them down."

"Hunt?"

"Hunt. I know almost all the redwood groves in the park and all over the Bay Area, too."

Lavinia loves holding his hand, as smooth as the polished stone with little grooves in his skin. She can't believe she's danced in a fairy circle with Mario in a mini forest in the city. Her cares drip off her, joining the mushy ground cover.

"I know why you come here," she says.

"It's alive. Can you feel its heartbeat?"

They walk in silence deeper into the grove, down a steep ravine that narrows like a canyon with the giant trees growing on each side. The world is deeper here—quieter, darker. As they make the descent, she becomes even more still inside herself. They walk slowly at times, supported by the cushion of pine needles and fallen branches, and at other times she slips a few steps, laughing softly like a kid at a playground. Together, these hundreds of small steps, equivalent to the length of three short city blocks, take them to the edge of the grove at Park Presidio, where they have to climb out of the mini canyon and up a steep hill.

Lavinia's shoes slip on the trail. Mario, standing uphill from her, takes her hand and pulls, then stands at her back for a last gentle push over the hump.

Like magic, they are now standing in front of the Rose Garden, which abuts the busy Park Presidio on one side and JFK Drive on the other. They stop in front of the largest roses; their pink faces glow in the night light like a baby's face smiling in glee at the young couple. They kiss in front of the roses. Mario's breath, warm and wet, brims within the fragrances of roses and pine, offering Lavinia another moment of bliss. She smiles to herself as she nuzzles into his shoulder. She swears the roses are dreaming her secret feelings of love.

"Let's go toward the museum. It stays open until ten o'clock on Thursdays," he says, plucking a rose and putting it in his buttonhole. He takes her hand and moves knowingly from JFK Drive to the Academy of Science, across the concourse.

They move gracefully up the Academy of Science's grand steps to the front door. It's all lit up and festive, and the foyer is filled with other patrons. It looks as if a party is going on, with music and a bar. Is she in a fairy tale? A sign in the foyer reads, *Thursday Nights: Music, Creatures, and Cocktails.*

"Amazing gatherings happen here on Thursday nights," Mario says.

"You knew," she says, poking his side, as they enter the hall.

"They even serve drinks—but first let me show you Claude, my favorite alligator." He guides her toward the swamp terrarium off the main hall.

Lavinia shivers at the thought of an alligator, but follows Mario off the main lobby to a large enclosure where the white reptile lives. She grabs Mario's arm, amazed at this albino creature, Claude, who lives in a swampy area of the museum.

"He has a missing digit," Mario says, pointing.

"No! I don't want . . ." she says, but peers anyway at Claude's missing finger or toe. When the thing stares back at her, she's reminded of Don, Nina's husband, that cold and sneaky man. She feels threatened by this creature, the way she does by Don, and wonders why she puts up with it, why she agreed to work at their house again tomorrow.

She imagines that Don has an evil twin, Claude, who lives at the Steinhart Aquarium in Golden Gate Park. Then she imagines pushing him into the pen to duel with his shadow. A sense of vindication runs through her veins as she clings to Mario's sleeve, catching her breath. They linger close to each other; she feels the warmth of his breath on her face. She turns away from the creature.

"They're frightening, aren't they?" Mario says, holding her tightly. "They have a reptilian brain."

"I know a lot of people who still have a reptilian brain. Most of my clients, in fact," she says half laughing, as they walk away, leaving the gator behind.

They wander toward the main foyer, where they order white wine. Most of the patrons are young—people her age. She stares at their gaiety and social expertise, thinking how much she has to learn about this beautiful city, despite having grown up here.

Outside the building, the soft taste of wine lingering on her lips, she queues up with Mario in a cab line. The fog mists their faces and moistens their kisses as they wait. The chill she felt earlier is gone as he embraces her.

Mario presents her with the pink rose from his jacket. He places it behind her ear. She has never had a man embellish her so lovingly before, and she looks adoringly at him.

"I'm a flower child in Golden Gate Park in 2017," she says with a thrill.

"Fifty years after the Summer of Love," he reminds her.

"Thank you for this magical evening. I love all of this, Mario—the walk in the woods, the fairy circle, the rose garden, and the museum," she says, adding his name silently to the list.

"You forgot Claude," he says.

"I'm not sure I can love him," she says, wondering if he wanted to say, "You forgot me."

They get into the taxi and sit quietly, hand in hand, as they head toward her apartment. It's maybe a twenty-minute drive before they're in front of her place. She waves bye to Mario and watches the cab leave, already wishing she had invited him in. But she's glad she's waiting. She wants it to be right. She wants to be ready.

She turns away and moves into her studio. It's 11:00 p.m. On the floor beside the outgoing letter she wrote to Uncle Sal, there's now another letter. How so? Then she remembers seeing the shadow of a man near her door earlier this evening.

She picks up the envelope. It's sealed, with no name or return address. Something personal, but from whom? She takes it back into her studio living space. Before opening it, she pours herself a glass of wine.

Dear Lavinia Lavinia,
I replaced the tarps you lost. So, no problem. Not to
worry. I hope we are back in business soon. The dust
from the clay needs to be washed out. I hope we can
settle as well. Give me a call. Thank you.
George

George's note disturbs her—or rather, not the note itself but the idea of his shadow lurking in her doorway. Why didn't he knock or use his cell, like a civilized person? This is downright creepy, and it confirms her fear that he's stalking her. She doesn't remember ever having given him her address. How did he know where to find her? She thinks about him circling her like a great ocean wave, leaving a foam in its wake, then returning to the great sea and pounding back again toward her.

"Whatever shows up on the potter's wheel has something to teach you." The thought, as clear as a chime, comes through to her as a wise voice. She looks out toward the back of her place. *No, I'm not ready to see George or his workspace or his art,* she tells the tree. Her eyes follow the darkened room toward its far end. She can barely see the shadow of the fig, but she feels connected to it at the root level. The nagging feeling of betrayal she feels toward George is loosening, not so sealed into stone anymore the way the memorial sealed all those names in Golden Gate Park.

But then, what kind of man lurks outside at dark? Not knocking on my door. She wonders briefly if George has a life other than his art. Who is he, anyway? The way he seems to lurk in every corner . . . a wave of loneliness spreads into her being.

She picks up her cell and dials.

"Hello?"

"Kinky, did I wake you up?"

"Still correcting some papers for tomorrow. Left them for the last minute."

"I came home from a glorious evening to find a note from the clay thrower."

"He came to your house?" Kinky asks.

"Like a rat, scurrying away in the dark."

"What does it say?"

"Just that he wants me to come back to work."

"Still no explanation of his behavior?"

Kinky's comment startles her; she hasn't thought of wanting or needing an explanation from him. She merely wanted to wipe him off her skin and watch the dirt go down the drain. But now he's reaching out to her and wanting to begin anew.

"Do I even want that from him? I'm working on my righteous indignation," she says. But then she adds, "'Whatever shows up on the potter's wheel has something to teach you.'" There's that saying again. *Maybe it's the wine*, she thinks.

"Are you all right, Lavinia? I'll keep my cell nearby, so call me if you like."

"You're a doll, Kinky."

"You forgot to tell me about the glorious evening," she hears Kinky say just as she's hanging up. She'll tell her all about it tomorrow.

Lavinia slips into her room, draws the covers up over her head tightly, and falls asleep, dreaming of the good fairies.

Chapter 16:

QUITTING DAY

At daylight she opens her eyes and sees the fig tree on the patio. The leaves reflect the golden rising sun. When she steps out onto her small patch of dirt, she remembers the redwood grove and dancing in Mario's arms among the trees. She lets herself imagine having made love to him and wishes they'd done it in the fairy circle last night.

With these thoughts she gets dressed, places the pink rose in her jacket pocket, and heads for North Beach, reminding herself that she must pick up Nina's blouse at the cleaners.

Just thinking of going into that house gives her the jitters. Chilled, she buttons up her jacket, questioning her judgment in working for them. *Am I stupid, or just afraid to quit?* More fearful, her heart races as she ponders this tangle growing inside her like the roots she imagines under the city streets. Walking toward Market, she decides to skip the bus and walk the full three miles in hopes of unwinding.

With her hand over her chest, Lavinia approaches Columbus Avenue and Falcone Cafe. She steps inside and walks up to Mario.

"Did we really see an alligator and walk in the woods last night or did I dream it?" she says, though she knows they did it all; she's holding the soft pink rose in her pocket, after all.

"The redwoods." His eyes caress her.

"My God, they're so impressive. Let's do it again." She hands him two pieces of Bubblicious in exchange for an espresso and a smile.

"Where are you going?"

"Russian Hill clients."

"On a Friday?"

"Yeah, she asked me to come a second day this week," Lavinia pauses, feeling that chill again. "The clients from hell." She wrinkles her nose.

"You don't have to go."

"I know, but I told her I'd pick up her silk blouse," she says, as if that's a sufficient reason to show up.

His eyes seem to see through her excuses.

She smiles.

"Do that again," he says, so she bares her teeth at him and growls. He puts his face next to her and whispers, "Let's go dancing tonight."

"I thought you'd never ask." She downs the last sip of the espresso, winks at him, and waves good-bye.

She heads up Chestnut Street to Hyde, loving the pull of her muscles working the hill, but again her heart begins to race hard. She covers it with her hand, feeling the thump-thump of it.

She stops at the cleaners to pick up Nina's blouse. She hopes Don won't be there when she arrives. Is he home on Fridays? She berates herself for not asking. She remembers the alligator and thinks about how Don looks at her, cold and predatory. When she gets there, Nina is at the door, waiting. She pulls the blouse from Lavinia's hands, inspecting it, as if this blouse is the most important thing in the world to her. Then she hands it back without commenting. Lavinia focuses on Nina's long nails.

"I know it's not the usual today, but there are some extra linens. We had twelve people here for dinner last night," Nina says, looking toward the dining room as if the crowd is still there.

"Pasta with tomato sauce," she says, gathering her stuff to leave for her office on the Embarcadero.

Lavinia watches her leave the house and hears her pull the door shut from outside. Relieved she's gone, she sets to work quickly, so she can leave as soon as possible.

Still holding the blouse, Lavinia walks past the hall to the master bedroom closet and hangs it inside, leaving the tag with *Lavinia Lavinia* scrawled on it attached. The bed looks like it's split into his side and her side, with triangular folds neatly creased to meet in the middle, unlike Sal and Rose's bed, upon which the blankets wrapped around each other. Lavinia wonders if they had sex after the party. She thinks, not for the first time, about how intimately she gets to know her clients through their things and being in their homes. In this case her musings make her not want to touch the bed where Don sleeps or has sex. She wonders how Nina can tolerate living with this man or more, sleeping next to him.

In the bathroom she opens the his-and-hers hampers, then goes to the patio to look at Coit Tower and the Bay Bridge off in the distance. She looks at the crooked street below, tracking her route from here to North Beach, wishing she hadn't come.

Twenty minutes later she hears the door open, making her jump. She jerks up and walks down the long hall, thinking Nina must have forgotten something but instead it's Don lurking near the front door, staring deeply into her face as she approaches. Just what she was dreading all along. The thought that he might have been waiting around all this time creeps her out. Surely, this was in the cards all along. It's just like a predator to trap his victim in this way. Suddenly, she feels threatened.

His presence scares her but she must not back down. She feels the heat of rage rising in her body, thinking how he has harassed her. She's had enough of him and snaps, "This is not part of my job, to stand here in front of you while you stare at me."

"Well, pardon me, but this is my house." He screws up his fist.

"I'm not here for your pleasure!" she screams, not caring whether she'll lose her job. "I'm sick and tired of you sneaking around when I'm here." She has a vision of her mother in that little kitchen in Napoli when she was four years old, standing up to her father. What was it she said? *"Lasciami."* She repeats these words now. Her mother's words become hers. *"Lasciami. Io non ci sto."* She looks at his fisted hand.

"What did you say?" he says, glaring sharply at her, moving closer so his angular nose is too close to her face. He stops short of her and stares at her birthmark. She thinks he might hit her.

"Leave me alone, I won't stand for this." She feels the strength of her mother in these words. She turns and walks to her station, begins to sort the clothes. She runs her fingers over a pair of pants, and, without thinking, she checks the pockets. She's startled to find another piece of paper. He catches her before she can unfold it, snatching the note from her hands. He crumples the piece of paper in front of her face.

"I don't appreciate your snooping, either," he growls.

"*Vaffanculo*," she says. *Fuck you.*

He looks at her, bewildered, and glares. He turns on his heel and walks away. She hears the front door slam, and she knows this is her moment to leave, too. Her work must be over for the day. She rushes to the window, shaken but steadfast in her decision that today is her last day working for them. She looks out onto the street below, where again she sees a car waiting for him. He jumps in, and the driver pulls away.

Lavinia turns on some music to calm her nerves, but it doesn't help. Her knees are shaking and her ankles wobble. She has to sit down. Her rapid breath seems to be galloping through her. It's as if the energy she used to confront him is stuck in her vertebrae, palpating, trying to get out. She sits, telling herself she is all right, safe now.

Anxiously, she rushes through the process of what she must do, dying to get out of there, *Why don't I just walk out? I don't have to finish what I came here for.* But then she thinks of Nina, and her responsibility to her, and figures she can just finish the job. Don won't come back for her.

She dumps a pile of clothes into the washing machine and adds detergent, listens to the water filling the basin. Then she takes the colored teddy, the silk panties and bras, and soaks them in the sink. With the spot remover, she sprays the tomatoes stains off the linen. The cycle of wash continues like the rise and fall of an ocean wave, offering some comfort—until the thought of Don's behavior agitates her in the way the machine now agitates the clothes. Her feet move to the staccato beat, stamping wildly, as she communes with the washer music.

She picks up her cash, lets herself out, and walks up Hyde, hunting for an ice cream shop that serves bubblegum ice cream on a sugar cone. On her way, she passes a Spanish restaurant on the corner. She comes to a dead stop, dismayed to see Don at the window seat in the company of a woman and two men. What were the chances? It is his neighborhood, but still.

His face is red and screwed up in consternation and malice. He doesn't see her but she runs anyway, like she's being chased by the devil. She runs right past the ice cream shop, no longer in the mood for a cone. All she sees is Don's red face, and she begins to wonder now for the first time about his business. He works in financial services, so maybe he's a launderer, too, but laundering money. She wonders whether she should tell Nina about any of this, but what does it matter if today's her last day?

Chapter 17:

VIA TOLEDO, #9

S he finally arrives at her apartment, spent and out of breath. In the mail slot is another letter from Via Toledo, #9. Damn! Foreboding grips her, the saying she heard entering the garden of trees pulses through her mind: *"Abandon all hope ye who enter here."* She's not ready for what will surely be another avalanche. She takes a deep breath, thinks of Mercedes, and picks up the letter.

Before she opens it, she pours herself a glass of wine. She walks outside, letter in hand, and hopes what she reads will not upset her as much as the last letter. She looks at the fig tree and its branches seem to nod, to say, *I'll provide a safe canopy for you.*

Toledo #9
November 2017

My Dear Lavinia Lavinia,
I couldn't sleep after writing to you, so here I go again.
I feel remorse for what you've lost. You deserve to know
the story of your life. I keep seeing you as the child I
scooped up and took home with me to America, away

from all you loved and those still left who loved you. I wanted to make a new home for you, to make it better for you. To get you away from the stinking tragedy of our family. That's all I could think of! Now I'm not so sure. Maybe I could have faced it here with you.

You remember the picture I left you of the two of us taken here in Naples? It was the first day I ever saw you, the day I introduced you to Bubblicious, and how excited you were when you learned to blow bubbles. When that thing popped, you were so surprised that you laughed and giggled and then made another and another.

I have no excuse for not telling you the circumstances of my taking you away from here, adopting you, and raising you in San Francisco. Only that I didn't know how to tell you about my dear sister Angela's untimely death at twenty-one years old.

I didn't know until I met Giovanni recently anything about the circumstances leading up to your birth or anything about your father. This year, Giovanni filled me in on the details of your mother's courtship with your father. Giovanni is your father's uncle. You probably won't believe me, but it's the truth. I only spoke with your father once, when he contacted me before I left to tell me he, too, was moving to San Francisco. I can still hear him say, "I want my daughter."

As I said before, you deserve to know about your early life. So here I am, good old Uncle Sal, halfway around the world, floundering. What I need to tell you I want to tell you face-to-face. Maybe sitting by the fig tree. You always loved that tree. But I couldn't ever tell you, could I?

Your parents met in a small village. Your mother was fifteen years old and spent part of every day with the other village women at the watering trough, a system set up in ancient times by the Romans long before washing machines existed. Our parents had a simple grocery store and Papa worked every morning collecting garbage. He was proud of his work, of his wife, his daughter and son, but the pride ate us all up. He insisted that I, as the oldest and the only son, take over the business. No way did I want to collect garbage in Naples. He wouldn't hear of my dreams to become an accountant. I never told him of my plans to leave because I was scared. He threatened me whenever I mentioned going to school, bettering myself, always saying, "On my grave will you leave me."

I left the old man and escaped the old country with Rose. That's when I lost touch with my beautiful sister, your mother. I never met her lover. Never saw her pregnant, and never laid eyes on you until that day I gave you the gum in the spring of 1996.

I left Naples in 1989, before you were born, for the United States to get away from my domineering and controlling father. When I left, Angela was a vibrant fifteen-year-old. Alive. When I returned five years later she was dead and you stood in her place, a young, inno-cent child who had lost her mother in a freak accident.

She was hit by a trolley car. Okay, here it is!

When your nonna called me to tell me my sister and father were dead, I returned to Naples immediately.

Oh, how can I tell you in one letter all that Giovanni has revealed to me in the year I have been

*living away from you, my dear Lavinia? Giovanni has
suggested that I send for you so that he can tell you in
person about the love your parents had for one another.
But then, it was always so difficult for me to tell you
anything in person. It still is.*

*Another friend I've made here has suggested we
set up something called Skype where we can see each
other's faces on the phone or something like that. You're
smart, you must know about Skype.*

*What do you think of all of this, Lavinia? We
could use the telephone, but this is such a precious
conversation to have by telephone. Please let me know
your feelings after receiving this letter. I still have my
same cell—you can reach me on it.*

I remain your greatest fan, Lavinia Lavinia.

Your loving uncle,

Salvatore

Idiot! Uncle Sal, as always, only telling half the story. Why
can't he ever just tell it straight? He spoke to her father once before
he left and didn't tell her. Wimp! He didn't even tell her he was
moving to San Francisco. And now here's this information—that
her mother was hit by a trolley car! Why didn't he tell her all these
years? Why were there two people dead at the same time? Who
else? Where is her father? Why the hell can't Sal just say who and
where he is? After all, isn't this story her story, too?

She throws the letter away from her body to get away from
its sting. The letter burns her in the way electricity generates a
charge. Like electricity, her uncle is jumping around, all over the
place, reminding her of when she brushes her hair and the static
pulls it in different directions. She thinks of his words, each a

strand of fine hair pulled by electricity, weaving the story of her life. But he just won't tell the damn story straight! Her hair is a charged mess, just like her insides.

Look at the space behind and before you, the DJ recommended at the dance. Lavinia sees many views and many rooms to explore. What will she find? Where will she begin? Is Sal's motivation to write somehow connected to the fact that he knows Lavinia's dad moved to San Francisco? She believes it is. When she reflects on his words, what remains for her among all these threads is the knowledge of her father saying that he wants his daughter, and the idea that he's living in San Francisco somewhere.

She will find him.

Chapter 18:

TIME TRAVEL

Lavinia takes a cab to Zack's. It's already been a long day. She is struggling to believe that it was only this morning she had the interaction with Don, now that the letter from Sal stands between that experience and where she is now.

When she arrives, Zack answers the door and Lavinia follows him into the living room. She watches the tall, orderly man smooth down his thinning hair and then put a black comb in his front pocket. He turns toward her, motioning her to sit. He looks nervous, and she braces for another request—or perhaps he wants her to commit to taking him to Ely.

"Have you given any thought to my proposal?" he asks. And there it is. He needs an answer. He stands by his wife's beautiful linen-covered table, directly across from her. "Please don't think I'm too forward, but I'd love your company."

"Thank you," she says, and just as she's ready to accept his offer, he interrupts.

"It's a long drive, maybe eight hours. So I'd like to pay you five thousand dollars rather than four."

Lavinia's eyes widen. She feels her mouth open. "Five thousand dollars," she repeats, astounded.

"Worth it to me. A few days of your valuable time."

"Yes." She laughs. "I'll do it."

Zack smiles at her warmly, quietly steps closer. His house slippers flap like dust mops. "I think you'll love the mountains and the bristlecone pines. That is, if you don't mind traveling with an old goat." He laughs when he says that.

She shakes her head and smiles back. He's becoming for her more of a curious goat than an old one. She's excited by his offer, but also for the adventure. She wants to get out of the city, away from the possibility of another letter from Sal.

"I'm going for my swim now," Zack says. "I'll leave you to your work."

After he leaves, she puts in a wash, rinses a pair of plaid swim trunks by hand, and thinks of traveling with Zack to see the old forest and the site of the clock. She can't wait to tell Mario—a whole thousand dollars more than the original offer. When the wash is done, she places it in the drier, sets the timer, lets herself out, and skips down the stairway.

She rushes down Columbus, dying to see Mario and tell him all the things that have transpired over the past twenty-four hours. She charges into the café line where Steve is on duty. Her heart skips when she doesn't see Mario behind the counter. But then she turns and there he is, sitting at a corner table with someone she recognizes—a friend of his she met at the club.

"Join us, Lavinia." Mario gets up to give her a peck on the cheek.

The man stands up, too, moves another chair closer, motioning her to sit. "Carmine," he reminds her.

"Thank you." She sits between the two men. "Yes, I remember you from the dance," she says. Then she looks at Mario, anxious to be alone with him. "I have a few things I want to tell you."

Carmine politely excuses himself, saying, "I'll see you both later. Dance again tonight!"

"Thank you, Carmine," she says. When he's out of earshot, the words gush out. "Mario, so much is going on. I'm freaking out. Nina's husband almost hit me today. And Sal told me in a letter that my father lives in San Francisco. And get this—I know I'll find him. And on top of all that, Zack offered to pay me five thousand to go on the trip with him. Can you believe it?" She hardly stops for breath, the whirlpool is spinning her around.

"Wow! This is a lot!" Mario says, reaching for her hand.

"My head is spinning, Mario. I feel like I'm exploding." She moves so close to him she can feel his warm breath on her forehead.

"Let's slow it down. I want to hear all the details." Mario kisses her forehead.

"Yes, that's what I need right now." She looks at him and shivers, thinking about what happened with Don.

"Where do you want to start?" he asks gently.

"I'm afraid of Don," she confesses, although certainly the information about her father has farther-reaching consequences. Still, she forges on in this direction. "He came back after Nina left today. He came right up to my face with his fists all tightened in a ball and scared the hell out of me."

"He sounds like a nut case," Mario says. "I wonder if you should press charges."

But Lavinia knows she doesn't want to bring that kind of energy into her life. She shakes her head. "I'm worried for his wife.

Maybe he abuses her. I feel I should tell her," she says, twirling a piece of her hair.

"I'm worried for you, Lavinia."

"I'm quitting, so I'll be fine. I'll tell Nina why I'm quitting, too."

Mario holds her, and she knows he'll support her decision either way. Satisfied, she moves closer to him, feeling his nearness, his body heat.

He reaches for her hand. "I smell something." Mario bends forward, cups her face, and kisses her lips. "Coffee and gum," he says.

"Not enough coffee today," she says, and Mario rises to his feet. "Let me make you a double espresso," he says, leaving to make the coffee.

When he returns, he hands her the warm cup, which she holds close to her face, inhaling the nutty aroma.

"I'm sorry." He puts his arm around her shoulders. They sit quietly. "You've had a hell of a day, haven't you?" He kisses her on the forehead.

"And it's only 2:00 p.m."

"So tell me about your father?"

"My father lives in San Francisco, and Sal just told me so in a letter. Can you believe it?"

"Man, that's incredible."

"I'm going to find him, Mario. I swear I will."

"I'll help you," he says.

"Maybe dancing will help," she says.

"Yes," he says, and then looks at her for a long while.

Lavinia sips at her coffee, feeling content and safe with Mario.

"Stay here with me after?" he asks, looking to the ceiling and his flat above the café.

"Maybe—or at my place," she says, standing up to leave.

She winks at him, giggling inside, and kisses him again before striding away.

As she walks toward Columbus, she gets a text from Kinky. "Dinner? Your place or mine?"

Lavinia strolls around North Beach, daydreaming about her childhood above the bakery. She stops and stares into the shop through the window, drooling over the scents of sweet dough and creams. She smells the rum in the *babas*, which overflow with yellow patisserie cream. Taken by the colorful meadow of pastries, like flowers on a spring day, she feels alive. She goes inside and buys an assortment: two *babas*, two cannoli, two *Napoletana*, and two *sfogliatelle*.

A text alerts her. Kinky again. "Come here. I'm home early today."

She skips away from the storefront with the Italian pastries, excited by her purchase, thinking about Uncle Sal's letter. It is coming in dribs and drabs how her pastry-baking mamma disappeared into thin air, while Lavinia left home to fly to San Francisco. He said she was hit by a trolley, but he is still not telling her the whole story. *Coward*, she thinks, and the bounce leaves her step.

With a heavy heart she walks the long walk to the Mission, thinking of Giovanni now, wondering when she'll hear from him—*if* she'll hear from him. She reaches into the bag, takes out a cream baba, and takes a bite, savoring the sweet cream and rum syrup.

Will Sal ever tell her straight? Or will he continue to drag it out forever? Will he really leave it up to Giovanni to tell her?

As she relishes her pastry, she wishes Sal weren't so guarded, that they could just sit and talk. *Why this secrecy? Was my mamma a* putana *who disgraced her family?* She dismisses that thought quickly, though, knowing in her heart that her mother was not a whore, knowing that her mother had stood up to her own father and had loved Lavinia at all costs. But what is the secret? And does she really want to know?

Lavinia stops by her house before going to Kinky's, and the answers to some of her questions come sooner than she imagined they would when she checks her computer to find an email from Giovanni Dellarosa.

My God, this day! Lavinia thinks, hesitating before clicking on the message. But she feels compelled to know, so she opens it up.

November 2017
Via Toledo
Naples

Dear Lavinia Lavinia,
You don't know me except for brief mention by your uncle Salvatore. My name is Giovanni Dellarosa. I have decided to tell you about your mother and father. Your uncle Sal has cautioned me not to do so, but I know he wants my help. He withheld knowledge of what I'm about to tell you because he always thought it best to protect you. But I can't be closed-mouthed any longer. Enough!
So I'm seizing the day, and the new century. Carpe Diem and Carpe Millennium.
I have lived and worked my entire life as a sculptor in this beautiful old part of Napoli. My studio is above the community water trough, which still exists,

though everyone has washers now. But then, when your mother was a teen, it was a vibrant place where women came daily to do their laundry and to laugh and to cry together. I used to go there to fill my water buckets to keep my clay moist, but mostly to see your mother, Angela Campana, who came daily to do the family laundry.

My sister Anna lives in New York. She left for America as a young woman and fell in love with an Italian American man. They had a son, Giorgio, who from the start had a proclivity for art. I suppose he took after me. I bow my head here. He drew everything he saw—people on the buses, cars and trees, little dogs, squirrels, everything. He kept a box of Crayolas in his pocket. Anna used to complain about getting the wax stains out of his trousers until she remembered to check his pockets before she washed.

You're probably asking, why this story? Giorgio wanted to be a fine artist and to go to the Art Institute in New York. Before art school, my sister sent him to Italy to study sculpture with me. He was a fine boy, so attentive to the clay. He could make that clay sing. His hands and the clay worked as one. He spent hours in the studio, sculpting, taking breaks only to fill a bucket to moisten the clay.

Pretty soon I noticed his breaks were longer and longer, and I began to understand that the teenage boy was at his turning. One day I followed him and watched him sitting beside Angela, your mother. He was helping her wash the family clothes, but mostly staring into her eyes. Angela had blue eyes.

*Angela was fifteen years old then, and Giorgio six-
teen. It was a first love for them. I think everyone in the
village knew about it and, like me, they were joyful to see
it and to remember such love in their own lives. Angela's
father, your grandfather Antonio, was very strict with his
daughter, jealous of anyone who paid attention to her,
and thought the only safe place for her was at the wash-
house with the other girls and women. But the women
didn't mind when Giorgio sat with her to chat. None of us
worried, because we were in love with love.*

Such a love as theirs enchants.

*Pretty soon they would disappear up into the hills
above our center for long hours each day. Beautiful woods
in the city near the great museum, Capodimonte, called
to them. When Giorgio returned to the studio in the late
afternoons he'd sculpt from memory amazing pieces.
First her head on an armature—she was so sweet. He
even included the little birthmark on her cheek like Mar-
ilyn Monroe. I understand from Sal that your birthmark
is similar to Angela's. Then he began to sculpt Angela's
nakedness. These sculptures are still here in my studio for
you to see someday. Your mother's torso was beautiful.
I can still see her innocent beauty when I look at them.*

*A blessed year passed, and then it was time for
him to leave for school in New York. Of course, the parting was excruciating for my nephew. He begged me not
to make him leave, but I'd promised my sister I would
not let him stay. That he, unlike her, would go to college.*

*I had to peel him away from your mother, not
knowing his child was growing inside her. She convinced him with her joyful ways that it would work out;*

that she would always be with him; and that someday, when he finished school, they would reunite.

Giorgio left and Angela kept her beautiful smile, washing clothes at the well. Of course, I had to intervene when your grandfather Antonio saw that his daughter was growing in the panza. *Do you know Italian, or have you forgotten? As she grew larger Antonio flew into rage, cursing the day, cursing me for arranging the boy's visit. He refused to speak to me ever again, in fact, and he disowned her on the spot, cursing, ranting, "You are not my daughter, on my grave." Oh, he was a proud man and his pride ruled. Your grandmother was helpless in the face of this.*

Angela had a beautiful pregnancy. She remained joyful throughout. We would see her caressing her roundness, circling her fullness with her hands as if in some communion with you and your father.

When her quickening came, Luciana helped to deliver you. It was an easy delivery, or that's how it seemed to Emilia, the midwife, who said you slipped out smiling. You were so beautiful, just like your mother. No shriveled face like an old man, but bright like the dew on grass, with that Neaplolitan dimple on your chin. For sure you were one of us. We were all there at your birth—except, of course, Nonno Antonio. Your first cry went through the house, sending out a call like the quack of a duck looking for her mother. You were pink like the morning light, with the little chocolate mark above your lip. We all loved it. Your hair was already long and shiny and soft. You had your father's brown eyes and her olive skin. Angela was so happy. She held you close to her breasts. You suckled immediately. Your little mouth searching, finding her nipple easily like a little bird. I'll never forget!

Angela stared at you with those same loving qualities she showed your father but even more. No words can describe it. "I'll name her Lavinia," Angela said. Your dad's last name—Lavinia. "Her name is Lavinia Lavinia. That is how I can keep him close to me all the time. Every time I call her, she will hear her father's name." She repeated "Lavinia Lavinia" over and over again. As she caressed you, she rubbed your cheeks, tickled your mouth with her fingers, pinched at your nose, and massaged your soft eyebrows and your forehead and your little ears as you suckled. Sometimes she twirled your soft hair around her index finger, around and around.

I decided to help Angela. We had a small apartment near the water—the place where you were born, Lavinia Lavinia. Angela lived with me and my wife, Luciana, God rest her soul, until Antonio saw you and fell in love with you on the spot. When you smiled at the old bearded man, he softened. Then you moved back to the family home with your mother.

I want to let you digest this before leading you to the day she died. Little by little, you will know the truth. I promise.

I hope I have not overwhelmed you, Lavinia Lavinia. I write what I remember so you will know you were born in love. You can expect another email in a week's time.

An old man,

Giovanni Dellarosa

Lavinia is bothered by something in Giovanni's letter. She can't put her finger on it. She experiences a quickening, a kind of rush of some idea, but it escapes her. She feels filled with an airy, yet an earthy, feeling. If it had a shape, it would be round—a circle, perhaps. But what is it? She touches her birthmark as if to make sure it's there.

Out on the patio, she sits by the fig tree and exclaims, "Oh shit!" aloud. It's George, the sculptor. With a deep knowing, stronger than she's ever had before, she knows the truth of it. He is her father.

Chapter 19:

FALLING INTO A GALAXY
OF CONNECTION

The letter makes Lavinia hungry for more of her story, but Giovanni said it would be yet another week before she'll get it. She walks toward the Montoyas carrying her Italian pastries and a growing warmth at the center of her hunger, knowing Mercedes will feed her. When she arrives it's almost 3:00 p.m., and she can see Mercedes through the window, fussing in the kitchen.

What is she making?

The gate is ajar, welcoming her inside the small front yard space.

The round woman yells through the window, "*Pasa adelante.* Come in, Lavinia. I'm making *tamales.*"

"I love them," Lavinia exclaims as she enters through the front door. "I haven't eaten today. Smells spicy in here." She has already forgotten the devoured rum *baba* from earlier.

"Pork shoulder and three kinds of chilis with garlic and onion." Mercedes lifts the top off her Le Creuset. Enticing scents flow into the space from the magic pot. "Five hours it's been slow roasting," Mercedes says. "Kinky went to the store to get some *queso.*"

"Can I help?" Lavinia asks, staring at the corn husks sitting in a steamer on the stove and a large bowl filled with corn *masa.*

"You rest, *mijita.* Once we start filling this soft dough, you can help me." Mercedes adds pureed chilis, broth, and melted lard into the soft corn mixture. With her small hands, she squeezes the yellow dough. It seeps, golden orange, through her strong fingers. Lavinia feels a pang of longing at the sight of this woman's knowing hands—hands so strong that know what to do and seem born of the earth, hands that touch Lavinia's heart.

Mercedes spends ten minutes squeezing the corn *masa*, her hands working, glistening with the oil. It reminds Lavinia of the clay she kneaded at George's, and she's overcome by her revelation from earlier—but she doesn't tell Mercedes.

Mercedes's eyes look to the corn husks. "Now, *mijita*, take one of these corn husks and follow me." She rinses off her hands and swipes them on her apron, then takes the rough side of a husk in her hand and, with a spatula, spreads the soft *masa* on the smooth side of the leaf, then heaps the *carnitas* in the middle. Lavinia picks up a husk and follows, her own hands bumbling, juggling the warm husk in her palm as she spreads the corn mixture on top.

"Fold the husk over and once under."

Mercedes makes two *tamales* to every one Lavinia manages, and soon they are through the mixtures and the tamales are safe in the steamer.

"We can put the dishes on the table now," Mercedes tells her. She walks barefoot to the fridge. With her hair tied back with a red ribbon, lips naturally pink, and arms bare, she looks to Lavinia like a young girl. "And to drink? *Agua fresca? Sandia?*"

"Yes, I love watermelon." Lavinia helps herself to the pink juice from a cool glass pitcher, pouring a glass for Mercedes as well. They sit at the table and sip the refreshing drink while waiting for Kinky. Quiet now, Lavinia sits contentedly, comfortable in the presence of this great *mamacita,* thinking as she often does of her own mother, Angela. Angela of the well; Angela of the wind; Angela, who named her Lavinia Lavinia out of love; Angela, who lives in the sky or the clouds, as far as Lavinia can see.

"You're dreaming. I can see it in your eyes."

"I'm dreaming of my mother and my father."

Mercedes gives her a compassionate look and takes her hands.

"I almost feel they exist, that I can touch them," Lavinia says, and tells her of Giovanni's letter. She longs to tell her that she knows who her father is, but she doesn't. She wants to absorb this loving moment, and the thought of it being George, of all people, is too much for her to bear right now.

Mercedes wraps her arms around Lavinia, who rests her head on the woman's bosom, feeling loved as she might have been a long time ago by her own mother. Lavinia cries and Mercedes rocks her. The warm woman hums, *"Ay ay ay ay ay,"* she was singing, *"ay ay ay ay ay."* The sounds of this song, though sad, are like a lullaby for Lavinia, who nestles deeper into her awareness of her lost family being complemented by a new family. Feeling the warm pillow of Mamacita's bosom, smelling her, she is overcome by what she's lost in not having a mother all these years.

Mercedes sings, about a sad bird.

Kinky comes home and Mercedes releases Lavinia gently. She keeps humming, holding the compassion in the room. Kinky gives her mother and Lavinia a big hug, and then joins in her mother's humming. *"Ay ay ay ay ay,"* repeats on her lips.

Kinky is still singing the refrain as Lavinia reenters present time. The tamales from the steaming pot are ready. The salsa and beans are held as side dishes on the table, the half glass of *agua fresca* is in front of her. They eat quietly. Lavinia feels wrapped in a tamale of love.

After dinner, Lavinia urges Kinky to come with her to the club. "Come on, Kinky, you can meet Mario."

Kinky readily agrees, and soon the two friends are on their way to the bus stop. Lavinia explains the rules of the dance—the five rhythms, the DJ's offering, the weird costumes, the strangeness of it, and the commitment not to talk.

"Two hours without talking?" Kinky says to Lavinia as they reach the bus stop.

"Yeah, that's part of it."

"What kind of dance is it?" The bus arrives and Kinky pushes herself next to Lavinia on the double seat. "Isn't that what you do at home?"

"Yeah, but only with my shadow. At the club there are at least a hundred dancers." Then she tells Kinky how Mario asked her today to spend the night with him.

"So it's time for you to do *the* dance with him?" Kinky smiles.

"Yeah." Lavinia grins, too shy to talk about the specifics of what she hopes will happen.

Kinky looks at her, seeming to want to broach another topic, and Lavinia braces herself. After all, Kinky came home to Lavinia being held in her mother's arms like a baby. "Something on your mind?" she asks.

"Yeah, so much today. A letter from Sal and an email from his friend, Giovanni." Lavinia takes a deep breath. "Kinky, my father lives in San Francisco. And he's a sculptor."

Kinky's face becomes alert. She grabs Lavinia's arm and pulls her in close to her and says, "Oh shit! It's George."

Lavinia watches her friend's face go from an open-mouthed gawk to eyes filling to the brim, shining with tears. This brings tears to Lavinia's eyes, too, but then she breaks it with a laugh. It's almost too absurd to be true. The stalker, the man who comes to her house at night to drop mail in the slot, the man who for one year has been letting her into his house and observing her through a lens, without telling her she is his daughter, the man who never came for her in all the years she lived with Sal. What in hell possessed him to live such lies? George the liar, the betrayer, the ant who lives around the corner from her, is her father. All the time he knew and she didn't. It pisses her off.

Kinky slips her arm through Lavinia's. Lavinia feels held by her as the bus travels through the downtown traffic.

The bus drops them on Columbus. They walk the few blocks to the café as the cable car pulls up and stops at Powell. Lavinia freezes.

"What's wrong?" Kinky asks.

"My mother got hit by a trolley."

"Oh my God!"

Lavinia stands in a frozen pose, not moving, until the cable car releases its brakes and rolls down the track away from them. "She died on the tracks."

"I'm so sorry," Kinky says, wrapping her arm around Lavinia, holding her up as Lavinia takes one step forward, and then another.

After a block of this, just from feeling Kinky's support and unleashing the feelings she's been keeping inside of her all day, she feels lighter.

"There's a twenty-dollar entrance fee," Lavinia remembers.

Kinky pulls out a check from her pocket, her paycheck from San Francisco Unified School District, and waves it around. "Maybe I should deposit this before I lose it."

Lavinia feels a little envious, until she remembers the five thousand dollars from Zack. And she's grateful to have a friend like Kinky—someone who rolls with the punches, who's not angry with her for forgetting about the fee, who listens and cries and laughs with her.

They stop at the bank. As Kinky finishes making the deposit, she looks at Lavinia, eyes gleaming. "I get to meet Mario tonight." She smiles.

"You'll love him." Lavinia increases her pace, pulling Kinky toward the café. "He's a steady person, not full of himself like Andy. That's the key for me now."

When they reach the café, Mario's eyes light on Lavinia and he offers a warm smile. He comes up to them and grabs her hand, giving it a little squeeze. Then he looks at Kinky. "You must be Kinky," he says.

The two friends look at each other—sizing each other up, it seems to Lavinia. Then she notices that Carmine is there, and Mario introduces him to Kinky. Carmine gives Lavinia a quick smile.

"Is Kinky your real name?" he asks.

"Since I was a toddler and my hair started getting long," Kinky says, pinching her tight curls.

Carmine smiles and tells them he and Mario have been dancing together once a week for three years. Kinky and Lavinia eye each other, and Lavinia can see that Kinky approves of her new friends.

They walk the few blocks to the dance hall, Carmine keeping pace with Kinky, talking to her. Lavinia hears Kinky telling him how they went to State together. "And you?" she asks.

"I work with Mario at the café. He hired me as the late-night staff. He's the best boss, gives me nights off on Fridays. We met in barista school."

"Barista school?" Kinky seems as surprised as Lavinia to hear of such a school, to hear that Mario hired Carmine. Mario catches up to them and listens.

"From roasting beans to steaming milk," Carmine says. "We learned to maintain machines, grind coffee in a hundred different ways for our customers. Like an Americano and espresso—they have different principles, different grinds." Carmine seems proud of himself as he explains, and Lavinia finds this endearing. "We went for advanced training and technique for preparing specialty coffees. I bet you never knew Mario's specialty is the double espresso and mine is frothing cappuccino." Carmine looks at Lavinia for the first time since they left the café.

"I know from experience," Lavinia pipes in. "Mario makes a mean double espresso." She winks at him, recalling the one he so lovingly placed in her shivering hands earlier today.

Now they're standing in the line, still talking coffee.

"You forgot to tell her about plant cultivation and fair trade coffees," Mario urges his friend. "You better get the story out before the music starts."

Kinky looks at Lavinia, bends toward her ear, and whispers that she thinks Carmine is nervous. Lavinia considers that he must think Kinky is cute. Who wouldn't, though?

They walk up a long, narrow stairway to the anteroom, where they check their coats. Lavinia knows the drill now, and leaves her tuxedo jacket in the cloakroom, exposing a slender-fitting tee. Then they enter a large dancehall. The open space, once a meeting assembly hall with an appointed podium, has now been converted into a dance hall with hardwood floors and high windows.

Slow music is playing. Kinky stands close to Lavinia, who moves toward the left corner, across from the DJ. "No talking," Lavinia mouths silently, making eye contact with Kinky.

She scans the room, fascinated by all the dancers in various positions. A woman lies on the floor doing back exercises; another curls in infant's pose; another "salutes the sun." Others stand by the wall doing yoga stretches or just bobbing. But most, as before, move slowly to the beat, their heads swaying softly on their shoulders and their hands waving. Beside her, a woman slides along the polished floor, doing what looks like slow breakdancing, while another man slices through the emerging crowd with purpose. Lavinia looks toward Kinky, silently wondering what she thinks. Her friend's expression is blank.

By the start time, five minutes later, the room is filled to capacity. Some know each other and hug, while others have soft eyes and move alone. Heads bob rhythmically on fluid necks, creating a sea of flowing waves. One man wears what looks like string pajamas and ballet slippers; a woman waltzes through the space with her arms raised above her head, floating a green scarf behind her. The costumes flow like colored banners and start to blend in with the music, an easy sound that flows around them.

Lavinia and Kinky stay close to each other as Mario and Carmine slowly migrate toward the center, finding their own way. Other dancers ease past them, weaving their own threads. Some dancers move quicker than others; all have their own unique pattern, as if each dance is a signature. Kinky and Lavinia face each other, moving in sync, gently bouncing their hips and arms, admiring all the costumes.

A woman in harem pants and a corset-like top that laces up her back dances beside Lavinia. Lavinia watches an older women, about eighty, doing intricate yoga poses. But what really stands out to her is the wave she experiences here, an oceanic feeling, as if all the dancers swim in one body of water.

Awesome. Being in this sea of people making waves, creating swells, makes her feel happy. Between each musical cut, just as last time, there's a transition where the last rhythm and the new rhythm interact, leaving her with a sense of suspension, like she's between two poles in a kind of uncertainty. Most of the music is unfamiliar.

"Consider the air as living space to join us in the dance of the greater space. Have a relationship with this space and dance the dance of life with gratitude," the DJ says.

"Kind of new age," Kinky whispers.

Lavinia puts her hands over her lips, reminding her to be quiet. The music begins again, and they each dance. Lavinia feels freer to explore the greater space, and she moves around the periphery of the room.

Mario dances by Lavinia in a serpentine light, his hands above his head, his bare feet grounded. He poses directly in front of Lavinia, and his hips rotate while his arms and hands invite her to join him. As he moves closer to her, she can smell his sweat. She inches toward him, and together they move as if connected by a great vibration.

The beat is building in a kind of crescendo where together they dance, bounce, gyrate, and sway their waists and torsos, but their eyes always face each other. Lavinia is so engrossed in Mario that she loses track of everyone else. Their two bodies and eyes long for each other. They pause. Then they dance toward the center of the room, where Carmine and Kinky dance wildly, joy in their faces. Lavinia feels laughter in her heart, and when someone hoots and hollers she joins in with her own voice. Joy feels to her a new emotion, precious and free. They play, splashing and diving into the music, swimming through the space like slithering fish flapping their tails. She hears her fellow dancers' silent voices sing of love.

When the music stops, silence comes into the great room, moving through the sea of humming souls. A vibration floats in and around, below and above. Lavinia hears the DJ say, "You are alive. Feel the hum in your connection. Take this with you into the night."

Carmine and Kinky sway toward them. They are humming their own vibration. The four of them huddle in a close circle, congratulating each other silently, heart to heart, beat to beat, arms around each other, before walking out into the night air toward the bus stop.

Carmine walks with them toward the 30 Stockton, where he says good-bye. Arm in arm, Lavinia, Mario, and Kinky wait for their own bus. When it doesn't come, they walk to Grant Avenue through Chinatown, flickering red lanterns lighting their way. Lavinia and Kinky smile at each other. After midnight, they reach the Mission and stop in front of Kinky's house, where Kinky leans into Lavinia for a hug and whispers, "I like him." The friends hold each other in a long hug before saying bye.

With Mario's warm hand in hers, Lavinia weaves seamlessly through small pockets of tourists and shopkeepers who are closing down on 16th Street. Their silence feels big and round, like the forest.

At her place, she unlocks the door. Mario follows her into the long, cave-like room and to the far end, where she leads him to her bed and darkened room. As natural as following the beat of the music, they undress each other, allowing their tongues to roam the wet spaces of their mouths and then move down each other's body. He kisses every part of her, finding hidden places that throb and seem to be laughing loudly.

"I like the way you move, Lavinia," Mario says. "You are on fire."

He slowly kisses her. She flows into him and melts. They dance as one great beat, yet also rooted, like trees. They fall into each other as his love releases and enters deeply inside her.

He whispers a love song as sweet as their embrace: "You are a perfect completion of a never-ending circle of my small life, Lavinia Lavinia. Lavinia, Lavinia," he repeats her name over and over while holding her in his arms.

As dear Sleep takes them in her embrace, Lavinia whispers, "Mario Mario, do you see we are falling into a galaxy of connection?"

Chapter 20:

THE DISCOVERY

Morning peeks through the slit in the curtain and watches Lavinia as she sits on her small sofa, feeling the sunbeams warm her memories of last night with Mario. She can still taste the sweetness of his tongue on her lips. She misses him and looks across the length of her blue-gray studio. He rose early this morning to open the café. Looking toward the back door, she sees the fig tree, its small green sacks absorbing the early sun, carrying seeds, reminding her of Mario's love pouch, the one she touched last night, smooth and soft. His poetry buzzes in her ears, whispering, *You are the completion of a never-ending circle, like the tree.*

Before leaving the studio, she rereads Giovanni's email and begins the long walk to Nina's house on Russian Hill, determined to face her and to quit. She's decided she must come clean with her about Don's behavior.

She pictures Mario's face—his voice, his encouragement. She smiles and walks up the steep hill. She looks at her watch; there's no time to go to the café before facing Nina. She takes the last hill slowly, her resolve waning.

How will I say it? In the timid way or the lioness way? Will I be the one who stands? The one who growls? The one who is in harmony with my own beat? Will I roar or smother my head in fear?

Before she even knocks, Nina yanks open the door, seemingly unsurprised to see Lavinia standing there. "What a morning! Don didn't come home last night." Nina's still in her slippers and her hair is in disarray; she's buttoning a silk shirt with her long nails, which slip around the button. The seam of her skirt is off-center. Lavinia hides her relief that Don's not in the house but feels disturbed to see Nina's body tremble as she steps aside to let Lavinia pass.

"What happened?"

"I don't know. This has never happened before. I'm worried that something terrible has happened to him."

"He's never stayed out before?" Lavinia can't believe this is the first time.

"The other times he's called." She finishes with her blouse and walks to the bedroom, gesturing for Lavinia to follow.

Upon entering the room, Lavinia notices that one side of the bed is still made and that Don's side table is clean. The charger to his cell phone is missing. His Kindle is gone, too.

"He took his stuff," Lavinia says, then walks into the closet. The hook where he keeps his running clothes is bare. The bureau top is clean, too. "A ton of stuff is gone!" she says.

"What?" Nina looks dumbfounded. She, too, notices his empty chair where his fleece normally would be, and the bureau. "Oh my God," she says, "he's taken all his belongings. His running clothes." She goes over to his closet and looks more closely. Lavinia watches as she runs her fingers along the empty hooks.

"Gone! He took everything." The drawer pulls Nina toward

it, and she yanks it open. "It's clean." She picks up a flashlight and an empty eyeglass case, a few pennies, and a photo of her. When she picks up the photo, she cries. Then she looks at Lavinia. "He left the picture of me. He used to look at it every day."

Lavinia remembers the morning Andy left—the morning he told her he didn't love her anymore. How shattered feelings cut into her own heart, fragmenting her. She feels the sharp edge of pain as fear creeps in—fear for herself and for Nina's well-being. Nina is crying now, and Lavinia considers how Nina has never shown weakness in front of her before. They both stand completely still, close in what seems like mutual sorrow. Except that Lavinia is not sad, not for Don and not even for Nina. She's pissed at her and her asshole husband, who groped her with his eyes, who harassed her and held his fist to her face. She backs away from Nina, her arms folded across her chest.

When Nina regains her composure, she looks at Lavinia. "Thank you for listening. I'm a mess."

"Yes, life is messy sometimes."

"Have you been through something like this?" Nina asks.

"I have." Although she relates to Nina, she feels almost no empathy for her. Anger has overridden any desire to connect with her former employer.

"Can I ask you a question, Lavinia?" It's the first time Nina has ever looked into her eyes or said her name.

"Sure."

"Is there anything you've seen—in Don's things, for instance—that would give us clues as to why he might have left me like this?"

Lavinia holds her breath, thinking about how much she dislikes Don, his hostile behavior toward her, how she decided to quit because of it, and how Nina still doesn't know that's the reason she's here. She believes that Don's leaving is more about Don than about Nina, but what should she say?

She sits in stillness for a few moments.

Then she tells Nina about what she experienced: the strange and confusing notes; his frantic return to the house after Nina left to harass her; the car that dropped him off, waited, and picked him up; the meeting at the Spanish restaurant.

"All of these things happened?" Nina looks shocked, but Lavinia knows she believes her. "Why didn't you tell me before?"

"I don't know," Lavinia confesses.

"He came back here after I left for work?" Nina yells now. "How many times? What did he say to you?"

"He mostly just stared at me." Lavinia fingers her birthmark.

"And that made you uncomfortable?"

"Yes. And the last time I saw him, he was aggressive and mad. I thought he might hit me."

Nina's shoulders drop. She seems to want to say something, but Lavinia imagines she doesn't have the words.

"And the notes, what did they say?"

"They were bizarre," Lavinia says. "The first said, 'Meet me at Velo Rouge.' I didn't know if it was for me, or what. Of course, I didn't go. I started to think they were an excuse for him to come back here and to harass me."

Nina looks away, deep in thought. Then she says in her formal voice, "Thank you, Lavinia. I'll call you about scheduling future days with you, after I find out what's happening."

"I'm sorry, Nina, I can't come back here under these circumstances," Lavina says. "In fact, the only reason I came here this morning, after what happened yesterday, was to tell you that I have to quit."

"Please come back one more time to help me clear out of here," Nina pleads. "He won't come back. He's gone."

"No, I won't be coming back here," Lavinia says firmly. "I quit."

Lavinia leaves the house, pops a piece of Bubblicious in her mouth, and runs down the hill toward North Beach. She enters Mario's café with her fingers knotted. Knowing this is his business, she runs to the head of the line, not even noticing the scowls of the other customers.

"Look at you, cutting in front of everyone," Mario teases. "Maybe it was the dancing we did together last night." But he stops joking as soon as he sees her face. He immediately abandons his post behind the espresso machine, much to the customers' chagrin.

He emerges from behind the counter, and she reaches out and puts her arms around him and squeezes him. He holds her tightly. He calls Steve to take his place. Arm in arm, they walk to the dark corner table in the inner part of the café and take a small table. She tells him what's just happened—that Don is gone, that she's sure he's done something bad.

"Nina asked me to return to the house one more time to help her clear out. I said no." She nestles into his shoulder. "Mario, I did it the way I wanted to." She feels his beautiful face, so close to hers, and her anxiety lessens.

Mario listens, holding her in his arms, until she calms down. Then he says, "This must be the day for surprises. When I left your place at five thirty this morning, there was a man lurking by your mail slot. When he saw me, he scurried out of the way."

Lavinia sits up tall. "The stalker!" she cries out.

"I grabbed his coat sleeve and he turned toward me. A guy about my height. Thin. Wavy hair, shoes that had mud stains on them—some fancy kind of leather shoes. I asked him what he was doing there. You're not going to believe what he said, Lavinia." Mario takes her face in his hands. "He said, 'My name is George Lavinia,' and then he pulled his sleeve out of my hold." He pauses. "Then we looked at each other, and I said, 'I know you. You're Lavinia's father.'"

Without any warning, Lavinia screams out, "The stalker is my father," and then covers her mouth, encased in stone, like one of George's statues.

Mario waits, his hands resting on the table, then he reaches for her hands, pulls her up, and leads her out onto the sidewalk.

"Oh my God!" she says. "You met my father. That coward never told me he was my father. Never even said his last name was Lavinia. He introduced himself as George Levine, and all this time he's been dropping off notes in the night like some kind of weirdo. He kept me from knowing who he was all these months—a year! He's been watching me, stealing from me, never saying who he was. I can't believe it! You met him before I ever met him. What did he say?"

"He just stared at me and turned and left. I think he was shocked."

"Oh my God," she says, "he was coming to my door hand delivering his notes for me to come back all these weeks and you found him."

"You know where he lives, right? I'll go with you so you can give him a piece of your mind."

"I don't know if I want to, Mario. What would I say to him?"

"Some of the things you just said to me," Mario says.

"But I'm furious." She feels so betrayed by George, mad he was secretly sculpting her face and body. She remembers Giovanni saying that when George lived in Naples, he sculpted her mother's face and torso. *Oh my God*, she thinks, *what if the statues were of my mother?* She jumped to conclusions about the sculptures in George's show room. *Those heads, those torsos, maybe they weren't me after all.*

"When shall we go to see him, Lavinia Lavinia?" Mario asks. "Do you want my company?"

"I don't know yet." All she can think about is checking out those sculptures again. She crushes Mario close to her in a long hug, so close she can feel his heartbeat and long breaths. They walk down the block, holding hands, as she gathers herself. She feels like she's spinning, like she might crash to the ground at any moment if Mario weren't here to hold her up.

Lavinia thinks of her father, George, who's always seemed to her so alone in the great studio, throwing clay. He's spent his whole life losing his loved ones. Dizzy and shaking, she cries a long, low moan—more like an animal cry, or is it a wound? Maybe she's crying for herself.

Mario holds her in his loving arms.

Chapter 21:

TELL IT STRAIGHT

At home, Lavinia racks her brain trying to picture her father's life. How did he spend his first days in San Francisco this year, and what of the days of the years before? Day after day spent molding clay in her image—her mother's image?—in some sort of trance she attempts to envision and yet can't imagine this life of a sculptor, hands deep in the black mud, squeezing and pulling and thrashing wet slabs of the earth for eternity. It seems like a relentless task, like the one given to Sisyphus. She can't presume to know the reward or the motivation. Is it to keep Angela alive? To keep himself alive? To keep Lavinia alive?

"Be open to whatever comes," says a voice too loud to ignore. She swirls around as if she's in a whirlpool. When she stops, she's facing the fig tree. Squinting, she imagines that she sees her father's round face, smiling joyfully. She feels her feet planted on the wooden floor, her toes grasping as if searching for a lifeline, a tight rope.

The face stares at her, a solemn mask. His wavy hair with the few silver threads is parted to the side; his eyes—brown, warm, mostly sad, deep, and inviting—tell of something old and sacred.

How can he have such sad eyes while he smiles with full red lips, as if he is sucking a cherry lollipop?

Her body starts to grieve for him, and some deep ravine of pain cuts through her heart and seems to break her open. She can't stand these feelings. She wants to run away, but she is stuck to the tight rope. One misstep and she will fall into the ravine and disappear. The spell is broken when she hears the Beatles music in her head, "A Hard Day's Night," and remembers when she was with him in the studio, watching him work the clay, waltzing with him, whirling around the great studio, stopping at his clay table. It seemed so natural to dance with him and then to learn what was on the potter's wheel.

It occurs to her she wants to tell him something—but what? What is it she wants to say? She waits; she listens. Nothing! She opens the door to her patio and goes outside and kneels by the fig tree, her sacred place. She begins to dig with her fingers into the soil, moistened by the early fog. The earth stuff loosens and becomes the clay she yearns for, the sculptor's diet. She squeezes it into a small clump and brings her hands to her face, smelling its rich mineral source before placing a speck on her tongue. The stuff melts away, leaving a pleasant, fruity taste in her mouth.

She looks up at the tree. *What is it that he wants me to know?* All is still, except for a small drop of milk that leaks from a ripening fig. Lavinia covers her face with her dirty hands and begins to cry. *He wants me to know the truth—yes, that's it. And I want to hear him tell me the story of my life and to tell me what happened. To tell it straight.*

Back inside the house she imagines how he'll say she looks just like her mother. That he'll ask for forgiveness that she will not be ready to impart. It's strange for her to think of such an intimate and honest meeting with him, having only ever seen him as a quirky New York artist who works incessantly, his hair flying as he works his clay. His East Coast accent, how inarticulate he is at times; his expressive movements compensating for his quietness.

She doesn't recall if she met George before Sal left for Italy. Didn't Sal tell her in the first letter that he talked to her father once before they left Italy? Was George here in San Francisco back then?

She's pissed at Sal all over again. *How dare he? How did he face me night after night with that cocky, lying face? He knew I was working for a sculptor. Why didn't he introduce himself to George before he left? The coward!*

She allows a scream to escape; its vibrations bounce around her head and then off the walls of her room. It occurs to her that one of her neighbors might call the police. But she is on fire, igniting feelings buried in embers. The heat rises in her belly like a volcano's fire show, ready to blow the top off the secrets and find the story of her life. No more rumbling around in a dark eternity for her. Lavinia expects an explanation. She stands on her tiptoes, making herself tall.

How dare they all deceive her? Why couldn't anyone in her family tell her the truth? Why was everything shrouded in some deep secret, leaving everyone tongue-tied? Even Giovanni waited until Sal returned to Naples to step up and talk about his nephew. And Sal, a million miles away, can barely say that his father killed his sister—and that's what happened, isn't it? It's like they're stuck in some kind of spell or curse that has put them all to sleep. Is she living in a fairy tale? Is she the sleeping beauty? Is a town waking up a generation later? And who is the charming prince?

Something is bothering her, something else she can't verbalize yet. It's so close to her awareness, yet it's unreachable. She has to see the sculptures. She knows they're Angela and not her, but she still has to see them. That feels key to forgiving George and for forgetting her belief that he was a pervert who was stalking her. She fingers her birthmark on her upper lip.

Sitting on the floor, rubbing her feet, she remembers how George laughed when she accused him of sculpting her without permission. How absurd it must have struck the man who expresses love in clay, if the only subject he's ever had is a woman who has been gone from him for years. Giovanni told her the boy of seventeen sculpted busts and torsos even back then, and he is still doing it now. She suddenly sees George for what he is—a lost lover who's pined his life away.

Her phone is blowing up with texts from Mario and Kinky. She texts, "I'm okay. I want to be alone. Thanks for understanding." Then comes a voice message from Zack: "Hello, Lavinia. How are you? I jus-s-s-t wanted to check in on you."

She lies on the floor, smelling her Raggedy and the dirt she hasn't washed off from her fingers. The thin layer of clay she rubbed on her face flakes off onto her doll, leaving a layer of dust.

When she wakes up, the street is quiet. It's the middle of the night.

She gets up off the floor and puts on her flannel pajamas, then gets under the covers, hugging herself under the warm blankets. Scared and yearning, she reaches for Raggedy, smells her, holding steady in her *querencia*, and falls asleep.

When she finally gets up, the pink morning sun is shining through the fig tree. She feels hungry and makes herself a breakfast of tuna salad with crackers and green olives and takes it to the patio, where she eats in the company of the warming sun and the fig tree. She drinks an old bottle of ginger ale she finds in the small outdoor fridge. Satisfied, she sits listening to the cadence of the birdsong, steady and sweetly flitting in the sun of a new day.

She sits outdoors most of the day, soothed by the birds and the whispering wind in the tree, listening to the neighborhood sounds and watching the changing light. Then the new moon rises on the low horizon, a sliver of a laughing moon. It smiles with her as she makes an intention to visit George tomorrow.

Chapter 22:

THE REVELATION

L avinia leaves her house and walks quickly down 16th Street past small groups of people chatting and drinking outside restaurants. A man with a grocery cart filled with bottles and cans stops to poke in a recycle bin on the sidewalk. Wearing her bomber jacket and a fresh pair of jeans, Lavinia feels confident, like she's gone through a dark tunnel and come out the other side. She crosses South Van Ness and heads to George's place. When she gets there at 8:45 a.m., she waits, knowing that he goes out for coffee around nine. She doesn't want to see him yet, not before she sees the statues. She positions herself in an alcove of a building diagonal from his so she can see him leave. She waits with her hand on her upper lip.

When he opens the front gate, he takes a look around before closing it. His eyes skim past her hideaway.

George turns right and walks toward the neighborhood café. She watches him walk away. His hips shimmy slightly, and his large hands sway gently by his side. She waits until he's far down the block before crossing the street.

She reaches inside her small purse to find the key to his studio. The door opens into the dark vestibule. A familiar feeling surrounds her. She takes the two flights of stairs, slips inside, and turns on the lights. The lighting is similar to that in a theatre, with different zones. As she walks she tips off sensors that light her path. It's as if she's starring in a magic play, with the spotlight on her. The indirect lighting is soft on the cinnabar walls, reflecting pale green and gold flecks of color. Has she ever noticed this before?

She walks through the studio space to where a sliding door is pulled shut. She knocks and waits. Convinced that she's alone, she opens the door and walks through. This alerts another sensor, which lights another large space.

Stacks of shelves hold ten-pound bags of white, rust, and dark brown colored clays, but it's the smell of wet earth substance, reminding her of rain and growth, that stirs her senses. She eyes the brown clay he prefers, Cassius Clay. The industrial-size kiln faces her from the farthest wall. As she passes she feels its warmth, but there are no figures on the drying racks.

She sees another door off the kiln room that opens into a display room. Again the magic lighting. Here, on white pedestals, Lavinia sees her own face.

She walks up to the statue and faces it squarely. The bust standing on a tall pedestal looks into her eyes. It's as if they're both alive, communicating, yet no words pass. Two beings fashioned of clay look at each other. She feels prickly, like electrical wave sensations are passing through her, generating a warmth on her skin, waking her up. If she touches the other, will she also be warm?

She walks toward the face of the young woman, marveling at how realistic she is. She closes her eyes and runs her hand over the hair, the forehead, and then down the slope of the nose, over to the cheek, stopping at the raised bump. The raised mark is on the statue's cheek.

"Oh my god!" she exclaims. "It's true." She pulls her hand away to her own face, stopping on her upper lip. She remembers Giovanni's recounting that Angela's birthmark was on her cheek, but still she is shocked. She rushes toward the other busts in the room and sees that all of them have a birthmark on their cheek. She feels stunned by this recognition. It's as though she is in the presence of her own soul, but it is the spirit of her dearly deceased mother. As she stands there touching her own heartbeat, she feels a double strand of heartbeat flossing through her. She waits, letting the fullness of the moment seep into her veins, and then she moves toward the other pieces.

More torsos, these with arms truncated, like you might see any museum or in Greek or Roman ruins. The full figure studies are as tall as Michelangelo's *David*. A beautiful woman stands naked. Her waist turns gracefully, her neck extends as if she is looking at something. The circular movement of the piece begs Lavinia to walk around the beautiful naked woman. Stunning! All she can do is keep spiraling this incredible statue of the central woman, Angela, her mother.

Beauty! She's in the presence of Beauty, and she can't breathe.

Behind the standing figure is yet another statue of the younger Angela. Lavinia walks toward the figure. As she gets closer she sees that the woman is pregnant, her body full and sensual. Clasping both hands over her belly, her chin rests on her chest. She's looking down. Lavinia circles her again, knowing that this is her mother, carrying her yet to be born child. She wants to jump up and caress her belly, the watery place of her *querencia*, the place where she once lived in an oceanic state, attached to her mother. She sees her life pass from in utero to nursing when she finds another loving statue of Angela with full breasts, nursing a baby Lavinia. She brushes against the suckling infant but her eyes are gazing at the mother. Lavinia stands in front of the loving dyad in a state of awe and stillness, watching for some time in the quiet room with the soft lighting. She touches the baby's puckered mouth. *That's me.* She's overwhelmed by emotion.

She is drawn to another sculpture, a hexagonal piece of stone in the shape of a large basket, different from the others. Horizontal, massive, it rests alone near the far wall of the studio. It's carved with Roman or Grecian urns; a ribbon of people six inches high graces the perimeter of the slab.

Lavinia walks carefully to the edge of the piece and finds a sleeping woman, her mother, among the figures. Her eyes, little smiling half moons, are fringed with fine eyelashes. *He's made each one. Which tool did he use?* She touches the cold face, resting her fingers on the cheek with the little bump—her connection to this woman, their coupling. Kneeling on the knee rest George has made, Lavinia focuses on the bouquet of roses in her mother's slender fingers. She follows the bent arm on up to her mouth with a slight upturn of her lips. Lavinia pulls her fingers away from Angela's cheek and covers her eyes, letting the warm tears wash over her own dissolving feelings—the ones she has carried for so long, which are now melting. She cries, letting the love drench her.

That George has been sculpting Angela and not Lavinia sinks in all the way. She doesn't know what to do with this revelation, and she realizes she needs to leave. But as soon as she turns around, she sees a man's form.

George stands opposite her, keeping his space, not coming too close. She looks at his face, his day-old beard. He's holding one hand in his sport jacket pocket. His woolen scarf drapes in perfect folds around his neck for warmth. Lavinia remains stunned, in disbelief, that he is her father.

"Hello, Lavinia. I've been hoping I'd see you again."

She remains silent. No words come to her but she doesn't avoid his eyes, which are warm and intense.

"You know," he says.

"I know."

"What a shock this must be for you. I'm sorry."

"I'd say an earthquake." Her throat tightens.

"I understand."

She looks at his eyes. Black pools reflecting the morning light. "Sorry I lost your tarps."

He smiles. "You're forgiven."

They stand in silence, facing each other. Time has stopped. What if she could go back in time and live a different life? Live as a child with her mother and father in New York City? She thinks of Zack Luce, who wants to go forward in time, to know that when he stops breathing, Time will still move forward into the next generations for 10,000 years.

She looks at her father. "I need time to process this, George. Should I call you George?"

"Yes, of course, Lavinia Lavinia." He smiles. "I love your name. It makes me happy to know you have carried me in that way. I'm sorry I didn't tell you the truth."

"Yes. That's for sure," she says, with mixed feelings. She looks at his face with its day-old beard. His eyes are deep and sincere, and bespeak his love for her mother. He has created a prayer in clay.

"I can wait a bit longer. Take your time to get to know me and love me. I know you will. I've always known we would be reunited. I have had this glorious year to get to know you." He reaches a hand toward her, then brings it back to his chest.

She loves what he's said, but she can't let herself take his hand. More than all her imaginings, he is generous, allowing her to take her time. And then the part about his knowing that she will grow to love him. *Will I? Do I?* "I don't know where to start."

"A coffee?" he offers.

"Thank you, but no. I'm on my way to North Beach to see a friend. I came here to see Angela's face." She touches her birthmark. "She's beautiful. I thought she was me."

"She is," he says, smiling. "May I walk with you, then, a short way?"

She nods, and they leave the studio. They walk silently down Folsom. When she takes a left at South Van Ness, they say goodbye. He takes her hand in a small handshake, and this time she lets him. They part and Lavinia continues on her way—then stops and turns, wondering why he doesn't follow her. She feels giddy inside. How can he just leave like that? She walks in the opposite direction a bit longer, stops again and gingerly turns to watch him go.

Then she yells, "Don't leave! I don't want to lose you the way Mamma lost you."

He's too far to hear her. She doesn't go after him. Instead, she walks toward her house, following her feet, step by step, feeling the pavement, knowing that something more awaits her at home.

She opens her door and rushes to her computer, and there it is: an email from Giovanni Dellarosa. She ponders the address, counting the days since the last email. She opens it.

Cara Lavinia Lavinia,

But before diving in, my hope is that the love story of your mother and father has given you a feeling of their love for you. A child born out of love is love herself. And you were a precious and adored child. Even if Antonio raged at

Angela's condition, he melted when he saw you with your sweet face and loving nature, your curiosity for life. You used to wake up in your crib and laugh at the reflection of the early-morning sunlight dancing on the ceiling. It was a pure joy to see. Your mother would come into your room and find you smiling, your eyes twinkling. Oh how she loved you. She took you to the water baths and let you watch and listen to the water as she did the family laundry. As you got older, you played and splashed in the water, and then you began to help her. First, she gave you little socks to wash.

You're probably wondering if your mother ever saw your father again, or whether he ever saw you as an infant or toddler. Sorry to say, he never did. Your mother was planning to take you with her to New York City to live there with him, all of you together as a family. Angela had been in touch with my sister Laura and her husband, Gregorio, Senior, and they had sent two tickets. Your father, George Lavinia, was named after his father, Gregorio, but the teachers called him George. I may have told you this already. Pardon the faulty memory of an old man.

Your mother was so excited to move across the sea to New York City. That day, she went to buy a beautiful dress for you in the center of Napoli, something for you to wear the first time you met your father. But she never came home from her shopping. When she was crossing the street, a trolley hit her. She died instantly. I told you that. But the strangest part of the story is that your Papa Antonio died the same day, in the same way, under the same trolley.

I'll stop a moment to think how to say this.

He was a vindictive man. He wouldn't let her leave. "On my grave," he ranted. But she was determined to leave with you. She told him not to worry. At the trolley, they argued. Some heard her say she refused to stay. Enraged, he grabbed her. They struggled. He pushed. She tripped onto the track. He grabbed to keep her from falling and then went down with her. It was a sad and strange day here in Naples—for you, for us, for your nonna. But also for the other people here. You see, we are superstitious and believe easily in the curse. It was said that someone had cast a spell on your mother and her love for the young man from so far away; otherwise, how could this all be explained?

Some went so far as to say that I had set the curse in motion by inviting my nephew to come to Naples. People here like to explain away the mystery of life and death as curses by someone jealous or envious. Nonetheless, we were humbled and silenced by the tragedy. Our penance was to never speak of it—partly out of fear of angering the gods, but more to protect the name of your proud grandfather.

You see, Lavinia Lavinia, loyalty is at the base of our not telling you. We were being loyal to your grandfather's honor. We were paying respect to the old man's memory by not talking about their death, not talking about how his rage killed her. I think your uncle Sal was being loyal to his father as his first and only son. How can a son tell someone about the awful atrocity of his own father? So it was easier for him to blame your father for what happened.

And your father may have believed it was his fault in some way. Crazy, I know, but that is the way we lived. Poor George devoted his whole life to his love for Angela, as a way to keep her alive, and to do penance. His love for her lives in clay for eternity.

Forgive an old man for overloading you.

You were with your nonna Caterina when they died. Instead of sending you to your father, we called your uncle Sal, who came here to mourn his sister and father and then to take you home with him to San Francisco. Your nonna complained, but she was in no shape to take care of you. Sal wanted to keep you safe from the curse, maybe. He adopted you on the spot, loved you. Salvatore and Rosa Compana became your parents. He let you keep the name Lavinia Lavinia, the name your mother had given you. I praise him for that generosity. But he could not be generous to your father, because he, like the village people, blamed him for the curse. They said, if only the boy named George hadn't come here and gotten her pregnant, both Angela and Antonio would be alive.

Not until Rose died did Sal decide to contact your father.

My nephew is a good boy—I should say man—and a great artist. I would like to see him again. When George heard you were released from Sal's grip, he moved immediately to San Francisco to be near you. How can he make up to you for all those lost years?

I regret that my friend Sal could not be honest with you and tell you your story, but then, who am I to stand in another man's shoes?

Telling you this shocking truth makes me feel more real and lighter, more than I've felt in all these years. Please know our home awaits you should you want to return to Naples.

With love from an old man,

Giovanni Dellarosa

Chapter 23:

NEW EYES

L avinia leaves her house with an aliveness that makes no sense in light of Giovanni's sordid tale. But his letter has freed her. The news, the discoveries, and his explanations give her a lightness much like the one he described feeling at the end of his email. It's as if she's never really walked this way before; something vital has taken hold of her, similar to how she feels when Mario smiles, or she loses herself in dance, or Mercedes rocks her.

The waltz in her step takes her across the avenues and over the streets, reminding her of her first playful dance with George. A bounce propels her through the Mission. She dances as she walks, connected to the new beat in her heart. *I've found my beat* runs through her like a song. Everyone who passes looks at her and nods or smiles. She can't believe this connection she feels with them. Before she knew the truth of the secret, they were strangers or ghosts. Now they are people with smiling eyes! A shade has lifted from her eyes, and now she can see others. She wonders if she's been walking around like a ghost herself—or just sleepwalking, not seeing or being seen? Maybe she has been fashioned of clay all this time, like her mother.

Lavinia walks and walks the miles to North Beach. As soon as she reaches the restaurants and smells the food cooking, her stomach growls. She rushes toward Mario's café, walks inside, and sees his joyful smile, that wide grin from ear to ear, so pure and loving, bubbling like a giant balloon.

He leaves his espresso, walks over to her, and kisses her hard. "I missed you. I called your cell."

"I went on silent mode. You got my text, didn't you?"

He nods.

"I needed to be alone. Zack called when I didn't show up."

"I figured something was up when you didn't pop in for your double espresso. No gum, either. Or dancing?"

"Was it really that long?"

"I haven't seen you for two days and nights. I missed you."

"It felt like an eternity." She inches even closer, feeling his breath on her face. Listening to his gentle inhalations and exhalations. She moves her lips close to his and feels his breath on her upper lip. She kisses the coffee-flavored lips of her barista. "You haven't shaved. I like it." She rubs her palm over his cheek. "I want you by my side," she says, kissing his neck where his flannel shirt opens to show a hairy chest.

He hums.

"Hey, I haven't eaten any real food in days, maybe weeks. Let's have lunch together. I'm starving."

"Sure, it's time for my break. Across the street?" He looks over his shoulder at his employees behind the counter. "Back in thirty!" He grabs her hand and they run out the door.

They eat at an Italian restaurant on the other side of Columbus. Lavinia orders eggplant parmigiana with a side of spaghetti. Mario orders a panino with prosciutto. They sit side by side, holding each other's hands.

"Did you see your father?"

She nods. "I went to his place to see his artwork."

"It's weird how he's been treating you."

"Words can't describe it. I'm so baffled."

"Coming home again?"

"Coming home to you," she says.

"You have some appetite."

She's conscious of him watching her ravenously eat the sweet tomato basil sauce and stretchy mozzarella cheese. "I'll say," she says, dipping focaccia into the sauce. "Hey, I never asked you. Are you close to your father?"

"Yes, very much so. I can't believe I haven't told you about him. He set me up in business. He's a great barista." Mario looks out the window toward his café. "This is where he worked and where we used to live until he got an offer at a fancy new hotel in Kona. Dream of a lifetime."

"Kona?"

"The Big Island in Hawaii." He looks out at the street, eyes wistful. "My dad and I are a team." He puts his hand on his chest. His voice catches sweetly. "I stayed here, obviously, but he trusted me to continue the business."

"I can't believe I've never heard this story." Thinking about Mario's father brings her back to images of her family, the mausoleum in clay in George's studio, and how he's created a living memory to her mother right here in San Francisco. She's enveloped in wraparound feelings, the same ones she experienced in the presence of his art.

"You're drifting away, Lavinia."

"Yeah, I was just thinking about my mother, and how George loved her."

Mario presses his leg into hers. She pushes her plate away, not telling him she was also thinking about how her grandfather's rage killed her mother. She doesn't want to talk about it.

The plates sit empty, and the waiter offers coffee.

"But today I saw her through George's art. She was beautiful, and she loved me so much. I saw George a little more clearly, too: how he's spent his whole life sculpting her, creating an unspeakable beauty. I couldn't breathe in the presence of his work." Tenderness and sadness accompany this lightness she carries.

Sipping the bittersweet coffee, she thinks about the unusual connections—time fast-forwarding, catching up with itself. She savors the thick coffee taste while an eternity of tears pass before her eyes. She sees the little girl and the big girl in one body.

"And now?"

"I don't really know, except that I feel free of some heavy burden. It's like the neighborhood thief took the sack of rocks I carried." She pauses and looks out the window at the people on Columbus Street, all of whom seem to have a direction, moved by the wind. Again she thinks to tell Mario how her grandfather caused her mother's death, but instead says, "George says I can take my time. He says he can wait for me. While I'm pissed off, I also can understand why he acted the way he did. I'm split. Part of me is like a little girl who's finally meeting her daddy. I want to jump into his arms and be a child. But I missed that. He missed that."

Mario has his arm around her.

She snuggles up to him. "What should I do?" She bends away from his hold.

"You'll be fine, Lavinia. You'll do the right thing."

"Want to go to your place? We can make up for lost time."
She winks at him.

"You can jump into my arms," he jests. "I like a girl who
asks for what she wants." He pulls her toward him. "Let's take the
back entrance and not cut through the café, though." They walk
arm in arm down Columbus to the entrance to Mario's upstairs
apartment, located in a narrow alleyway beside the café. She's
never noticed it before. Up an enclosed stairway they go before
entering a small flat, cozy, full of the rich smell of coffee. The sink
has a few dishes stacked on the sideboard, waiting to be washed.
A half-empty bottle of beer sits on a small wooden table, seasoned
with water stains and spots. A *Chronicle* sits on the floor. A long
couch has a plaid skirt like a grand dame.

"Wow! So retro! How cool is this place." Her eyes widen to
take in the whole view.

"This is my mother's old furniture."

The floors are bare, stained with watermarks, just like downstairs. The windows, covered with plaid curtains, match the sofa.
They walk into his bedroom, where a double mattress rests on the
floor. Soft flannel sheets, a solid, dark green, and a blue comforter
with matching pillows are all ruffled up together on the bed in
a heap. Mario puts on some slow music and faces her, searching
her eyes. The music flows in and around them, and they begin to
dance, moving slowly. He takes each hand in his, gently presses
each of her fingers. She takes his fingers in her mouth, one at a
time, feels a shiver go down her back.

Their hands and arms become entwined as they move down
to sit on his flannel-covered bed. She welcomes his hands; she
glides them over her breasts and torso, toward her hips, and then
she lets him undress her. Their slow rhythms give rise to a kiss.
They lie down on the bed.

He's kissing her lips, then sucking them with urgency. She feels aroused, a 10.0 on the Richter scale. His head is no longer on the pillow beside her but buried under the heap of blankets somewhere, heading down, his tongue tracing the contours of her neck, down her shoulders, and sliding slowly over her clavicle, over her small breasts. Then he moves from her belly button down to the lower torso and navel, where he stops briefly before tenderly caressing her other lips.

She ignites with his gift of pleasure, kept a secret from her until now. How has her lovemaking always been so standard? *Where have I been? Can this be how it is?* Though she'd been intimate with Andy, it was never like this. Sex with Mario is reciprocal and generous. Lavinia feels empowered, as if Mario has just initiated her into her own sexual awakening into the Kingdom of Eros.

"Please don't ever stop, Mario," she says.

Chapter 24:

IN-THE-EARTH PARENTS

The morning light wakes her. She's in Mario's apartment alone, savoring his scent, which is mingled with hers and the coffee aroma from downstairs. Dressing, she admires the place with its heaps of comforters. She considers the grand initiation, that rite that took place last night, and smiles. Before going down into the café she makes a sweep around the flat, imagining Mario growing up here. She conjures up an image of a playful but focused child, then a strong and friendly teenager, sure of his place in the world.

She uses the back stairway, the way he showed her in, which leads to a small kitchen much like the one upstairs. Sacks of coffee beans in special bins line the walls and lead her to a small door. She opens it and finds herself behind the bar. She doesn't belong there! Awkwardly, she scoots out, kneeling and slipping herself under the hinged counter. Mario is too busy to notice that she's slipped past him; he's focused on making an espresso. She takes him in as if for the first time.

From this vantage point, she can see how his muscular body—torso, waist, buttocks, calves—work as one. Those well-developed arms just held her to him. She feels giggly. She sees new things in his face—a man's face, mature and handsome; how gently he handles the espresso machine; how attentive and confident he is; the kind smile he shows to his customers. He dispenses two measures of coffee and flushes steaming water through the machine, cleaning it, before he sees her.

"Good morning," she says, moving to the front of the bar.

"You look beautiful, Bubblicious." He hands her the espresso he just made.

"Thank you." She takes the coffee. "You're super duper." She giggles.

He laughs.

She takes her coffee to the corner seat and, to her surprise, sees Zack reading at a nearby table. He looks up just at that moment, and their eyes meet. He touches the seat next to him. "S-sit down, please," he says so softly she can barely hear him.

"So sorry I missed our laundry day, Zack."

"Just more for next week."

"Yes."

"You're okay," he says. "You look happy." He looks toward Mario and smiles.

"Very!" She blushes. She sits across from him as time quietly passes. She's happy to be in silence with him, with no pressure to talk or share with him. He just silently takes her in.

"Are we still on?" he asks after a while. "Thanksgiving break?"

"A few days from now." She nods.

"All packed?"

"Not yet."

"Time waits for us." His long, thin fingers play with the knotted string he wears around his wrist.

Lavinia stares at the bracelet of white silk threads, wondering if the three knots signify anything.

Zack fingers the knots, seeming to read her question. "These are promises I've made to myself. Do you ever set intentions, Lavinia?"

"Not really," she says, though maybe there is something brewing. She thinks about the exhilaration of seeing the statues of her mother, the incredible sex with Mario. "But I am receiving some sort of intentions from the universe."

"You're doing your work, Lavinia," he says, touching her wrist with his bracelet hand.

"Yes, I am." She trusts that she is. She feels more grounded having seen her mother holding her, nursing her, loving her. She left George's yesterday remembering how dearly Angela had loved her.

Outside, rain pours down, the first of the season. An amazing burst of energy hits the sidewalk, slashing the windows, the roof. Lavinia thinks of Mario's bed and how the rain might sound upstairs. She watches him spin from customer to customer, pulling shots of steaming coffee into cups. In her mind's eye she sees George pulling clay; it's a similar movement, a pulling and thrusting of energy like the slashing and abating rain. All in a flash, these images come to her. She imagines the dry earth under her fig tree sucking in the moisture, fulfilling its thirst after the long dry spell, just as her own body did with Mario—a quenching after a desert spell not only in her sex life but in her imagination, and her faith in herself.

And now another richness for her: an offer to go to Ely, Nevada, with this kindly gentleman who wants her company and wants to give her five grand, too.

She looks at Zack. "The knots?"

"Intentions, as I said." He fingers the first two. "I want to visit Mount Washington, where the 10,000-year clock will be buried, and I want to visit the 4,000-year-old trees."

"And the third knot?"

"I wish for s-snow," he whispers, letting the soft *s* sing.

She nods as the rain pours down hard, puddling near the door, where Mario has placed a rolled towel on the floor. *Noah's Ark*, Lavinia thinks. Though this talk of snow and the pouring rain outside make her shiver, she feels safe in this cozy café and sets her own intention: to cultivate her friendship with Zack.

"Clothes for snow, then," she says.

"Do you want to borrow some of Margaret's ski clothes?"

"That would be perfect," she says.

Zack sits quietly, furrows his brow. "You know, they killed the oldest living tree—WPN-114, they named it," he says. "They killed her to see how old she was. The stupids."

"WPN-114 sounds so alien," she says, "like ET or Obi-Wan Kenobi."

"True," he acknowledges. Then he tells her the scientists first called the tree Prometheus, for the God who stole fire.

Lavinia remembers her mythology.

Now he's telling her that WPN-114, like Prometheus, was sacrificed, cut down to be studied. But Lavinia's thoughts gravitate toward her mother, who was cut down by her own father. Talk about stupids!

Lavinia remembers an old dream she once had about seeing the lights of Las Vegas. That dream seems so distant to her now and so much less interesting or meaningful than the trip she'll take with Zack. Surrounding herself with people she loves is shifting something in her—toward better and more positive intentions.

Mario is walking toward her and Zack, who's now opened a California/Nevada map on the café table. He's routed the trip to East Nevada via Route 50, and he's pointing this out to Lavinia. Ely, Nevada, is speck on the map.

"A small town of about four thousand," Zack says.

The road looks long, and she notices that their trip will take them nowhere near Las Vegas. She's relieved. She doesn't want to be burdened by old dreams. She wants to focus on her new life and new dreams.

"What's it like to drive to Bishop in November?" Lavinia looks toward Mario for the answer.

"Long. Cold. And boring until you reach the incredible Eastern Sierra." Mario fingers the map, tracing a line to Bishop at the eastern end of US 50. "The road may even be closed because of snow."

"I'll have snow shoes in the Subaru," Zack says.

They laugh, and Mario pulls out his phone to check the weather. "Average high 48 degrees," he says, "average low 18.7 degrees, average snow days in November is 4.4 to 5.7 percent."

Mario and Lavinia's eyes lock as Zack slowly recounts a day he spent among the ancient pine trees fifteen years ago, when he was investigating the old forest as an environmental engineer in water management for the Owens Valley.

"The path moving up to the highest elevation was dus-s-ted with snow," he says. "A light snow, and it was-s-s beautiful. Early morning in June. I was the first imprint on the trail. The sun was barely up, so the white powder wouldn't melt for an hour or so. Just me in the bristlecones, me and a light wind. As I walked toward the altitude where the living bristlecones-s-s still breathe, our breaths deepened, seeming to mix with each other." His fingers twist his bracelet as he takes in a deep breath. "It was late spring, the time when the wildflowers bloom—mostly those luscious penstemons. Mountain blue jays sang raucous songs; I even saw a golden eagle soaring above."

"Wow! That sounds incredible! I'm so excited!" Lavinia says.

"I'm so happy you're coming, Lavinia," Zack says.

"You're making me jealous," Mario says.

"I'm off now," Zack says. "Got some packing to do."

Lavinia readies herself to leave, too. Mario has to work, and she has errands to run.

As Zack leaves, he says to her softly, "It's winter I'm interested in now. It's the season of my life." He pats her on the shoulder. "Thursday, 6:30 a.m."

"I'll be there," she says. She bids him farewell and gives Mario a light kiss good-bye.

The rain is still coming down outside, but only as a light drizzle. She walks up Columbus Avenue to the financial district. The pyramid building seems out of place until she thinks of the limestone mountain in the desert where time will pulse for ten thousand years. If that is not out of place, what is?

Ten minutes later, she's on the bus, headed for the Mission District and Kinky's house.

She finds Mercedes in the kitchen, messing with lunch. It's early afternoon, and the rain has stopped completely. The sky lightens up, the air is fresh, the spices that Mercedes blends are intoxicating.

Mercedes lights up when she sees Lavinia. "*Mijita,* come and sit with me."

Moving to the now-familiar chairs, they sit together.

"Kinky should be home soon," Mercedes says. "I bet she can smell lunch right now."

Mercedes reaches out a hand to Lavinia. As she sinks into the puffiest cushioned seat, Lavinia imagines she's sitting in her lap.

"*Gracias, Mamá.*"

Mercedes sits erect—spine straight, feet flat on the floor, naked and strong. Her hands rest on her thighs. Her skirt forms a flowing cup between her legs.

"*Mijita*, you look happy today."

"I am."

"*Sí*, I see much joy in your face."

"I have come out of my cave—love has visited me. His name is Mario. And I have found my father, too. He was near me all this year, and I never knew."

"*Qué bueno.*"

Lavinia looks into Mercedes's eyes, focusing on the dark pools—reflections of love, of joy. They are so unlike George's eyes, which reflect melancholy. "I have mixed feelings about him. He's a good guy, a little sad, and he really loved my mother. But he betrayed me."

"The pain is back, *mijita*. I can see it in your eyes." Mercedes leans in close to her.

"Yes, *Mamá*, it is terrible. He has kept me in the dark, kept me from seeing his love for her—and for me, too."

"It's hard to trust him?" she asks.

Lavinia nods.

"Do you want to have a relationship with him?"

"Yes, I do, but I'm scared. What if . . ." Lavinia pauses, falls into her arms.

"*Sí, sí, entiendo*, but you can go slowly, *mijita*, little by little you can let him in. *Despacito. Despacito.*"

"*Sí, Mamá.* Little by little," she repeats, unfolding from the older woman's arms. She wipes her eyes, remembering Mercedes's chant the last time she sat here—deep, dark sounds, hauntingly sad, like her father's eyes. Mercedes sang with her eyes closed, sang the savagely sad song as if to add another presence.

Mercedes, as if reading Lavinia's mind, begins yet another song. "We will celebrate," she says. "I have a lighter song for you today. *Una canción chica, una alegría.*" She closes her eyes and moves her arms and hands in a circular motion. "*Ay ay ay, lie lie la, hi hi lee, la lay, hi hi hee, ya ya hi ha,*" she chants. Her hands, small and firm, cup each other as she claps a one-two-three rhythm with an accent on the third clap. She sings *puertacita*, the little door opening and closing, opening and closing. She sings *la campana, tiene cariña* with some *ba ma pa pa, pero ba-ma-pa-pa*. Jubilantly, she claps and sings. Lavinia keeps to the beat with her right foot tapping the floor.

"*Olé!*" Kinky is opening the door to the house.

"*Arriba*, Kinky."

After many *olés* and clapping and stamping, they get up and begin to tap their feet and wave their arms, circling each other around the room as Mercedes sings her *alegría*. All thrilling! And Kinky is an incredible dancer, full of poise and attitude and soulfulness. She enchants Lavinia. What a pair, the flamenco artists, mother and daughter—*la cantante* Mercedes and the dancer Kinky.

"All that is missing is the *toque*." Mama and Kinky look into each other's eyes.

"*Toque* is the guitar," Kinky explains, looking at Lavinia. "My father used to play for us."

Mercedes sings, "*La puertacita, aah, oh, aah, way; da detta a da; ba-ma-pa-pa; pero, ma ma pa pa.*"

"She's singing that he's at the doorway, playing for us," Kinky says. "I feel he's right here."

"Mine, too." A wide smile breaks across Lavinia's face. "Oh, I have so much to tell you."

"Well, yeah, it's been so long now," Kinky says.

"Yes, the long now." Lavinia starts laughing, thinking about the Long Now Foundation and Zack Luce and all she has had going on since she last saw Kinky.

"*Comer, niñas!*" Mercedes commands. She's beaming, refreshing her face at the sink, washing her hands before preparing her famous tamales.

"Hot tamales for lunch, *Mamacita*?" Lavinia beams.

"*Mijita*, today you are our hot tamale, and a happy one, too." Mercedes places two tamales on each of the girls' plates.

Chapter 25:

THE UNFINISHED PIETA

Early morning, Lavinia wakes to the sounds of birds. Convinced they are singing an *alegría*, she drops back to sleep with the humming of Mercedes on her lips and tastes the colors of the flamenco dance in her dreams. When she wakes again, she's ready to see George. She dresses, leaves her place, and in fifteen minutes is standing at George's studio door.

He greets her with a large smile and those dark, penetrating eyes. "Come in, Lavinia. Tea? Coffee?"

"Yes, thank you, but first I want to visit her again."

George moves aside as Lavinia lets herself into what she now thinks of as the Temple of Love. A sculpted casket, holding Angela, draws her attention. She kneels down on the padded knee rest in front of her mother, caught in repose. Lavinia can't believe the detail he has carved into the clay. Softly creased folds flow like currents.

Currents. She stares, convinced the folds are moving, the statuesque figure is breathing. She undulates. Lavinia squints at what seems like her mother's pulsing heart radiating waves, or maybe breaths. She's still alive. Lavinia rubs her eyes, her face, pinches her cheeks, and looks again to see the vibrating woman. Maybe she's dreaming. So strong is her desire for this beautiful woman to be alive. George has created an homage to his love, and Lavinia wants her to wake up.

But Angela sleeps in the folds of a beautiful garment, her hands resting on her full bosom, a rose between her long fingers. Lavinia touches the smooth face carved in clay and closes her eyes, letting her fingers find the raisin mole, so similar to her own—a kind of umbilical connection that grounds her. She cries into the folds; tears run down her cheeks. The soft-lit room is a memorial to her mother, another Taj Mahal. She cries, letting the beauty of the sadness soak through her pores.

She doesn't move away when she feels George's strong hands on her shoulder. Instead, his touch grounds her further in the moment. Tears stream, but now they are tears of sadness for this man's love for her mother. It occurs to her that they have shared this connection all this time: they both love and long for Angela. He's never moved on from her. He too has been paralyzed in some block of stone, himself an unfinished pietá, solidified in time. She considers how she was perhaps on track to follow in this unwanted tradition, and she's not interested in being encased in stone.

She wipes her nose on her sleeve and turns toward George, He reaches for her hand and walks with her through the great sanctuary of love and death. The lights dim as they move toward a smaller light, where she sees a wooden table, two chairs, and a stovetop. George puts some water on the small burner, and they sit down.

"You have built a temple of love for her."

He pauses. "You have seen my heart." He places his hand on his chest.

"Your heart?" Lavinia searches his eyes.

"Yes. She rests in my heart, and these are the stations of my love."

Lavinia thinks of the scenes on the church walls on Good Friday when Christ is on the road to his crucifixion. She shudders, thinking of the times she must have sat beside her mother in the church as a toddler on Good Fridays, and then with Sal and Rose in front of all the mortifications of the dead and dying Christ. It leaves her cold. She shivers.

Responding to what must be a morbid look on her face, George says, "I don't think about this as the stations of the cross but as stations of my love for her . . . and you." His face is soft and relaxed.

"For me?" she says, feeling the sting of betrayal again. "Why didn't you tell me who you were when you first saw me? Why did you wait so long?"

"I don't know," he confesses. "I couldn't grasp the reality of it."

"Which part?" she asks.

He fumbles with the teapot cover, not answering.

Lavinia continues, "But you knew it was me, and I didn't know it was you. That was unfair." She hears a demand for answers in her own voice.

"I had been thinking of you for so long, thinking I might never meet you, and then when I did, I felt lost. Afraid." His eyes drop. The crease between his brow intensifies.

"Afraid?"

"Terrified you might reject me!" He opens his eyes.

"Why have I been so excluded from all of this?" she cries.

"I agonized over it for years." George looks sheepish, like a dog with ears that hang down to his side. When he comes up for air, he says, "It wasn't until Uncle Giovanni told me Sal was returning to Naples and Sal called me himself that I seriously decided to find you."

Lavinia couldn't understand why he waited so long. If he had only come to her in San Francisco, she would have known her dad: he would have taken her to school and picked her up; he would have told her of her beautiful mother's love; she would have known her grandparents from New York. They would have loved her. He had the power to make her life different. What kept him away? Another family? The curse Giovanni mentioned? Was everyone's lips sealed?

Fear? George said he was afraid. Maybe all he could do was hold the torch for her mother so he could keep her alive. Was all this obsessive creating related to his guilt about not returning for her? Lavinia can't help but wonder how her life might be different if he had returned to Naples the next summer to see his new baby, to spend that summer with them, even take them back with him to New York.

Her mother would be alive in real flesh, instead of this damn stone.

He was making up excuses!

"Sal called me and asked me to wait until he left. He said he would arrange for you to call me. He said he wanted to tell you first." George sits down again. "I guess he didn't."

"Why didn't you insist he introduce us before he left?"

"I don't know. I thought it would be better if he did, but he said he couldn't do it. When you called, I realized you didn't know." He fumbles with the cups and saucers.

"Why didn't you tell me then?"

"I thought it would spill out. It didn't. Then I thought you might cut me out of your life. At least this way, I could see you twice a week. I know it was cowardly."

"I'm pissed at you!" It feels good to admit this out loud to him. She looks into his dark eyes, which soften her outburst.

"I've known you all your life, Lavinia Lavinia. I've imagined how you look, your smile, your eyes, your gesture—but when I first saw you I was stunned! I froze when you were right here in my home."

She tries to remember that first moment, but nothing seemed out of the ordinary to her. She knows that Sal and Rose also kept their emotions from her, and now she understands how she learned to keep her own feelings packed in stone.

"I wanted to tell you how beautiful you were; how you looked like your mother; how sad I was when she died; how I went to look for you in Naples as soon as I heard about her death; how I found a shrine with her picture; how I visited your nonna, pining away in a darkened room. But everyone was sworn to silence. No one would tell me what happened or where you were!"

"That seems to be the story of my life," Lavinia cries. She wants to break something—the cup, the saucer she holds—but realizes what she really wants is to break this pattern of keeping secrets.

"I'm sorry, Lavinia."

"You didn't even tell me your last name."

"I know. I agreed to keep that secret, too."

George gets up, walks to the cupboard, and returns with a cookie tin full of a dozen chocolate-covered biscotti. She takes one and dips it into her hot tea before biting into it. She lets the chocolate melt on her tongue.

"Your mother loved dark chocolate, too."

"Bittersweet."

"But her life was sweet, too. It was filled with joy and love for you and me and everyone she touched."

"But then she died at twenty-one."

"I know it's not fair, Lavinia."

"It's not fair. We both lost her." Now it seems she is grieving for the man, her father, who lost his love and his daughter, too. Lavinia tenses up; her rib cage seems to float up toward her shoulders as her neck stiffens, and now her jaw feels contorted. Her mouth twists in some weird, silent cry. But she does not cry.

"Angela has always been with me, maybe even before I set eyes on her at the well." He looks out in the distance. "And she's with us now."

"I don't see her."

"You will see her through me. I'm not going anywhere now that we have reunited."

She feels a damp clump of breath emit from a hidden vault inside her.

"We knew when we made love that you were there with us. Your mother felt you deep inside her womb. We saw you before you were born."

Lavinia fidgets in her chair.

"And I feel her presence as if she's deep inside me, guiding me to you, Lavinia." George looks off in the distance again, as if he is seeing Angela still alive. He is no longer speaking to Lavinia but to Angela, to the memory of her. "You placed my hand on your smooth olive skin and kept it there. You wanted me to feel the pulse of her sweet blood. Bless you, Angela, for giving me a daughter. She's here, can you see her, Angela? She's beautiful like you. Lavinia Lavinia is twenty-six now." George is smiling, tears of joy collecting in his eyes.

Lavinia sits stunned by George's words, enthralled by the images they evoke. When he sees her looking at him, he smiles.

"You lit up your mother's life."

They sit in silence for a long moment. But still she wonders why he never came back to Italy to see her as an infant.

"Why didn't you come back to Naples? You knew she was pregnant. Why didn't you come to meet me?"

"It's the biggest regret of my life," George says.

Lavinia looks in her tea for the answer, but the tea leaves are gone. All she sees is the biscotti floating, a ball of mush. Everything that might have been was interred in a mausoleum. Her mother, who might have seen her daughter grow up, lived in cement. Angela had missed the first grader reading both Italian and English; the girl who made her first Holy Communion with bubblegum in her mouth. What if, as a preadolescent girl, Lavinia had walked hand in hand with her mother in Manhattan, heading toward her artist dad's studio in Greenwich Village? What if they had taken the boat to the islands near Naples?

Now Lavinia sits at her father's small wooden table, mourning her losses, all the little deaths, thinking how she missed her mother's baking. Angela would have baked to celebrate Lavinia's milestones. Her mother would have made her famous honey-topped *struffoli*, and cakes with patisserie cream, and hard biscotti that would be worthy of a hearty bite, not like these soft ones George served. There would have been many celebrations, including her graduation from college; she would have made meals for Kinky and Lavinia.

Here in her thoughts she smiles, reminded of Mamacita Mercedes, who has done a good enough job.

When she gets up to leave, George says, "I'd like to walk you home. I need some fresh air."

"Okay, we can walk the few blocks together."

They silently walk to the Mission toward Valencia Street. In step with her father, she stops and turns; she's silently asking him not to disappear. She lifts a finger to tell him that, but feels faint, dizzy. He guides her as she wobbles toward her flat. When they get there, he holds a hand on her shoulder lovingly.

"Lavinia, I'm sorry for not coming back . . . for you and her."

She feels sad, not sure of her ability to forgive him, though she wants to. She points him away.

Inside, Lavinia goes into her room and pulls her blankets over her head against the daylight, then closes her eyes to nap, as she smells Raggedy and whispers to her doll, "I think everything's going to be okay."

Chapter 26:

MOURNING

At the first dull light, Lavinia wakes to the sweet black of sadness, like the rich espresso she has come to love. So full is the bittersweet feeling that it's almost a delicious yearning.

Peeking out from her cave, she sees it's still dark; she has slept through dinner and into the night. She doesn't want artificial light. She has to plant each foot securely on the floor in order to get up. That accomplished, she makes her way into the dark room to find her jeans, shirt, and jacket.

Pulling her clothes on feels challenging today. *Why these straight-legged jeans? Why can't they make stylish pants for women be more comfortable?* she asks herself as she contorts her feet and extends herself to get into the tight legs. She promises herself some new flowing clothes soon. She's only ever worn black, but maybe now it's time for something with a splash of color.

Finally dressed, she finds her way out to the fig tree and sits in contemplation with a gentle wind on her face, thinking of George. She has let him touch her heart, seeing his love for her mother. Again she experiences their shared love and sorrow. She bows to the tree for holding her in these moments of clarity. When she opens her eyes, a spider web glistens in the first rays of light. Tiny drops of dew cling to the web, bursting with the light of dawn, dripping from the threads of silk. Lavinia lets her eyes jump from one diamond to the next, convincing herself they hold the image of the tree, her mother, the sun, and her face, reflecting them like the facets of a diamond.

When she leaves her apartment, the street is quiet with early dawn just arriving. The shops are closed on 16th Street; few people are about. She walks. A screeching trolley on Market startles her. She pictures herself, not her mother, sprawled out on the pavement. She flinches as the trolley comes to a stop, covers her eyes, not wanting to see these pictures—and a desire to live bursts forth.

Sunrise brings with it an orange glow to the day. She walks down California to Market and then up Grant to Chinatown, where shopkeepers are opening up stores or moving garbage bins to the rear of their places. One man is hosing down the sidewalk. In North Beach, the cafés open early, with patrons straggling in before work. The smell of coffee soothes her mind. She can taste it and feel the rush of her favorite medicine.

As soon as she enters Falcone, her own falcon, Mario, looks up. "You're out early."

"Couldn't wait to see you." She leans across the bar and kisses him.

He sets to work making her a double espresso and a plate of fresh croissants.

"I was up this morning contemplating by my tree," she tells him.

"Wish I could've been with you."

"Me, too," she says.

He smiles and reaches out a hand.

"George told me about their love for each other. My mother was in love with life, and me, and him, until she died on the day she planned to leave with me for New York to be with him." She sighs. "My nonno pushed her, and they both fell under a moving trolley."

"Oh, no! Man, was he some kind of wacko?" Mario moves in closer. "Come here."

Lavinia lets him hold her. She sobs on his shoulder, saying, "Why'd they have to die together on that day, Mario?"

"A waste. How could he do that?" He pulls her in closer. "What happened, exactly?"

"They were fighting. He pushed and grabbed and they stumbled, fell into the oncoming trolley. He didn't want her to leave him." Her eyes widen. "It's all some kind of dark magic steeped in secrecy, and loyalty. They didn't tell anyone because they wanted to keep my grandfather's honor intact."

"That's why they didn't tell you?"

"I don't know," she says, gazing off. "Giovanni said people were scared. They thought a curse had been put on them with these horrible deaths. They didn't want to further tempt the gods."

"I'm so sorry." He kisses her wet cheeks and hugs her. She bends her head and neck into his chest.

"What if my mother lived here and could meet you and Kinky and Mercedes and Zack, and live with my father, and see me so happy?" She laughs, realizing she's wetting his shirt with her tears. She answers her own question silently, feeling the tragedy deep within her but also the sense of resolution in having spoken about what happened with George and feeling gratitude for her own angels.

"I'm eager to hear about your visit with George," Mario says. "What happened?"

She slips out of his arms, takes his hand, and walks with him to her favorite table in the back, grateful Falcone is still empty. She tells him about George's working showroom—how he's chronicled her mother's life in clay, solidified now in stone.

"It was all there for me to see, Mario. My beautiful mother in the stages of life—as a youth, as a young girl in love, as a woman pregnant, as a mother nursing me." She has to catch her breath before telling him how she kneeled before her casket. "She's a dead angel," she says.

"And this is what George has spent his life doing?"

"All of it. He devoted his youth and adult years to Angela, living to keep her alive. Can you imagine? He gave up his life to make clay images of her. It seems we are both still mourning these deaths. You know, spending that time with him yesterday made me feel a lot better. Seeing his heart like that has made me feel closer to him."

"Did you say 'heart'?"

"Yeah. I guess both his art and heart were exposed. We both lost her. We both feel the grief."

Mario and Lavinia sit quietly. She's thinking about George, the sad clay thrower, and his devotion to her mother. But somehow giving up his life to a clay image seems wrong, too sacrificial. "He's been recreating what he lost. With each statue he mourns my birth, my infancy, and Angela's death." She looks at Mario. "It also occurred to me that he's doing some kind of a penance for leaving us behind."

"Maybe he feels responsible for her death?" Mario says, holding her hand.

"But aren't we supposed to live our lives as well?" she asks. "And what about me?"

"Maybe he's into sacrificial living."

She sees Iphigenia carried to her funeral pyre by her king father, Agamemnon, and she cries for her own sacrificed mother, her rage-filled grandfather, and George, who she now sees as scarred by this loss. She cries for herself, too, and for all the children, the soldier boys, who have been sacrificed by their elders for some sin of pride and hubris. *All of us!*

"Bubblicious, I'm here." Mario places two croissants in front of her. She eats one and gives the other to him.

"I want to have a relationship with George," she says.

Mario puts out his hands to her. She takes them. They sit in silence.

"It's only been a day since yesterday," she says eventually, feeling the world has turned.

His warm eyes invite her to continue.

"And such an amazing day. Encompassing everything. Starting with you and me and now circling back to us. It's like I've been around the world in twenty-four hours."

"Lavinia. I need you to be by my side." His eyes sparkle. "Let's dance tonight."

"Okay." She smiles back at him.

Lavinia takes a corner of his croissant into her mouth and feeds him the rest. When he's finished, he has to return to his counter. The place is filling up with eager customers—quiet, thirsty-for-caffeine customers. He waves good-bye.

"I'll be back after I see Zack," she calls to him before slipping out the door.

Leaving the café, she heads down Chestnut Street to Zack's. He doesn't mind that she missed her Monday. He greets her just as eight cuckoos sound off, along with other chiming bells. On a long coffee table he has set up maps, guidebooks, a compass, a Swiss Army knife, water bottles, and rain gear. Hiking boots with heavy socks sticking out the tops sit on the plush carpet, next to a series of open maps.

"Aren't you going swimming today?" Lavinia asks.

"Later. Let's look at the maps together." He points to Bishop, California.

She's never heard of Bishop, but his slow speech grounds her as she takes a seat next to the outstretched maps, upon which he has made many circles. On closer inspection, she realizes the circles are depicting the gradations on various altitudes of forest and mountains. Bishop is the closest town to the bristlecone forest. It's not flatland, as she imagined. The Eastern Sierra, where he plans to visit, has high altitudes.

"You're so organized," she says. He seems like a Boy Scout to her, a mountain man for sure.

"That reminds me." He gets up, grabs a navy duffel bag from the couch, and brings it over to her. "Open it."

Inside is a brand-new rainproof down jacket with a hood trimmed in fake fur, tags still on. "Ripstop nylon fabric," the label says.

"I hope you like red. I ordered it from REI."

"It's beautiful, Zack. Thank you."

"There's more in there."

She feels around the cushioned bottom of the bag and finds a soft cashmere scarf. She pulls it out and puts it up to her face. The wool is softer than her Raggedy. She covers her eyes with the scarf, to dab the tears growing in there. No one has ever given her such a thoughtful gift.

"Mario said it could get as low as 18 degrees," Zack says, chuckling and not commenting on the tears that have sprung to her eyes. "The weather will be a crapshoot, but I thought you should be prepared."

"Thank you, Zack. You are so kind." She gets up, unzips the jacket, and tries it on.

"Beautiful," he says. "Red's your color."

Her eyes fall to the map with the route he's highlighted, expanding in concentric circles as the cuckoo sings the half hour. She watches his steady hand drawing with a Sharpie a straight line easterly toward the Sierra, and then south. Her pulse rises and her skin prickles, like when Mercedes sings her beautiful, deep *rondas*. His dream, his three wishes, pull her in and toward this ancient forest adventure.

"Where will we sleep?" she asks.

"I've reserved motels for us. Two rooms."

She looks around at all his gear. The maps of the Owens Valley, the White Mountains area, and Highway 395; the socks, the boots, snowshoes, poles, hats, and gloves. She touches the front of her new jacket.

"I have things around here of Elsa's or Margaret's, and what you don't have we can rent. There will be lots of mountaineering stores in the mountains for tourists."

"I have hiking stuff, too. I'll get everything together this afternoon," she says, "and be ready. It's two days from now."

"Good, sounds like we're on our way."

Zack gets up and begins to gather his swim bag and leaves the apartment with Lavinia sitting in her shiny red jacket. *Whenever have I been treated so kindly?* she thinks. It feels like Christmas morning to her.

She opens the door to the room holding the replica Millennium clock with its tungsten parts. The moving parts—a wheel of time. The books call out from the library shelf—*The Oldest Living Things in the World, Deep Time, The Story of Time*.

"Time and more time," Lavinia says aloud. *It's time to live the good time, to open the door, to face my beautiful life.*

She looks in at the machine with the pendulum at its base in the form of a three-pronged wheel, at the clock dial on the top, made of multiple spirals of solid tungsten. Zack said tungsten, of all metals in their purest form, has the highest tensile strength, even stronger than uranium. Her mother did not go to high school or college to learn about the periodic table of elements. Her mother was not indestructible like tungsten but in George's mind she lives. Carved in stone, if not in blood.

Lavinia closes the door to the room where the model of the 10,000-year clock resides. The cuckoos in the living room sing out ten.

She washes the swimsuits by hand and places clothes in the washer and then the drier. She can hear the noon bells of St. Peter and Paul's in North Beach chiming in the distance as she finishes.

It's time now. She grabs her money and puts a now dried fig leaf on the blue linen tablecloth, which Elsa used to fuss over in her life. People and events from the long past seem to rush together in her life, emerging with new vigor as people rise from the dead. She lets herself out into the late-morning sunshine of North Beach.

When she reaches Falcone, it's quiet. Mario is standing at the counter, looking at his cell. When he looks up, he smiles. "Lavinia, you look beautiful in red!"

"A Christmas present, she says. "He wants me to be warm in the mountains as well as help with the driving."

"That's Zack."

"I'm ready to go."

"You'll love the high desert. The open, vast spaces of stars and mountains, deserts like an ancient ocean—there's an openness there that clears out the cobwebs."

"And I have some cobwebs to clear." She laughs, considering the idea that her cobwebs were made by the spider whose web she saw glistening with diamonds in her yard this morning. "It's settled, then. I'm leaving on Thanksgiving morning. Only two days away."

"You can stay at my place on Wednesday night, and I'll walk you over to his place with your stuff," Mario suggests.

She smiles and nods. "And tonight we'll celebrate—go dancing. But first I have to pack. I'll come here tonight about seven o'clock." She gives him a kiss, kicks up her heels, and heads for home.

Chapter 27:

LONG DISTANCE

A note in her mailbox from George. His writing is very small and legible, like he took time to write it. She reads it at the entryway to her long room.

> *Yesterday. Thanks for your questions. I wonder how you're sitting with all this. We'll talk some more when you're ready. I may have gone too fast. Please forgive me for not starting this conversation earlier, but I didn't know how. Not sure I even can do it now.*

Lavinia sticks the note in her top drawer next to the photo of five-year-old Lavinia with Sal crouched over her as she examines her first-ever bubblegum. The fig tree is whispering—or is the wind swishing the leaves?

She closes the drawer and searches for some heavy clothes from her closet—woolen socks, corduroy slacks, a North Face pullover, a raincoat, a ski hat, and mittens. Hiking boots. Sunglasses and case. Eyeglass strap for them. A bandanna, a sunhat,

and sunscreen. All stuff she's used hiking on Mt. Tam. She folds
the new cashmere scarf and the red jacket on top of her gear.

Leaving town now, just when what seem like harmonic con-
versions are occurring with the loves of her life, must be some
kind of ritual.

But Sal, he's missing. She wants to talk to him before she
leaves. She picks up her cell. She looks at the world clock: time
in Naples, 10:00 p.m. She dials his old cell phone number, not
remembering whether he's given her a new number.

He picks up the phone. "*Pronto, pronto,*" he says.

"Uncle Sal?"

"Who is this?"

"Lavinia Lavinia. Where are you?"

"What?"

"You sound so near, Uncle."

"I'm in bed in Naples. What time is it there?"

"Early afternoon in San Francisco."

Sal seems to be waking up now and sounds less hassled.
"How are you, Lavinia?"

"Why didn't you tell me you kept the same cell number
sooner?" She can't believe she never tried it before.

"Is that why you called?"

She can see him wrinkling up his nose. "You never told me
I had a father, Uncle Sal. Why was Giovanni the one to tell me
about George? Did you know that George lived on Folsom Street?"

A long silence.

"Sal, answer me! Did you know my father lived here in our
neighborhood?"

"I could never find the right time to tell you."

"That's so lame, Sal."

"Did you meet him?" Sal says.

"Of course, I met him. I bet before you left you arranged with Dr. Brady for me to work for him."

More silence.

"Well, did you?"

"I'm a coward, Lavinia. I couldn't tell you. I couldn't even introduce you to him. I never wanted to see George. I blamed him for what happened to my sister."

"Excuse me, Sal." Lavinia's voice rises to a fever pitch. "What, exactly, did he do to my mother?"

"He loved her and that made her do strange things," he says.

"Like what?"

Again, silence.

"Answer me!"

He doesn't answer.

"Sal! Sal, what did his love make her do?"

"Die."

Stunned, she shouts, "But he still loves her."

"That love killed her, and our father, too. How could I ever let that happen to you?"

"Sal, that doesn't make any sense. It was your father who killed them both, not George."

He doesn't answer. She hears some hissing or gasping sounds.

"Lavinia, can we talk about this later? I'm exhausted right now. Please, Vinnie, calm yourself down."

She hates when he closes down like he just did. Just like when she was a kid and he said, "Stop asking, stop asking, Vinnie."

She hangs up on him.

Continuing with her packing, she thinks of Zack and his kind gestures toward her. And what was it he told her? Didn't he say she has something to do—fill in the pieces of the puzzle, or something like that?

Chapter 28:

BEAUTIFUL SAD EYES

She walks out to the patio and touches the earth mulch beneath the tree.

"Lavinia Lavinia, come upstairs," she hears. Is that the fig tree calling her now? She ignores the voice, worrying that it is Aunt Rose waking up from the dead. A bird chirps and chirps again. A wind breezes through the fig tree. She succumbs to its call and takes the key and once again heads to the upstairs apartment.

Why am I going upstairs today? She doesn't know, but she's begun to trust this voice—and yet she fears seeing Rose on that deathbed again. She wants to think she's finally departed and is resting in peace now that she's returned Raggedy. The whispering leaves of the fig cancel the voice of Sal cussing, accusing George of killing her mother, and soothes her as she enters the upstairs bedroom.

She stops at the foot of Aunt Rose's bed, clenching her eyes shut, scared, half expecting Rose will stick out her finger and point her to where she needs to search again. But Rose has gone away now, having redeemed herself. She is finally at peace.

Lavinia looks at the bed. "I forgive you, Rose. Thank you for providing a home for me."

On the opposite wall from where Raggedy lived all those years stands a unit with fifty-odd small drawers—more like an apothecary cabinet, with rectangular pullouts of varying sizes.

She doesn't know where to begin and takes a stab in the middle. She opens the small drawer, pinching her nose at the odor. Musty dried hair clings to a white pearl comb, hairpins, a hair net with strings of gray hair, Q-tips. She searches quickly through several more drawers until she finds what she's looking for—a small discolored photo album about two by three inches sits at the base of the drawer. Sal must have taken it from Italy. Who gave him this album? Nonna Caterina?

She leafs through the little album of tiny photos and stops at an early picture of her mother. Angela is truly beautiful, just as George described her. Her auburn hair reflects the sun. She wears a sundress, showing off beautifully rounded shoulders. She is voluptuous in a classical way. The faint smudge of her birthmark on her cheek seems to accentuate her beauty rather than detract from it.

Then Lavinia sees a picture of her pregnant mother with joy in her face; next, a picture of George as a young boy, sketching as Angela dances. *Who took this picture?* They're in a park with white flowering trees. Having never seen it before, she wonders how this picture is in Sal's possession. Was it meant for her? Did her nonna Caterina ask Sal to give it to her so she could see her parents and their love? She snatches the book, closes up the dirty-smelling room, and leaves it—for eternity, she hopes.

She places the photo album in her small purse and heads for Folsom Street to show George. She wants to erase Sal's nasty accusation that her father killed her mother. How could such a pure love kill her mother? What killed her mother was a maniac.

Arriving at Folsom Street, she enters the studio, remembering those innocent days when she came here to pick up tarps and then return them and collect the money. That seems so long ago now, yet it has only been a few weeks. She watches George working in his hot clay room near the kiln, throwing clay the way he showed her. He's in his shorts, shirtless. She stares at the man she doesn't really know, the man who is her birth father. He works the clay with quick movements—a vertical, a swift diagonal, and then a horizontal throw, like some exquisite tai chi move. Then she hears the music: "The Merry Widow" waltz. She listens to the lyrical melody, which ascends and descends, creating a bittersweet mood. She walks closer. He stops throwing and looks at her.

"Lavinia!" he says, clearly surprised to see her in his space. "Let me put on something, and I'll meet you in a moment."

She turns toward the larger room from which she entered and walks across it to the center. She is the hub of a wheel that is her mother.

"Hello, Lavinia." George returns dressed in slacks and shirt and walks toward her, following the circles she's making. He stops beside her in the middle of the room. He reaches his hand out to her with affection.

She looks into his soft eyes and accepts his hand. They stand in the center of the great room, holding hands gently. She lets herself accept the warm, loving affection.

"I found a picture of you and my mother."

She drops her shoulder pack onto the cement floor. Crouching, she removes the small, faded album. She opens to the page where, on a sunlit summer day, a fifteen-year-old Angela poses for a sixteen-year-old boy.

He takes the photo and brings it to his nose, smelling it. Then he brings it close up to his eyes, steadily stares, and bursts into a joyful smile. He kisses the photo and returns it to the album.

"She didn't pose for you in the nude, did she?"

"No," he answers.

Lavinia feels a sense of relief, not liking to think of her fifteen-year-old mother posing naked. "She's more beautiful than I even imagined her."

"Yes." He touches his heart. And stays still, seeming to be in his own world.

"Do you know who took this picture? Could it be him?" Lavinia asks.

A shadow crosses George's face, accentuating his aquiline features and intensifying his dark eyes. At first, he doesn't answer her. Then, as if the shadow has passed by, he says, "Her father. Well, he stole her life, didn't he?" Their eyes stay glued to each other for some time before he offers, "Let's have some tea and cookies."

She follows him to the multi-purpose room he uses as a kitchen, where she watches him fill the teapot and put it on the gas burner. This time he sets out some clay mugs on the table. They sit and wait for the teapot to call its readiness. She doesn't feel as jittery this second time.

"Do you want to see the other photos?" she asks as he pours hot water into the mugs.

"No, I want to sit with you, Lavinia. I've waited so long."

"Me, too. Only I didn't know it."

Lavinia fingers her hair as George gets the cookie tin. They drink slowly. She dips the biscotti and watches the chocolate melt, just as her own heart is melting for her father.

"I called Uncle Sal today. It's true he wouldn't let you see me before a year ago." She tells him how Sal accused him of being responsible for Angela's death; how she told Sal he was wrong; how he didn't want the knowledge that Papa Antonio killed Angela; how she hung up on him.

"Bravo," he says. He sips his tea, his face softening. "Who could bear that fact?"

Fingering her lips, other cheats come to mind: Aunt Rose, who stole her Raggedy, the one tangible connection to her mother; Don, who taunted her; Nina, who acted cold and bitchy toward her. All jealous, nasty, rageful people, or some combination. Her grandfather must have been like that.

George looks at her as if waiting for her to complete her wandering thoughts.

"My mother is beautiful, just the way I remember her," Lavinia says. Then she tells him her recollection of the flowing sheets on the line and how the clean, fresh air carried her mother's love song call, "Lavinia Lavinia."

George smiles. "My sentiments. Truly beautiful and still beautiful." He takes Lavinia's hand. She feels his rough sculptor's fingers. His voice lowers solemnly, as if he's confessing. "Your mother didn't meet me at La Guardia as planned, so I called Giovanni, my uncle. All he would say was that she wouldn't be coming to New York City. Nor would you." He looks into Lavinia's eyes and bites his lip as if to hold back some sound.

"You didn't know she'd died."

"No, they didn't tell me then."

"But why?"

"*Omertà*."

"What is that?'

"It's a Mafioso pledge. The law of silence."

"Isn't that Palermo?"

"You know, then, about the Mafia. But it's also throughout Southern Italy—the entire boot, the heel and the toe. Even Roma. Your great-grandfather had those proud ways."

"Do you think Papa Antonio was actually a Mafioso?"

George shrugs. His shoulders rise up like question mark.

"Did you know him?"

"He was the scary one in the village. Possessive. One day when he saw me sitting with Angela at the laundry pools he came and pulled her up by the armpits from where she sat washing the family clothes. 'You can't do that, you can't do that,' I yelled. But he kept dragging her away with brute force, his steel blue eyes bulging out of his thick face."

When George says this, his own eyes widen with what seems like rage, but just as quickly they become as clear as a still night.

"Your mother looked at me with an expression saying she would be all right, and then she told Antonio, too, that everything would be okay. She left with him, but not before he scowled at me as if he wanted to do bad things to me."

"The secrets, even Sal's, kept me away from you . . ."

"Remember, Sal is Antonio's son, and loyalty is sometimes stronger than love, Lavinia."

She looks straight into George's eyes. "Another law."

"You've got it, girl. I often think it's the first law, loyalty. Followed by silence."

When he calls her girl, she folds toward him again, recognizing herself as his child—not Sal's, not Papa Antonio's. She smiles. George is breaking the silence.

"When the news came to New York that you and Angela would not be coming, I was furious with Giovanni. He had let me down by not getting you and your mama safely on the plane.

Then I was furious at Antonio, knowing that he must have had something to do with it. That he'd found a way to keep her from leaving him."

Lavinia drops her biscotti in her hot tea and watches it dissolve.

"So the plans changed suddenly, and there was a big hole in me where there'd been joy and anticipation. I had just finished art school and had some great shows under my belt—galleries in New York City. I jumped on a plane to Naples in search of your mother and you, only to find, when I arrived, that the funeral had passed. The only evidence I found was a placard near where she'd died. Like the ones you see in Mexico, planted on the side of the road, when a loved one passes tragically. I never saw you, either. They had sequestered you away from me." A shadow passes over George's face. "The women in the streets spoke in whispers, lowering their eyes when I passed by. I searched for you, but you were nowhere to be seen, and Giovanni's lips were sealed. He knew nothing. He spoke to me with his eyes lowered. I walked by the restaurants and pizzerias through the old labyrinth of streets, hearing her laughter at every turn. I walked to the gardens on top of the great hills to the place behind a tree where we made love. I walked to the waterfront where hydrofoils take passengers to nearby islands, wishing we had done that together. But everywhere I turned I longingly looked for you as well. Every four-year-old girl was you but attached to a different angel. Not Angela."

Lavinia stares at him.

"I even went to the kindergartens, the *scuole materne,* waiting for the children to be let out for recess or after school. I knew I'd know you if I saw you, but no, you were not there. Once I followed a little girl with T-strap sandals, thinking it was you. From the back, with her auburn hair glistening long, she was how

I imagined you to be. But then she turned . . . and I knew. No. You had disappeared from me."

Lavinia feels her anger with Sal rising in her again.

"Yet I wasn't convinced then that you were gone from Naples. I needed to find you. And I needed to visit your nonna Caterina. I entered her house, and next to the front passageway I saw a small memorial altar encased in stone. There was a small statue of the Virgin Mary and a picture of your mother smiling, the angel she was. Angela Campana, and then the dates of her short life—1975 to 1996—were inscribed in the stone. Someone had put a pink rose in there. A votive candle was flickering. All day. All night." He puts his hand on his heart. "There was no picture of your dead grandfather."

Lavinia can hear his voice cracking. Seeing that his own cup is empty, she offers him some of her tea and watches his lip quiver as he sips.

He goes on. "The silence they showed toward me was remarkable. Even Giovanni and Luciana, my aunt and uncle, buttoned up. I knew your mother was guiding me, though. It was as if she took my hand, accompanying me up the steps into the darkened chambers of her mother's heart. Caterina Luisa Campana. It was like walking into a dark tunnel, a cave, the old woman bleeding in deep contemplation or catatonia, wearing a shroud."

"How did she survive?"

"I don't know. In one swoop, she lost her daughter, her husband, and her beloved only grandchild, you. Outside her house, a pulley was attached to the second story that allowed her to lower a basket for the local grocer to place bread, cheese, fruit, vegetables, and chocolate in, almost daily. For the first week I spent hours hanging out by the door each day, watching, hoping I might see her, talk with her, see something of Angela in her features. But no.

She did not emerge. So I went up the dark stairwell carefully and slowly. I took each step thinking how your mother walked this same passageway during her short life. This was Angela's stairway. Not grand. Full of shadows, except for the brightness she brought to it with her own inner light. At the top of the stairs I stopped at the front door. There was a small white button—the doorbell—and a peephole. All quiet, inside and out. I pressed the button. A long time passed before I heard slow shuffling, like slippers, across the floor. I felt as though someone peeked out. I wondered if Caterina would recognize me, and, if she did, whether she'd even let me in."

Lavinia wishes she had a piece of gum to chew right now. She twirls her hair tightly around her finger and takes a deep breath.

"Then I heard the slow turn of the lock and a slower opening of the door. The apartment was even darker than the stairwell. The older woman squinted and winced, her hands covering her eyes, as if even the minimal light from the hall was blinding her. In comparison to when I'd last seen her, she looked ghostly—like a cadaver. Her black hair had turned gray. She wore a black sweater, a loose-fitting cardigan with small buttons, a long black skirt, and old lady shoes. She was shorter than I remembered and stooped over."

Lavinia sees this image so clearly, it's if she's standing there next to George.

"She let me in. I followed her to a chair by a closed and shaded window. Maybe she opened this window daily to let down her food basket; I hoped she got some air on occasion. It was stuffy. I sat across from her in a chair with side wings, sweating. Caterina sat silently, chewing her gums. She had no teeth, and she hadn't put in her dentures. With her hands on her lap, her fingers opened and closed. She let me sit there beside her. I wondered where the signs of a little girl were. Did she keep any of your toys or shoes or clothes in her apartment? Or had she renounced everything? I began to think that she was mute, even wondered if she was crazy. Then my thoughts left her for a bit and I wondered where you'd slept—where you'd eaten. Where had you taken your first step? When had you said your first words? You must've called 'Mama.' 'Dada,' too. All babies say 'Dada.'" He smiles. "As if Caterina were reading my mind, she looked up at me slowly, which reminded me of the time when I looked into the eye of a whale at Provincetown. I saw something ancient in those eyes, something eternal—only her eyes spoke to me. She didn't say anything." He pauses. "She just gave me that look, that whale-eye look, then smiled, an upturn of her lips, like a smiling moon."

"That's all?"

"It was the smile of your mother."

He gets up and goes to the shelf above the biscotti and takes down two tiny shoes. Hands them to Lavinia. "She gave these to me."

They don't speak for many moments. Then Lavinia cries into the soft leather T-straps, big enough for a four-year-old. And she thinks of her grandmother.

"My poor nonna," she says, thinking how life took its toll on her. She lost her granddaughter, her daughter, and her husband—all in a fraction of a second. And then Sal reappeared and disappeared again. "My God." Lavinia bows her head in sorrow for her grandma Caterina and for her own losses as well. For the first time she realizes she has not only lost her mother but also her grandmother and her grandfather.

She clutches the soft Italian shoes in her hands, thinking of the four-year-old, still a little girl, who never got to wear the T-straps her mother picked for her; who never knew her family, because it was snatched away from her; who lost everything dear to her before she was even five years old. She cries into the cup of the soft animal's skin.

Chapter 29:

BREAKING THE CURSE

"**D**ancing tonight?" reads the text from Kinky with a happy face emoji, waking Lavinia up from her reveries. She just left George's studio, and she almost forgot she made plans with Kinky and Mario to go to a special pre-Thanksgiving dance.

"I don't know," she texts back at first, but Kinky convinces her to get out and to meet her at the pizza place near Falcone.

Kinky is sitting at a back table of the long, narrow pizza parlor when Lavinia arrives. She smiles and waves when her friend walks in, then stands up and embraces her. Lavinia falls into her arms, grateful to have a friend like Kinky—someone who listens but also keeps her from falling into the abyss.

When they sit down, Kinky's eyes stay glued to Lavinia's. "What happened today?" she asks.

"George told me the whole story today. Even his part in it."

"No way, Vinnie!"

"It's a kind of crazy story, beginning with Mario finding George in front of my house in the early morning. George was leaving me another of his notes before sunrise." Lavinia smiles, no longer disturbed by this mail-dropping habit. "But now the truth is coming, just like I've always wanted, Kinky."

"Tell me everything," she says.

Lavinia starts with the letters from Giovanni and the story George told her about going back to Naples to find out what happened, finding her grieving grandmother, and what he learned about out why they never made it to New York. "I heard it first from Giovanni and now from George, who wove the story around his love for me and my mother. Today he gave me a tiny pair of shoes that my mother bought for me before she died. My grandmother gave them to him. Can you believe it?"

"Ahh," Kinky hums.

Lavinia watches Kinky as she processes this last bit of information. Her face is twisted, and now Lavinia has some insight as to how she might have looked upon hearing the news. She loves her friend for her reaction. "Yeah," is all she can say.

"That's wild and weird shit, like a novel. What do they say about true life being weirder than fiction?"

"There's more. I called Sal." Lavinia tells her how Sal blamed George for what happened to Angela and how he still can't come clean with Lavinia.

"And the barista?" Kinky asks.

"Kinky, I think I'm in love. He's so precious to me, so there for me, like I've never had."

"You know"—Kinky smiles at her—"my mother told me today that you are happy, and I can see it now."

"She knows everything," Lavinia says.

"About her girls," Kinky says, placing her hand in Lavinia's. "You're my sister, Vinnie. Should we get a slice of pizza and a beer?"

"Just what I need. I'm starving, and"—she looks at her watch—"there's still time before we have to meet Mario."

While Kinky walks up to the counter to order, Lavinia remembers the *alegría*, the one Mercedes sang on the day Lavinia and Mario first made love, and she begins to hum it to herself. When Kinky returns with the beers, Lavinia sings, "*Ay, ay, ay, ay, ay.*" They both laugh and toast each other with their mugs. And then they eat their pizza.

Lavinia and Kinky cross over onto Columbus, arm in arm, singing, and walk the few blocks to Falcone, where Mario is standing at the door with Carmine close behind him.

"You look divine," Mario says, giving them each a hug before they all move outside and walk down Columbus toward the dance hall across from Washington Square, only minutes away. The queue is moving from the street into the building. It's almost ten thirty, near to when the music will start.

This time the venue feels celebratory—a gratitude dance. Lavinia is more at ease with all the costumes people wear, the hugging, and the "stay quiet" rule. In fact, she loves that there's a place where you can experience two hours of dancing and no one is allowed to talk. She's getting used to a room filled with more than one hundred people, all moving slowly to the flowing music. She and Mario face each other; music thumps around them, but Lavinia is only aware of their internal silence. Slowly, she begins to let the rhythm of the slow beat move her. As she and Mario sway gently together, she smiles, taking pleasure from his eyes that seem to mirror her joy. She knows he is happy to be with her, in this room, in this time.

The two of them respond to one another in kind, rooting their toes and feet into the earth while flowing and swaying. They move like two waves in the great ocean, not noticing the people jumping and playing around them. They stay glued, and their eyes switch from still presence to joy. They dance through the openings in the crowd like ribbons blowing in the wind. They are heating up—and then the subtle rhythm signals a change and pulls them to dive in more deeply, spiraling, even jumping, swirling, and spinning. When has she ever danced like this? She hears herself hooting and singing like Mercedes hoots and hollers when she sings. Then they are waltzing across the long room, their arms and hands circling each other, creating a world that holds them within its galaxy.

Yet again the sound shifts. Calmer and quieter now, it's a kind of pause. Lavinia and Mario stand close, sweaty, sparkling, bathing each other in warm breaths. Like stars in the night sky, they twinkle. When the music finally stops, they are encircled by its after-hum, which wraps around them and spreads through them. They cannot move; the soft caress of those vibrations holds them hostage.

They carry the feelings from the dance outside into the city, where the moist San Francisco air raises goose bumps from Lavinia's skin. Mario puts his arm around her and pulls her in.

The silence is broken by Kinky. "What a workout! I'm thirsty," she says.

"Let's get a beer," Mario says, moving them toward a bar where kids hang out on the sidewalk. A teenager spins a yoyo, its orange glow like fire.

"I could use a tequila," Kinky says.

Lavinia mostly wants to swaddle herself in these vibes and listen. She misses the silence of the dance hall, where she doesn't have to use words to relate. "Let's keep dancing," she says, and her friends comply. They dance down Columbus toward the bars, stopping at one and then another bar.

They stay out well into the early morning. Carmine and Kinky hold hands. Mario and Lavinia hold each other around the waist.

"This is how the world should be," Lavinia says, breaking her silence.

"This is how the world is, Lavinia." Mario kisses her. "Did you guys know that Lavinia is going to the mountains for a few days?" Mario says, turning to their friends.

Kinky looks at her friend in surprise.

Lavinia says, "I didn't tell you? Sorry." Did she really forget to tell Kinky? But of course, so much has been happening lately. She tells Carmine and Kinky about Zack and the mountaintop in Nevada where a clock will beat and ring deep in the limestone mountain for ten thousand years. She tells them how Zack needs help driving; how he has a replica of the Millennium Clock, a weird space-age contraption, in his spare bedroom; and how he's paying her five thousand dollars.

"But the real reason I'm going is because of his kindness," she says. "He wants my company to help him drive in the High Sierra. To tell you the truth, I'm looking forward to it."

"Sounds groovy," Carmine says.

"He's dear," Lavinia says. "He wears a string bracelet with three knots, each representing a sort of wish."

"What are they?" Carmine asks.

"I'm a bit superstitious about wishes, so you'll have to wait 'til I come home before I tell you." She hugs Mario.

Mario moves her away from her friends. "Did you know it's almost two in the morning?" he asks. They hug Kinky and Carmine good-bye and watch them walk toward the bus stop. Then

Lavinia and Mario walk toward his apartment above the shop, entering through the back door.

"Let's talk about windmills." Lavinia pulls on his shirt.

They take the steps two at a time, entering the apartment from the back porch. The fog drifts lightly over the full moon, exposing the fullness of the bay. They slip into the apartment, past the cluttered desk where a map of Nevada lies open.

"You've been studying our route." She sees the line from SF to Bishop in Sharpie.

"I have a different route for you to follow right now. Come with me." He gives her a long, wet kiss; the beer and the tequila they've been drinking merge like some colorful ballad. He dances her into his bedroom, where they move slowly and sensually to a rhythm only heard by them, where the staccato builds to chaos and then returns to stillness. She thinks of her mother and knows that she felt this with George, these incredible rhythms of love that move in and around like a great spiral dance. Or, is it an inner spiraling, one into the other? She smiles.

All is quiet outside. The three-in-the-morning stillness is like a blanket covering them as they fall asleep in each other's arms.

They sleep with their legs and arms wrapped around each other: tangling and untangling, folding and unfolding their limbs and fingers and toes; lips and tongue twirl around each other. She doesn't want to leave him. What if it is the last time? She thinks of her mother and George. Their parting was forever.

"What's the matter, Bubblicious? You look so sad." Mario kisses her quivering lips.

"I don't want to leave you, Mario."

"It's not forever. You'll be home in less than a week, in time for the next dance."

"You promise?"

"I promise—cross my heart and hope to die."

She bursts out in tears.

"What'd I say?" Mario holds her as she cries on his chest.

"Hope to die. Why'd you say that?"

"It's just a saying, Lavinia. It means I promise. I give you my word."

"It's just that it feels too close to home, that's all. I'm scared to lose you."

"Don't worry. You won't lose me. I just know it. Take my flannel pajamas with you to keep you warm." He cuffs her gently on the chin. "And besides, my love, you're not reliving your mother's life. You don't have to be held hostage by this curse."

He winds his fingers through hers. She squeezes back.

The spell is breaking. They hug, and she knows he will be there when she returns.

Chapter 30:

MILES TO FLY

Zack opens the door. "You're a day early," he says.

"Just checking in to see if there's room for these flannel paja-mas." Lavinia laughs, holding them up, and glances at an empty backpack he's placed up against the sofa. "Anything we need?"

She looks around the cluttered living room, seeing his tent and the two sleeping bags, the camp stove, and the lantern. He sees her question before she asks.

"Just in case," he says, assuring her that he's prepared. "Let me show you the car."

She follows him down the back stairs to the garage, where his hatchback is already full and ready to go. Zack takes inventory out loud. "Water containers, flashlights, tarps, walking boots, trekking poles, sunhats with a tube of sunscreen stuck inside . . ."

"It's all here," she says. "You've thought of everything."

"It could be a long drive. The shortest route, over Tioga Pass or Sonora, closed mid-November," he says, "so we'll have to go the longer way—northeast through Truckee before heading south on 395."

"Looks like you're prepared," she says.

"There'll be lots of driving, Lavinia," he says, heading back up the stairs to the apartment. "You're sure that's okay?"

"That's why I'm here—to help with the driving," she says, entering the flat behind him.

Zack looks around the apartment. "Ah! Here's what I've been looking for," he says. "Some snacks I put together to munch along the way." On the kitchen counter are Peet's coffee, dried fruits, assorted nuts, packs of hot chocolate, canned tuna, a can opener. He gathers them into a blue stuff bag.

"Are we camping?"

"The camping stuff is in case of emergency." He looks at his tent. "We're staying in a motel in Bishop."

"Were you a Boy Scout?"

"Still am." He puts on a wide-brimmed hat and lifts his bony knees up and down as if he's in a parade.

Lavinia laughs.

"Are you ready, Lavinia?"

She looks again toward the empty backpack sitting on the floor by the couch.

"For you," he says.

She walks toward the pack, and carefully places Mario's soft pajamas on top, and smiles. The red parka and the cashmere scarf will be tucked in the middle pocket with the gloves she has. These clothes give her comfort.

"By that smile, I see you're excited. I can almost hear your heart beating."

She laughs, thinking how funny he is to frame her excitement as heartbeats. It reminds her of his fascination with clocks.

"Or maybe it's my own ticker I hear," he says. "I can't wait to be with you among those ancient trees and the mountain."

The cuckoos burst into song, first the grandfather clock and the others join in concert. Lavinia counts to ten as other various bells whistle and chime. They no longer faze her like they did when she first stepped into this apartment. Then she could only think of spirits. Now they represent this spirited man. Lavinia focuses on his soft slippers as they move over the plush carpet around all the stuff he has accumulated. She sits, quietly watching his movements, smiling inside, admiring how his excitement rides so close to his orderly ways.

"You're ready," she says.

"I've never been more ready," he says, standing tall, as if he's saluting.

At the sight, an eerie feeling passes through Lavinia, along with an image of the great pyramid in Egypt with its entombed pharaohs. The sound of silence is broken by the light ding of the quarter-hour, and Lavinia realizes that fifteen minutes have passed as she's sat here in contemplation.

"Tomorrow at dawn," she says, getting up.

"Wait, Lavinia . . . before you go, I have some sad news to tell you. I don't want to tell you tomorrow, on the day of our travels."

She turns on her heels, feeling instantly worried. That eerie feeling returns. Zack looks upset.

Zack pulls out the morning paper and shows her the news about a local murder-suicide. At first she feels confused. She doesn't absorb the words she reads in the article. It's all scrambled in her mind with her grandfather and her mother.

Zack explains what the article says—that Nina White was killed this week by her crazed husband before he shot himself. "A murder-suicide," he says.

Lavinia can't let it sink in. She doesn't understand. Something is not right. She goes numb. "Nina was alive! No, it can't be!" She lets out a gasp. "I can't believe it, Zack. I just saw her a week ago. She asked me to help her move her stuff from the house. Don had left her, and she didn't want to stay there. Maybe she was afraid of something like this, though she didn't say."

"He came back."

"No, not Nina," she says again. She has never experienced this sense of disbelief and knowing at the same time. Of course it's true, even as she yells, "Noooooo, this is not possible!"

Her mind conjures up the heinous act. Of course Don was capable of murder; she sees his disturbance more clearly now and wishes she could have somehow managed to tell Nina sooner about how weird he was acting. She feels responsible. She looks at Zack, wanting to expel her guilt. "What if I had done something . . ." She sobs.

"Lavinia, this has nothing to do with you," Zack says softly as he reaches for a Kleenex box.

She receives the tissue gratefully, wiping her nose and tears—and then gasps. Instead of Nina and Don, she sees her own mother sprawled out on the trolley tacks, splayed like a baby lamb, splattered before her. Her body convulses and folds over, her heart breaks open. She thinks she's cracking apart. She grabs her chest at the center of the stabbing pain. Her lower lip quivers, as it did earlier today with Mario. The shudder. The chaos. And then the silence.

"Welcome back," Zack says as his face comes into Lavinia's blurry view. "You were out for a minute. You fainted."

Lavinia looks around at the room as Zack ministers to her.

"I revived you with some smelling salts."

"You did?" She sits up from her bed on the couch. He must have lifted her up here. "I'm sorry."

"Please, don't be sorry."

"I need to get some fresh air," she says, standing up.

"Let me call you a cab," Zack says.

"No, it's okay. I'm okay. I need the walk. Thank you. Six o'clock tomorrow."

She leaves and begins her walk downhill on Chestnut Street, her feet and legs wobbling, less grounded than when she climbed the stairs. It's as if she's floating on a cloud. She bypasses Falcone, wanting to be alone, to walk through the neighborhoods to the Mission. Her attention moves toward the rare clotheslines where white sheets blow in the wind, like ghosts of people gone by. She takes an unusual and hilly route toward her home. Though her pack is empty, it feels heavy and full, carrying this new burden. She's grateful for Mario's pj's, tucked inside the top pocket.

She enters her studio and walks through to the back, where she sits by the window facing the fig tree—staring, immobilized— until she hears a thump on the window and then sees a tiny sparrow fall onto the outside patio, its wings spread, paralyzed from fear or shock or pain. She stands up and peers out the window, looking down where the bird has landed. With her heart racing, she opens the door and walks toward the little thing, resting on its back with its tail feathers up in the air. The feathers on his head wave slightly in the breeze. She can't take her eyes off the little bird, keeps watching as its tail feathers become stiff. The bird leans diagonally on her resting head, supported by her belly-breast, which is puffed out like a pillow.

Lavinia quietly kneels beside it. "I hope you are breathing, little bird," she whispers. "Please fly again." When Lavinia is convinced that she sees its chest rising and falling ever so slowly, her heart lightens. The bird looks like a Christmas ornament you could hang on a tree limb. Its face now lies on the patio cement at a slightly different angle, resting on point like a ballerina. Oblivious, it doesn't mind Lavinia's gawking.

She only has eyes for the little diver, this bombing bird. How long does it take to revive after such a blow? The bird rests before her—a little ball of feathers. *Yes, that's it. It takes rest to revive oneself. It takes time. Doesn't it, dear God?* She prays again, "Oh, little bird, please come to. You have more worms to discover, and figs to peck, and miles to fly."

The bird lies still, its tail straight in the air, still resting on its chest and pointed beak. Stillness. Stillness. Lavinia's own heart rate seems to slow down, mimicking the bird's.

"Oh, little bird, I know you're still alive. I know you will come through this." She watches quietly, then prays again, "I know you have come here to teach me, little bird, I know. Thank you. I want to pick you up and hold you in my hands to feel your precious life beat, but I'm afraid. Now your head is off the ground, and you are the ballerina who comes off point and flattens out her feet."

Time stands still, not moving. Does it matter whether it moves? She thinks of Zack and his obsession with time. But this is eternal, like the end of time. She is fully alive in this moment as she watches the bird slowly turn, tuck in its tail, and sit on the floor of the patio. Its beak looks like a thin sliver of white in the sun. White light reflects on its breast. It rests its head under its left wing, as if in a deep sleep.

Lavinia watches, feeling very protective, like a mother hen. She watches its feathers flurry in the wind as it tucks into itself to save its life energy. It is so vulnerable in its frozen position.

Just then, the little sparrow perks up and faces Lavinia. Seconds later, it is flying diagonally up like an arrow into the fig tree.

Lavinia feels lifted, ready for flight, too.

Chapter 31:

THE SIERRA NEVADA

The car is ready to go. Fresh fruit—bananas, apples, pears, strawberries, a pomegranate, and a persimmon—sits on the backseat in a straw basket. A small ice chest holds some cheeses and soft drinks. By six thirty, Zack is in the driver's seat, backing out of his garage, heading east toward the Bay Bridge. The morning sky lifts an enormous shade, revealing an orange horizon line. Lavinia has never seen the streets as quiet as this, with barely any commuters. It's Thanksgiving Day, she remembers. The new span of the Bay Bridge sits like a grand wing of a white bird.

"Incredible," she says.

"Some engineering," he says, driving over the bridge as Lavinia takes in the sights, all new to her. She realizes how cloistered she has been living, how small her world has been.

Soon she is fast asleep, her head gently bobbing as if she is at sea. Zack drives smoothly through the East Bay and toward the foothills of the Sierra Nevada as she dreams.

She opens her eyes frequently, catching the California hills—still tawny from the summer sun—Zack's hum to the soft classical music on the radio, road signs where new developments are springing up, and the multiple exits for Sacramento. A kaleidoscope of images breeze in and out of her consciousness. When a sign announces Davis, she perks up. "Is this UC Davis?" she asks. "Isn't that where Margaret works?" Zack nods and smiles.

She closes her eyes and disappears again to some suspended place, like the one she experiences just before falling asleep at night. She feels far away with Zack's soft hum like a chant in the background.

She comes out of her trancelike state when Zack makes a stop in a small historic town called Auburn, just two hours away from San Francisco. He pulls up in front of a corner café with a side patio. No one is sitting outside in the brisk morning air, and this is where she and Zack have their coffee and a blueberry muffin. The cool air wakes her up, and she wants to talk with Zack about his relationship with his daughter. Though he's told Lavinia before why Margaret didn't make the trip with him, she asks him anyway why his daughter isn't spending Thanksgiving with him.

"Ahh! Margaret." He mentions her name softly, affectionately. "Margaret is on-call this holiday weekend."

"But wouldn't she want to join you in the bristlecone forest?" Lavinia wonders at her not wanting to be here on this momentous occasion. He's fulfilling a dream for himself, and Margaret is not here to witness it. But Lavinia feels honored to take her place.

"She's pretty dedicated to her work right now." He sips his coffee and bites into the muffin. Lavinia watches how his eyelids flutter as he chews.

"Do you see her much?" Lavinia is curious, not really knowing what might be normal. Growing up, Uncle Sal was a father to her, but they never spent one-on-one time together. Rose was always there.

"We speak every week, and she comes to visit every other Sunday."

"She knows you're going on this trip?"

"Yes, she knows." He switches quickly. "But this is our trip, remember? Are you up for driving a stretch over some exciting mountain passes?"

"Yes, I'm very much awake now." She looks at her empty coffee cup. "I'm ready to drive. You already put in two hours."

They're back in the Subaru by nine o' clock. Lavinia adjusts the seat back, checks the rearview mirror, and pulls out past shops as old as the Gold Rush. Soon they're winding their way through the foothills with pine trees clustering on the side of the road, while the elevation increases quickly. At Emigrant Gap and Donner Lake, they're above seven thousand feet and the air is crisp and thin, the bluest she's ever seen. In the distance, she sees snow-covered mountains.

About fifteen minutes later, Zack breaks the silence. "Would you like to stop for lunch in Truckee?" He points to the exit where Lavinia will bear right into another western town, a railroad running parallel to the road. Lavinia takes the direction and rolls into the quaint town.

"Pull up at that old hotel. They'll have a brunch today," he says. "Likely turkey. It's Thanksgiving, after all."

"But it's just after ten," she exclaims. She parks in front of the hotel.

"Must be this mountain air—makes me hungry," he says, sniffing the air. "Do you smell the scent of a roasting turkey?"

She doesn't, but she can imagine many ovens in town roasting their turkeys. Maybe at the next place they can have Thanksgiving lunch. She pulls out her cell and finds Bridgeport, the halfway point between Truckee and Bishop, their destination, just two and a half hours away. "Let's see if we can make a reservation in Bridgeport."

"Sounds good," he says as they walk into the hotel dining room. "Maybe we can get a piece of pie here as a mid-breakfast."

She nods. They walk into the place. It's empty except for the wait staff setting up a buffet table. A woman in a black skirt and white blouse approaches, a red flower in her hair.

"Good morning! Happy Thanksgiving," she says. "Do you have reservations?"

"Ahh, no, miss," Zack says, looking hopeful.

"It's still early, we don't open for an hour."

"Yes," he says, "but I'd love a piece of pecan pie." His gaze slides toward the dessert table, where several pies sit waiting.

"Do you mind sitting at the bar?" she asks.

Zack looks toward Lavinia, smiling, and gives her a thumbs-up. They follow the middle-aged hostess, who wears comfortable shoes, out of the formal dining room and through a door to a mahogany bar. After they're seated, the woman takes their order.

"You already know I'm a nut for pecan pie," he tells her.

"Well, you're in luck then. Ice cream or whipped cream?"

"I'll take whipped cream."

"And for you, miss?" The waitress turns to Lavinia.

"I'll have apple pie and a coffee, please. No ice cream."

The woman leaves to get the desserts.

"I love this stuff. Since Elsa died I rarely eat pies," Zack says.

"What do you eat?"

"I'm a tuna and saltines man. I keep it simple with an occasional beer. Sometimes a pizza. All easy stuff now. I don't eat too much. And you, Lavinia?"

"I chew gum and have an occasional tequila." She laughs.

"No kidding," Zack says.

"If it weren't for my friend Kinky, who brings me her mother's tamales, enchiladas, and tacos, I'd starve. I don't like to cook."

"You're like my daughter—not domestic."

"No." Lavinia runs her fingers along the edge of the smooth wooden bar top.

"Actually, of course you are," he says, taking it back. "Sorry to speak out of hand, Lavinia. You lovingly do my laundry."

"Thank you." She blushes. "I want to be a teacher. I only have a semester left to go." A spark of hope gnaws at her. It's not too late to go back.

"Yes, I can see the teacher in you."

Lavinia appreciates the compliment and, remembering her teacher training, feels a little pang for her profession. How did she get so off track? How did she let her history derail her so? For the first time, however, sitting here with Zack, she's thinking about something other than her losses. It seems to her the jaws of time are relaxing their bite.

Zack accepts his pie and tucks in, humming after each bite. They eat their mid-morning desserts in silence.

When they're done, the woman wearing the black skirt and white blouse returns to the bar with their check, and Zack settles the bill.

"So what's next?" Lavinia grabs her hair and twirls it around her finger.

"We'll bypass Reno," Zack says.

"And the slots?" Her voice goes up a pitch.

He looks at her in anticipation. She figures he'd stop if she really wanted to. But she wants to focus on his dream, and she already knows that her own dreams have shifted to something much more important than gambling.

"Never mind," she says.

"Okay!" he says, and she senses his relief. "We'll take the fastest route to Bishop through Bridgeport, where we'll stop and get that turkey lunch. It's about two and a half hours away."

They look at the map, making a plan to go through North Lake Tahoe without stopping, then south on 28, then east on 50 to reach South I-395 and Bishop, their destination for today.

"Good plan, lunch at one thirty," she says. She checks the weather on her phone. "Forecast clear, sunny, cold."

Zack makes their Bridgeport reservation on his cell. Lavinia hops into the driver's seat once again, and they're on the road.

She drives the 117-mile route to the Bridgeport Inn while Zack rests. Soon after they are underway, she hears him snoring softly beside her in the passenger seat.

North Lake Tahoe is beautiful. She rolls down the window and smells the fresh pine air. She wonders what it would have been like if she'd been raised in the country. The miles of national forest enchant her. The two-hour ride is smooth and peacefully nurturing.

As soon as she pulls up and stops the car at Bridgeport Inn, Zack wakes up. He looks around and then at his watch. "Why, we're already here for our Thanksgiving brunch, and with a half hour to spare."

They climb out of the car, and Zack recommends a short walk around the place. Lavinia can't get enough of the natural beauty of the eastern slopes of the Sierras.

"Zack, this is truly beautiful. Thank you," she says as they stroll through the pines.

"I thought you'd like it. Let's eat, shall we?" He takes her hand.

They enjoy a traditional Thanksgiving meal of turkey, stuffing, brown gravy, sweet potatoes, cranberry sauce, and more. Though this type of food is not part of Lavinia's Thanksgiving tradition, she loves the way the creamy potatoes slide down so easily, the tangy taste of cranberry sparks on her tongue. She feels a part of an American tradition. Rosa always refused to cook a turkey, insisting instead on an escarole soup with tiny meatballs, a simple pasta, and a small roasted chicken with potatoes. But Lavinia feels happy about this now. There's no Thanksgiving traditions for her to miss, just new ones to be formed.

After they eat, Lavinia gets back in the driver's seat to begin the last hundred-mile segment of the desert drive to Bishop. The blue skies are softening to dusk, and the snow-covered sentinels are smiling in the distance. Zack, too, is smiling, no doubt as moved by the silent landscape as she is.

Chapter 32:

SWEET ARE THE USES
OF ADVERSITY

L avinia wakes up early in a strange bed. How far did they drive yesterday? Four hundred miles? Did she really drive six or seven hours to reach Bishop? The last daylight stop she remembers before Bishop was outside of Bridgeport.

The dark sky casts a silver light across her bed. Shadows of tall, heavy furniture seem to assail her as she pulls the blanket over her head, listening to an old heater chug along like a steam engine. She hides, holding herself under the wooly blankets, not ready to face any more lonely mountain roads on the Eastern Sierra desert highways.

Last night they checked into the Best Western after sunset and got two adjoining rooms. She slept soundly until now. She gets up and uses the restroom and then puts her ear to the opposite door. She hears the old man snore with his characteristic hum. His breathing is deep and slow, a steady buzz. He's still asleep.

Cold, she runs back to her bed and rubs her hands on her new, soft pajamas, grateful she had sense enough to jump into them last night. She wishes Mario were here. Silently, she waits in the dark room.

When Zack begins moving, it's predawn, the blue hour, when a deep blue hue floods the room. She gets up and starts to move about, getting dressed.

"Look, Lavinia. Come see!" he calls to her.

When she enters his room, he's standing by the window, peeking through an opening in the curtain.

"Look," he says, fingering his bracelet, "a deep blue sky with a hint of orange toward the east. A new day." He pulls the curtain and she stands beside him. "Let's go! Methuselah is waiting."

"Who is Methuselah?" she asks, looking at the light.

"Methuselah lived to be 969 years old. The oldest person recorded."

"Is that for real?" Lavinia asks, never having heard of Methuselah before. "Is it a legend?"

"Yes, based on a biblical figure in Judaism, Christianity, and Islam. He was supposed to have the most longevity of any figure in the Bible. And the tree we're looking for is named after him."

"Let's go get a coffee," she says, satisfied with the explanation.

"Good idea. The Erick Schat Bakery is less than a mile from here and opens at six o'clock. Let's walk."

In a flash they're dressed and outside with eyes cast toward the changing sky. At Erick Schat's, Zack selects a loaf of sheepherder's bread from stacks of thousands of loaves—the labels read, "Fennel," "Golden Raisin," "Pinto Bean Bread," and "Cranberry Chocolate Chip." Lavinia grabs a raisin bread to have with a steaming cup of coffee. They eat at a table crowded among the thousands of loaves.

"Who made all these breads?" she asks.

"The early-morning bread elves," Zack says, his eyes twinkling.

They retrieve their luggage from the room, and by seven o'clock they're in the car with Lavinia driving again, heading south from Bishop on I-395 toward Big Pine. Zack sits with the hunk of bread at his side. The road opens up with acres of puffy sage fields against a dark, looming mountain. Lavinia's eyes follow the white line while Zack munches on the end of the sheepherder's bread like a contented grazer.

"Four thousand feet elevation," he says, looking toward yellow cornflowers that seem to smile back at him in the light of the setting moon.

Lavinia resumes looking at the white line where tall electric poles stand. Then she counts the poles, preferring to think of them as windmills. Behind the lower dark mountains rise the white peaks of the Sierra Nevada mountain range, with lines of snow encrusted in the ridges like ribbons in time. "New or old snow?" she asks.

"Maybe a little of both. Glacial," he answers.

She begins to slow down as the trees lining the road grow taller; she feels as if she's entering an enchanted forest. In the field she sees a low hump, which turns out to be a sleeping cow under a tree. She follows the signs to make what seems like a sharp left at Big Pine, leaving I-395.

"We're almost there, Lavinia," Zack says, his feet tapping a little tune, making her consider what he must have been like as a kid. "Follow this road heading northeast, and we'll be there in a jiff."

They are cruising toward the White Mountains and the Ancient Bristlecone Pine Forest.

"What's that?" she asks, looking at a sign for Scotty's Castle.

"It's in Death Valley. Have you ever been there?"

"No. But to me this looks like Death Valley, with this vast bowl of desert."

"A bowl of sage, Lavinia," he says as the car climbs higher and higher.

She likes his reframe but feels caught in the sagebrush, a small child in a tiny car in a vast sky of desert carpet. A chill runs up her spine. Is it the vastness that makes her feel so small? Her back muscles tense up. She wants to hide, to curl herself into a ball with her knees touching her chin, but she drives on, letting Zack's humming and foot tapping soothe her. She looks at him and then returns to viewing the curvy road, narrowing in its ascent. Suddenly she feels lulled by the delicious smell of desert sage, sweet and earthy like Aunt Rose's pasta with burnt salvia and butter.

"What's the color you see, Lavinia?" He is asking about the changing hue of the desert floor, which seemed purplish just minutes ago.

"The color is butterscotch," she answers.

He laughs. "You don't really see butterscotch, do you?"

"No, but I smell spice and sugar in this dusty earth." She looks out, sees sage plants growing next to an orange brush like a checkerboard. The new sunlight has given them a life, reminding her of candy in a crinkly package.

"God's country," Zack says, rolling down the window and inhaling.

Now tall canyon walls with their rocky outcrops bar the rising sun. Stratified layers of rock make her feel heavy, as if she's entering downwards. When they move out of the narrow gorge, the sky lightens and she begins to see pines. Smells like the red-wood grove in Golden Gate Park, where she danced in the fairy circle with Mario.

"Are these your trees?" she asks. "We should be near now, according to that sign." She points to a sign announcing, "The Ancient Bristlecone Pine Forest Reserve."

"No, no," Zack says, "these are piñons!"

Ten minutes later the road picks up again, passing open fields of small trees. As they approach a scenic overlook, Zack suggests that they stop the car for a stretch. Lavinia pulls off the road and they get out.

"Listen to that silence, Lavinia." He walks to the overlook.

But the silence is deafening to her ears. How can silence be so loud?

Back in the car, they pass the 7,340 feet elevation mark at a ranger kiosk. When Lavinia sees no one in the booth, she feels disheartened, fearing the park is closed for the season. Two shiny ravens soar in front of them, orange sun glinting on their bodies.

"Do you think we're the only ones here?" Suddenly, she feels like a lone piñon in a dusty plain.

"It's not tourist season," he says.

"I have to go to the bathroom," she confesses.

"Up the mountain there's a rest stop," he assures her.

They drive to ten thousand feet and pull into a rest stop where a woman is standing by her car door, ready to get in. Lavinia breathes a sigh of relief to see another car. They won't be totally alone in the park. She rolls down her window. "Is there a bathroom around here?" But the woman can't hear her; she's already in her car. She drives off with a wave.

Lavinia worries she won't make it.

They get out and Lavinia finds the toilet door is locked. She finds a place to go next to a piñon. She hears the soft flow of urine against the dry earth and wonders if her caffeine-filled pee will hurt this tree. She hopes not.

She reads info on a board near the rest area. "Bristlecone pines live on precipitation alone, moisture from snow, hail, and rain. Their roots are shallow and spread out in search of moisture. They have no taproot." Learning this, she feels assured of her pee contribution.

A small plane buzzes overhead, reminding her of civilization. It feels to her like a miracle to be in this high desert with Zack.

They get back in and head toward Schulman Grove, where the old trees live.

"Almost there, then Ely tomorrow," Zack says, sniffing the air from his open window.

Ely, Nevada, miles further on, where they'll see the place where the 10,000-year clock will be entombed in the limestone mountains. Zack is looking ahead, chin nodding.

"Maybe from this higher elevation you'll see across the horizon to your mountain?" Lavinia suggests.

"You mean so we won't need to go there after all." He laughs, looking across to the top of the mountains in the direction of Ely.

Lavinia hopes this first stop will suffice. Another 287 miles of high desert driving sounds dreadful to her.

He chuckles. "You'd rather not drive those three hundred miles tomorrow?"

"I'd rather not," she says, sighing, looking over to the last stretch of barren White Mountains, which look more like an ocean of wavy green lines. She can't imagine the route from here.

The parking lot at Schulman Grove is empty. They get out, gather their gear, and walk up to the information at the trailhead.

"We have a choice to make here," he says, looking at her. "The Patriarch Grove, twelve miles farther on a dirt road, or Methuselah—right here."

She hears "Patricide Grove," though she knows that's not what he said. Her chest jumps and heaves. "I choose Methuselah, right here." She looks toward the trail.

"Best not to drive another twelve miles. Anyway, that grove always makes me sad." He looks down. "That's where Prometheus, the old tree that was cut down, grew."

She shakes her head. "So awful."

"Methuselah, it is! And the oldest living tree is here in this forest. It's 4,848 years old, and besides, it's wonderful to have the place to ourselves." Zack hefts his small but heavy backpack to his shoulders and starts walking—but when he glances at her, he stops.

"You're crying, Lavinia," he touches her shoulder.

"I'm thinking about fathers." Her heart wants to jump out of its protective sleeve. Her throat constricts and more tears come.

"Your father?" he asks.

"Yes, him too. But more about what my grandfather did to my mother." She struggles to tell Zack about the joint deaths. "You know . . . what happened to Nina and Don White?" she reminds him.

He stops. "The suicide-murder?"

"Yes. . . something like that happened to my mother." She stifles her cry.

Zack faces her, reaches for her pack, as if to ease her burden.

"You know, it was my mother who gave me my love of doing laundry."

"Bless her," he says.

Then she tells him about how she died. "I was four, and she never came back from buying my shoes for the trip," she says, her eyes filling. "My nonno, in a fit of rage, killed her and himself so that she wouldn't leave him." Seeing Zack's attentiveness gives her permission to feel her sadness. "Nonno pushed her and then somehow in the scuffle they both got hit by a trolley."

He lifts his eyebrows in surprise, his jaw falls open. "No wonder Nina and Don's deaths hurt you so, Lavinia."

She buries her face in her hands.

"You know you're not responsible for these crimes. This is not your fault. This is not your story," he says tenderly.

"How could it not be?"

"Listen to me, Lavinia. You don't deserve that legacy. You have to find your own beautiful story inside you." He puts both their packs down, takes out a hanky, and gives it to her. She wipes her eyes, yet her tears fall. They wait.

When she stops crying, she hears the silence and it doesn't scare her, because Zack is waiting beside her, his arm around her shoulder, his face openly caring. How comforted she feels by his words and the way he just lets her be. She feels his quiet presence hum inside her.

She blows her nose, breaking the silence. "I'm ready for Methuselah."

"We'll begin our walk here. It's a four-and-a-half-mile loop. We'll make it back to the car by noon."

The narrow path holds an earlier snow. They begin in the soft light of the new day. It's cold—the sun hasn't yet warmed the trail. Lavinia can't believe they've had breakfast and made it here all in two hours. It's only eight thirty. The half moon is still visible behind moving gray clouds. With each step, she hears a crunch, like crystals beneath her feet. She imagines Zack's liquid crystal that he spoke of, now frozen and supporting their steps. This sound eases her mind, gives her a focus, and adds a dimensionality to her surroundings.

"By nine thirty the sun will warm up this ridge . . . just about the time we pass the old tree," Zack assures her, his feet crumbling ice on the frozen path.

They walk by young healthy bristlecone pines about fifty feet tall. The branches are covered in waxy green needles that look like bottle brushes. Each needle is a cluster of five—a peculiarity of bristlecones, Zack tells her. At the tips of some branches, purple or green cones seep with sap, giving off a butterscotch smell. The white dusting of snow sticks to the branches, reminding Lavinia of Christmas.

"That's a two hundred-year-old tree," Zack says, pointing to one.

She follows the old man up the hill, listening to the crisp sound of their feet on the crystal path. Cold air grips at her face and hands. She stops to zip up her red parka, pulling the hood up to cover her ears. She can feel the warmth of her own breath around her nostrils as she inhales and at her mouth when she exhales. Actually, she feels lightheaded; she wants to take more breaths than usual. If only she could catch a deeper breath! Zack tells her they'll be climbing eight hundred vertical feet of elevation to be in the company of the old trees, but assures her that this walk is a steady winding switchback with ups and downs, not a straight vertical ascent.

She paces herself, following his steady, slow footsteps like she's keeping time with a metronome. Like one of his clocks, he is steady and consistent. The smell of pine is primal and seems to enter through her pores and mix with her own blood. She imagines the smell being carried through her blood vessels to her heart. The sun rays warm her face.

The partially sunny sky casts a soft light. When they reach the moraine an hour later, Lavinia sees the oldest naked trees standing in dolomite stone, shaped by thousands and thousands of windstorms, hail, rain, sun, and moonlight. She stops before the most ancient living, breathing organisms she's ever encountered and faces squarely these living trees. Silence prevails.

Never having seen such nakedness before, Lavinia gasps. Her eyes widen and her heart opens while everything else seems to stop, except the smell of resin.

Living stones like sculptures chiseled by nature's hands appear in front of her. She thinks of George and his stone-cut mausoleum for his beloved Angela; how her mother, too, seemed alive in stone. As the sun rises higher, the air warms, reflecting the wash of color on the body of the trunk, orange and red dripping for thousands of years like the tears that have been cried over her stone-struck mother.

"Limestone and dolomite with ice particles," Zack whispers.

"So shiny, like gold and silver—reminds me of tears." She pats her gloved hand over her lips.

"I see that, Lavinia, the way the sun is reflecting on the dolomite." His eyes glisten in the low sunlight, catching the brightness.

They listen silently to the gentle wind that rustles the pine leaves, the gentle crackling of the light snow cover beneath their feet. Sounds mixing with their breathing and heartbeats make their own music.

"So this is the great rhythm of stillness," she says, beginning to appreciate it. "Zack, what is time?"

"It is this moment, nothing more," he says, reaching for her hand. The moment is prescient.

They stand together in the midst of the family of trees, the dead ancestors clinging next to the live younger trees, all of them holding each other in their own majesty. She watches the old dead and the old alive hand in hand before her. When the wind picks up, Lavinia moves in closer among the trees, using their trunks as a protection from the cold. They are not much taller than her. Zack hovers nearby, touching the great skin of the tree trunks—cold and naked, yet clothed sparsely by the pine foliage. Enchanted by the family group, which stands solidly together yet alone, Lavinia stares, wondering if the spirits of the dead trees feed the spirits of life or whether they are a drain on the living. Pine needles glisten on the naked bark, calling her attention.

They walk farther on. When they come to the grove of the oldest trees, she asks Zack which is the Methuselah.

"Not marked for fear someone will take a chunk of it," he says, his eyes still searching for the old one, the one older than time. "Maybe it's the one on his knees," he says, moving toward a tree whose trunk curves, resting on the ground, in a penitent pose.

She prefers to think the oldest living tree is the one she now finds in front of her, standing tall, a flamenco dancer dressed in vivid red and burnt orange and a deep brown. A flowing wood sash of stripes hangs down its leg, and green plumes of life grow out of its side. She stops in her tracks, leaving an imprint on the crusty snow on the path. Right in front of her she swears she sees an ancient Mercedes, dancing her *alegría* with her arms and legs twirling and swirling.

"Is that you, Mercedes?" she asks. She hears, "No, *mijita,* that's you. Lavinia Lavinia, you are an old and beautiful soul. This tree is within you to give you strength." Tears come to her eyes. She crouches down on the narrow path, resting on her knees on the crispy snow, and looks up into and through the old branches. She sees a myriad of antlers crisscrossing. She sees a great stag.

"Who are you?" she asks. She hears, "A woodland deity. A god of plenty and the voice of the spirit." She doesn't feel so alone.

When she stands up, a long, waxy branch brushes her face. She turns, half expecting to see Zack smiling, but he's not there. How long has she been here, huddled in awe among the ancient ones, engrossed by their twisting swirls and turns like the people on the dance floor, like the clay torso of her mother in George's studio, oblivious to the passing of time? How long has she been standing in the place where there is no time, like when she was with the littlest bird?

Worried about Zack, she steps out of the grove and into the colder air, but she doesn't see him. She retraces her steps, feeling frozen. The cold stings on her skin and she wants to get out of here, but where's Zack?

Should she stay put? Should she return to the place where they last spoke? What's the rule? They haven't spoken about a plan in the event of getting separated. She looks around before and behind her and sees footprints in the dust of snow. She traces a circular path until the prints disappear. The sun rises higher, melting the snow. She tells herself that he has wandered into a smaller grove the way she did, so she follows a path to where a stand of the eccentric trees breed. She wanders within the circles, and there, at her feet, she sees Zack lying face up, his eyes closed, his mouth open. His hands rest one over the other, as if he's in a deep sleep or . . .

She stares at him. "Oh no, not him, too."

He's just lying there with his hands crossed, the way Angela's hands rested in her casket in the mausoleum.

She yells.

Listening to her own echo dissolve into the thin air, she drops to her knees before the outstretched man. He looks stunned, like the bird that flew into her window. He lies on a bed of crushed bark, eons old, in this small, sacred, butterscotch-smelling grove in the sky. *But who is more stunned?* she asks herself. *Me or Zack?*

She sits with him in the same way she did with the bird, like she must have done with Nonna when Angela never came home on that fateful day. She feels paralyzed. She cannot move, though she wants to help him. She knows she needs to do something, but what?

The sun disappears behind the clouds. She hears a slight hum on the distant wind and imagines an oncoming storm. How long has she been gloating over these tree images? An hour? Ten minutes? Time has slipped away. What is this thing called time? He said it was this moment.

She considers that he might be hypothermic. *I can't let him get any colder,* she tells herself. She takes off her jacket to cover him, but it barely does, so she covers his body with her own, lying down on top of him and listening for his heartbeat. She feels his breath with her fingers. His gentle exhalation is moist and warm. Outstretched, her head reaches to the top of his shoulders and her feet touch just below his knees. Her heart rests above his waist. *We have to be heart to heart.* She adjusts herself and feels the pulse in his neck—slow, like the softer roar of a distant wind, but at least his heart is beating. The great clock nestled within his long, thin body ticks, sending out blood to his limbs and back again. Lavinia stays, transfixed like the stone princess, reminded of the sleeping princess on Mount Tamalpais. She listens to his heartbeat, hoping for courage, hoping he will wake up.

It begins to snow, and just when Lavinia is beginning to despair, Zack begins his own hum, which feels like a bright vibration—first on his neck and then moving on and pulsing through his veins. He sticks out his tongue, lets a few flakes fall there. He opens his eyes. They twinkle like the snow.

"S-s-sweet s-s-snow," he whispers, a light wind song to her ears.

She's not sure she has heard him, so she lets her body tilt to see the old man's eyes.

"It's s-s-snowing, Lavinia."

A wide smile like the moraine itself crosses his face just as a white eagle soars over them from the top of the bristlecones. She rubs his forehead with her hands and then slides off of him. She takes off her parka and tucks it around him. Lovingly, she cups his head in her hands.

"Look, Lavinia, look." He points to the eagle. "You see? There's nothing to fear in this puzzle of life."

Lavinia on her knees beside him, with his head in her hands, feels an urgency to go back downhill toward the parking lot. She begins to lift him at his neck and shoulders.

"Wait, Lavinia, listen to the wind. Look at White Eagle. Do you hear him?"

She strains to hear and just makes out the whirring sound of its wings.

"I dreamed that death is sweet," Zack says. "The eagle is confirming this truth. You saw it, didn't you?" he asks, lifting his head, now free from his stupor.

She nods.

"Wait. And there's more, Lavinia. The great clock ticks. I have seen it, buried deep in the mountain, across the way." He looks in the direction of Mount Washington, near Ely. "It rests deep inside the cavern of the earth; it's buried deep in the inner heart of the dark mountain like a great god, breathing into eternity."

His beatific smile radiates, making her feel she is amid something sacred. She holds still, realizing that this experience is holy.

"I've seen this through the eyes of the eagle," he says. "He showed me. It's as clear as a bell."

"Yes, and now you must rest, please, Zack. You fainted, and you need to save your energy for the steep walk down. We must get down to our car before the snow falls heavier."

He has a dusting of snow on his eyebrows and nose. He ignores her, instead wanting to tell her about the transitional pendulum, the equations of time, the horizon, the sun, the moon, the good morning star. He goes on, not making any sense to her, which is concerning.

"I have seen and heard the clock tick once a year, seen the hand that advances every hundred years, and the cuckoo that comes out once every thousand years. Only it was a great white eagle singing, and you saw it, too. No need to be afraid, Lavinia, of time, or death. I have seen the long now, *carpe millennium*." He rests his head back down on the ground.

"Zack, you need to sit up," she insists. "Do you think you can stand?" Getting to her feet, she helps the old man up to a sitting position. She holds his arm as he gets his bearings. They look over the ridge to where Mount Washington and the excavated site for the millennium clock might be. Cirrus clouds mark the great blue of midmorning in the form of a giant bird.

"Maybe it's the plume of the Great Eagle," Zack says.

She nods, standing beside him, reaching for both his hands. "Let's go before more snow and wind come, Zack. We can talk about the plume later."

She brushes the needles and chips off his clothing and takes the pack he still wears on his shoulders, with water for two, off of him. She gives him some water.

Zack winks at her. "We have time," he says.

They rehydrate and walk slowly down the curved path to the lower elevations.

"You saw it, too, Lavinia, didn't you? You saw the limestone mountain and the eagle." He stops, wanting reassurance before they go on.

"I saw it, too," she says with conviction.

She will not crush this moment for him, and besides, she asks herself, how is his seeing these visions any different from her seeing Mercedes and the stag? Or listening to the fig tree? All she's doing is affirming. She's just validating his dream. This is what they've come for—to fulfill the pieces of the puzzle. Didn't he once tell her in his apartment that she would fill in the pieces? Her life is beginning to make sense to her as he, too, is filling in the pieces of his life.

"Look, a new dusting of snow, Lavinia," he says with child-like wonder, holding her hand. She squeezes his long, thin fingers in her tiny hands, thinking about the miracles she has experienced in recent weeks.

But he's coming out of his daze and wants to talk. He tells her how the old trees stay upright for one thousand years after they die.

"That's fifty generations, a long time after death!" she says. She finds herself thinking of her grandfather again. "How do the trees die?" she asks.

"Heart rot." He pauses and then stops to look into her eyes. He takes her hand in his, his eyes penetrate her being. It seems to her that he is giving her his heart. Her heart feels like it might crack open, as this gentle being sends his beams of love right into her. His eyes seem to see her pain.

"Heart rot?" she asks.

"Yes, trees die when their heart core is diseased."

"Like Don's?"

"Yes, like Don's, and perhaps like your grandfather's, too." He seems to be reading her mind, and they walk in silence through the grove. Then he says, "You, Lavinia, have heart-love. I could feel it the first day I saw you. Your heart cannot rot. I see the beauty born into you as a child." He pauses. "You have more opportunity than your mother did, and her mother before her; you don't have to carry the burden of the family legacy anymore; you don't have to fear this past. You are glorious. I have seen this. Now you have a chance to take your place."

"Like Margaret has," she says.

"Like Margaret has."

"But—"

"'Sweet are the uses of adversity,'" Zack cuts in. He lifts his eyebrows. "Shakespeare."

They look at the old trees in this adverse condition of their lives.

"That's me," she jokes, feeling lighter.

"That's you, a fine laundress-teacher who could resuscitate this old body. Thank you for bringing me back."

Thinking now only about getting him down safely, she helps him along. "Let's go home, Zack."

"That works for me," he says. "No need for Ely."

"I'll drive," she says, feeling *la querencia* pulsing straight from her core.

They walk, holding hands, letting the deep silence comfort them.

Chapter 33:

GOING HOME

It's midnight and Lavinia is sitting with Mario, who'd minutes ago met her at Zack's place and walked her back to Falcone and his upstairs apartment in North Beach. It was a poignant moment with Zack, saying good-bye after their two full days together. Tears and blessings came from the old man who, as he gave her a gentle hug whispered, "You are worthy of seeing your many gifts, Lavinia. You are a blessing to me."

Now Lavinia, content with a satisfying fullness, feels happy to be in Mario's arms, telling him about her adventure, laying out the story about the white eagle and how they retraced their steps down the trail, arriving back to the car at noon; drove down through Bishop for another loaf of bread and to gas up; stopped for late lunch in Bridgeport; and made it to Truckee for dinner. How, after a double espresso in Auburn, they drove two more hours toward the wing of the East Bay Bridge, that looked to her like Zack's white eagle.

"Eight hours of driving," Mario says. "You're amazing." He squeezes her close to him.

"Yeah, but with Zack beside me, talking and humming all the way, it was a breeze." Before she knows it, a heaviness descends upon her and she's in a deep sleep.

In her dream, Lavinia stitches a bracelet with colored yarns, each loop a gratitude. One is for Zack's revival and his trust; two is for Mario and their love dance; three is for Kinky and her sisterly love; four is for Mama Mercedes and *la querencia*; five is for George, the keeper of his love for Angela; six is for Rose and Sal, who gave her a sheltering home; seven is for the fig tree, who speaks to her; eight is for the redwoods and the bristlecones, which have survived time; nine is for her mother and grandfather, and their strange dance; ten is for Nina and Don, may they rest in peace; eleven is for Nonna Caterina and her suffering. And finally, twelve is for the glimpse of Time Eternal. She knows each moment is made of the past, the present, and the future. The present is already the future, and the past is gone.

When she wakes up, it's morning and Mario is next to her, still sleeping. How new he seems to her. He is beautiful, like a living tree. She wants to tell him all her secrets and to know his, to sleep in his bed and in his arms forever. He rouses and reaches out his hand to her and she takes it, staring into his eyes. She sees his inner beauty. He makes her laugh and makes her cry at the same time. When has she ever known such love? She looks into his face and kisses him.

"I'm in love with you," she says.

He moves closer to her and says, "I want to spend my life with you."

Their arms and legs move in unison, mirroring each other. They rock and tumble from side to side like joyful babies.

They dance the kind of dance that's not hers, not his, but theirs. The dance they make together is both the beginning and end of time, like eternity.

He doesn't have to go into work. He calls Carmine to relieve him so they can spend the day in bed together, talking and giggling and playing like kids, interrupted only by the peak coffee times, when rumbling voices and coffee fragrances drift up into the apartment. Every now and then she hears a release of steam from the machines; it reminds her of Zack's beautiful hum, like thousands of bees making honey.

Mario and Lavinia stay together the whole day and through to the next morning, when he goes downstairs for work in the café. Then she nests into the comfy, warm spot he's left behind, breathing in his scents, until the sun is up.

She texts Kinky: "All is A-OK. I'm home."

Soon a response comes: "Already?"

"Yup! It's all a miracle. Dinner with you and Mercedes tonight?"

"Super, can't wait."

She calls George, who answers on the first ring. He's happy to hear she's home safely, mission completed, and tells her he has some great news, too.

"But not on the phone," he says.

"I'll be right over. I can't wait anymore. No more waiting!"

"Okay, then. I'll put up the tea."

Lavinia gets dressed and pulls on her red jacket as she makes her way toward the door. She calls an Uber and in fifteen minutes she's in George's small kitchen, sitting at the wooden table with tea and biscotti set out for her, her red jacket on the back of her chair.

"Okay, tell me," she says, "I can't wait another minute."

"The Museum in Naples, Capodimonte, has invited me to show my work in their beautiful botanical garden as part of their permanent sculpture art."

"Which pieces?" She recalls the heavy, large rectilinear piece of stone with the reclining sleeping woman—her mother—in it.

As he tells her which pieces are to be shown, she sees clearly
how her mother's memory will live on in the secret garden where
she and George made love, and this makes her happy. Then she
sees her grandfather Antonio's love—a possessive and vengeful
love like Don's—and this makes her sad and angry. In a moment
of clarity, though, she wishes for both her mother and her grandfather to rest eternally in the long now, as the clock does buried
deeply in a limestone mountain, ticking and ringing for ten thousand years, showing that we have time to balance and foster a
less impulsive thinking. *Maybe we can hold the long view.* She
knows love can take many forms and sometimes can even kill.
Her grandfather's stark beliefs—what Zack called heart rot—
killed her mother.

She shivers, rubbing her hands on her face.

"Will you come to Naples with me next summer?" George asks.

She stops cold at this invitation, goes inside herself. She
considers that this is the invitation she's always longed for. There
are many reasons to go to Naples—to see where she was born,
to find Salvatore and forgive him, to see the garden where she
was conceived, to meet her grandmother Caterina. And yet she's
confused. It feels like she's stepping back—back two steps and
one step forward, back two and one forward through time, never
really progressing.

George is staring at her. Lavinia sees love in his eyes and feels
blessed, but she cannot give him an answer right away.

She pictures her nonna as George described her, the then-
forty-six-year-old ancient woman, sitting in a darkened room in
a catatonic state, growing old in her chair, looking at him with
the eyes of a great whale. The ancient sea creature must be similar to the bristlecone pine. She fantasizes for a moment that her
grandmother is waiting for her.

As if reading her mind, George says, "I have a letter from your grandma addressed to you."

"What!"

"Uncle Giovanni sent it to me to give to you since I last saw you. And a little package, too," he says. "Uncle Giovanni wanted me there when you opened it." George reaches into a small drawer in the wooden table and pulls out a letter on silky paper and a small cardboard box wrapped in brown paper and hands it to her.

Her fingers slip over the paper. She opens it and looks for a long time at a pair of tiny brown gloves, fingers rubbed smooth by someone's hands. Lavinia touches each soft leather finger, which has clearly been caressed repeatedly over a long period of time. Her tears fall onto the brown, leaving a spot that's almost black, as she touches the old woman who has held her for all these years.

George hands her a Kleenex box after taking one for himself. They sniffle together. Then she opens the letter and stares through blurry eyes at the small, well-formed letters. She notes the way the g's sit on the line with their tails wagging so gracefully below; the way she addresses her, *Cara Lavinia Lavinia*. She wants to read it, but the whole letter is in Italian.

"Please read it to me, George."

She squares herself in her seat and closes her eyes.

"Here goes. Bear with me my translating, Lavinia."

Lavinia sits in her *querencia*, the place she's discovered with Mama Mercedes, the still place where she is safe, waiting, protecting herself.

Cara Lavinia Lavinia,

What would I tell you if I could see you? How I've prayed for your well-being every day of your life. Have you heard me ask you for forgiveness for what I did? Your nonno was a proud man, strong, and willful, too. Strong in his body and mind. He could do everything— help others and even kill our Angela. He let his vengeful pride override his goodness.

You probably can't understand how he could love your mother and do such a horrible thing. I've asked myself that, too. There he was screaming at her on the tracks, cursing in rage. Pushing and pulling at her bags with the new dress and shoes she bought for you to wear on the plane. He pushed her, she slipped, and he fell crashing with her.

I see it as a crime of passion, committed because of his impulsive rage—not a suicide to save face. We call those honor killings. Some here would think him honorable for taking his own life with hers and not just hers. But that was not his way.

What he took was my life, and yours.

The day your father came looking for you, I wished you were here with me so I could hand you to him. But you were already gone, safe away with Sal. Maybe I could have told him where you were, but I didn't. I was so afraid of the curse that had taken Angela away from me. But I secretly hoped your father would find you and you'd be united, like in the dream I dreamed every night.

I must have looked like a scary old lady when he came here. I was only a shadow of myself. Lost and confused, with only my prayers. I promised myself I would someday give you the shoes your mother carried. They are yours.

Each bead I prayed, and still do, is for your uniting with him. I pray for forgiveness for what I did to you. I don't even pray that I will ever see you, because I don't deserve that. I do pray that your mother's presence is somewhere, guiding you. In the trees, in the water, doing the laundry, baking. She loved all those things.

I let Sal take you away from me. Why I didn't follow you there so I could be part of your life and tell you about your parents, I don't know. Why didn't I get Giovanni to call his sister? I ask myself these questions every day.

Why didn't I see to it that George got custody of you? My complacence makes me as guilty as your nonno's act of violence. I am sorry for my passivity. I let my self-pity and self-indulgence keep me from helping you.

All of them in this village played along, wanting to protect the prideful vengeance of our people. We were all guilty of the sin of pride. How did I not see this at the start? Wasn't I a part of this? I think so. I am sorry. I hope you can forgive me. I give you back your hands.

Your nonna, Caterina
Molti Auguri, Baci

So many feelings compete in Lavinia's heart. A whirlpool of contradiction—love and hate, sadness and joy, feelings of being both lost and found. She feels sucked into that tidal wave, like her grandmother, rolling and churning, and wants to be free. She doesn't want to face the same fate as her nonna, trapped in the past. She remembers Zack telling her that what happened to her mother was not her fault, that she has her own destiny.

She remembers her dreams of being in the dark womb of her mother and spinning; how Mercedes told her spinning can turn things around for us, not to fear them; how she has danced forward and backward, getting closer to her place; how she has danced the dizzying 180 degrees to the right, 180 degrees to the left, back and forth, around the room, spinning forward, taking her place in the physical world with her new family by her side.

Now she has her feet and her hands and she's spinning on that thermal, going up on a vortex, circling, circling, circling like Zack's bird, going through multiple vortexes and finally reaching a hot spot where she sees a new family and a new future. She wants to go to back to school; to teach alongside Kinky; to play drums with Mama Mercedes and eat tamales; to dance with Mario and marry him; and to get to know her father here in San Francisco. Now she has time to do so.

George is waiting. She hears him say her name.

"Yes, I'm here."

"Will you come?"

She pauses as a crystalline thought burgeons from deep within. "No, Dad. I cannot come. Not now." She calls him "Dad" for the first time. He is her dad. The thought makes her happy.

There is a pause. They look into each other's eyes.

After a long silence, he smiles. "Maybe another time. For now, I hope we can get to know each other here in San Francisco."

"I want that," she says.

"There's time, Lavinia Lavinia."

ACKNOWLEDGMENTS

Without Brooke Warner, my coach and publisher, who believes in me, there would be no Frances Pia or Lavinia Lavinia. Thank you and the staff at SWP, especially Shannon Green, Krissa Lagos, and Julie Metz, who helped make this a beautiful book.

November and the glorious days between the autumnal spirit world, November 1 and the shortest day of Winter Solstice, lend me a creative spirit. In November, anything is possible, including the unfolding of plot and story inspired by my inner fire and Chris Baty's *No Plot No Problem*. November is novel-writing month.

Many thanks to others who inspired the particulars of this novel. Peter Schumacher introduced me to The Long Now Foundation in Fort Mason, San Francisco, where the real Millennium Clock originated from the efforts of Danny Hillis, Stewart Brand, and others. Thank you.

Others I owe thanks to:

Cary Pepper, professor at The Fromm Institute for Lifelong Learning at the University of San Francisco, in whose class the characters Lavinia Lavinia and Zack Luce were born.

Gabrielle Roth's 5Rhythms and The Open Floor Dance, Sausalito, where dancing brings me closer to my best self. Dancers and teachers Kathy Altman, Claire Alexander, Lori Saltzman,

Jennifer Burner, and Andrea Juhan, as well as Flowing, Staccato, Chaos, Lyrical, and Stillness, inspired this work.

Miriam Philips, who first brought flamenco dancing to Marin County.

My Sicilian and *Abruzzese* grandparents, who found their way to America. This ancestral heritage appears in all my works to date.

Thank you to my parents George and Gloria Indelicato and my sister Catherine Kurkjian for your love.

The Ancient Bristle Cone Forest, which I first visited in 1999 with my husband, and which has stayed with me into the Millennium.

Tebby George's sculptures, which, like George Lavinia's, are eternal.

My love for my dear husband, Peter Sapienza, informed Lavinia's relationship with the barista Mario.

Lavinia Lavinia would like my gum-chewing, African-dancing daughter, Elisa Sapienza, and my granddaughters, Isabella and Milla, who dance every day. My son, Peter Sapienza, is a storyteller whose skills I admire. His wife, Valerie, is an incredible chef who inspired the great dishes on Mercedes's table.

Thank you to my teachers at San Francisco State and the Fromm Institute, who gave me the gift of craft, which I tried to apply here to balance my more open style of writing.

And thank you, dear readers: Kathy Andrew, Sue Salinger, Marsha Trent, Janet Constantino, Clarice Stasz, Ann Ludwig, Sharmon Hilfinger, Susan Shaddock, Marlene Douglas, and Marie Greening. Thank you Sister Mary Neill, Chris Durbin, and Laurie Schubert.

ABOUT THE AUTHOR

Barbara Sapienza, PhD, is a retired clinical psychologist and an alumna of San Francisco State University's creative writing master's program. She writes and paints, nourished by her spiritual practices of meditation, tai chi, and dance. Her family, friends, and grandchildren are her teachers. Her first novel, *Anchor Out* (She Writes Press, 2017) received an IPPY bronze medal for Best Regional Fiction, West Coast. Sapienza lives in Sausalito, CA, with her husband.

Author photo by Chris Loomis

SELECTED TITLES FROM SHE WRITES PRESS

She Writes Press is an independent publishing company founded to serve women writers everywhere. Visit us at www.shewritespress.com.

Size Matters by Cathryn Novak. $16.95, 978-1-63152-103-4. If you take one very large, reclusive, and eccentric man who lives to eat, add one young woman fresh out of culinary school who lives to cook, and then stir in a love of musical comedy and fresh-brewed exotic tea, with just a hint of magic, will the result be a soufflé—or a charred, inedible mess?

Beautiful Garbage by Jill DiDonato. $16.95, 978-1-938314-01-8. Talented but troubled young artist Jodi Plum leaves suburbia for the excitement of the city—and is soon swept up in the sexual politics and downtown art scene of 1980s New York.

Cleans Up Nicely by Linda Dahl. $16.95, 978-1-938314-38-4. The story of one gifted young woman's path from self-destruction to self-knowledge, set in mid-1970s Manhattan.

To the Stars Through Difficulties by Romalyn Tilghman. $16.95, 978-1631522338. A contemporary story of three women very different women who join forces in a small Kansas town to create a library and arts center—changing their world, and finding their own voices, powers, and self-esteem, in the process.

The Lucidity Project by Abbey Campbell Cook. $16.95, 978-1-63152-032-7. After suffering from depression all her life, twenty-five-year-old Max Dorigan joins a mysterious research project on a Caribbean island, where she's introduced to the magical and healing world of lucid dreaming.

Tzippy the Thief by Pat Rohner. $16.95, 978-1-63152-153-9. Tzippy has lived her life as a selfish, materialistic woman and mother. Now that she is turning eighty, there is not an infinite amount of time left—and she wonders if she'll be able to repair the damage she's done to her family before it's too late.